REIGN OF
DARKNESS

REIGN OF

DARKNESS

THE STORY OF THE FIRST ARCHIMAGE

BOOK 3

MICHAELA RILEY KARR

Rye Meadow Press

Published by Rye Meadow Press, based in Emporia, KS.
ryemeadowpress@gmail.com

ISBN (paperback): 978-0-9986065-5-2
ISBN (hardback): 978-0-9986065-6-9
Library of Congress Control Number: 2019906339

Cover Design © 2019: Magpie Designs, ltd.
Photo Credit: Pixabay
Texture Credit: Sascha Duensing
Author Photo Credit: Jordan Storrer Photography
Interior Map © 2019: L. N. Weldon

Printed in the United States of America.
First Edition, 2019.

DEDICATION

To my husband, Olin,
my one and only.

NERAHDIS

TREDENO

JOSHUUA'S TREE

LEONAR

RHYDIN'S PALACE

THE KINGDOM OF
MINERALTIR

CADEN'S

MINERALTIR CASTLE

DEMORA

TRANINI

THE
GREAT DESERT

IONDRIA

IVANN'S DELTA

N

★ CAPITAL
● CITY
■ CASTLE

CHAPTER ONE

Lunaka was thawing. The mountains were balding as their icy caps slowly receded, and it seemed the prairie grass grew inches every night. There was still a slight nip in the incessant Lunakan wind that had brushed my cheek since my birth, but most of winter's traces were all but vanished. In some ways, it felt like Lunaka never changed. However, I couldn't say the same about much else.

I walked slowly along my well-worn path back toward the Rounan compound from my daily escape. Kylar toddled before me on his awkward, ever-lengthening legs. Rayna watched him intently from my arms, jealous of his ability to be mobile. My two children were growing like weeds, and yet most of the time I couldn't look at them with the joy of a mother. Instead, I always felt the worry of my precarious position.

Rhydin had been emperor for a year now. I was an Allyen, and yet I couldn't stop him from slaughtering Archimage Dathian and turning the people of Nerahdis against us. They

1

all believed Rhydin a hero for liberating them from the made-up tyranny of an Archimage who controlled all of the Royals' abusive actions. I had hoped they would have realized otherwise by now.

While Rachel insisted that we needed to leave the Rounan compound as soon as possible, Sam and I had done our very best to stall that decision. We needed to get our children to safety, but we couldn't abandon our people, even if most had already abandoned us. I could feel it in my very bones that we would have to choose between the two soon. I refused to even ponder which of those parties I would consider. And so, while Kylar and Rayna continued to grow by leaps and bounds, every time I saw them, I was only reminded of the situation I dreaded. Thankfully, Rhydin recently seemed too busy establishing his reign to begin hunting for us and the Rounans.

The Ranguvariian feather hanging around my neck jingled against the warm metal of my Allyen locket as we continued our walk back to the Rounan compound, our home. It hid my presence from being detected by any mage, most important Rhydin, every moment of every day and night. Kylar and Rayna both wore ones as well, even though technically Kylar, as a Rounan, couldn't be sensed unless the mage saw him. Our whole compound was actually protected by an entire wind chime of these special feathers, but I knew the day was coming when it would not be enough.

When we came to the top of the last grassy hill between us and home, the compound came into view. It was a rather small settlement compared to the other established cities and towns in Lunaka, but it had been growing in recent years as Rhydin began spreading his message of revolution during the war and ultimately came to power. A few dozen small shanties were now sprinkled across the plain. No roads connected them, only a general sense of community and some trampled grass. Over the last couple of months, Rounans had started leaving the compound. They seemed to sense the same thing I did.

Our tiny shack was still on the very edge of the compound. It made things easier when we first moved here since the Rounans very obviously hated my guts. I was Gornish and belonged to the class of people actively persecuting and executing them, so I guess I couldn't blame them too much. After I brought Sam home from the war last year, a fraction of that hatred seemed to have dissolved. The men still viewed me with dislike and the women only made small talk with me, but it wasn't quite loathing or disgust like it had been before. I took it as my one victory from the entire war.

I knew from one look at the house that Sam wasn't inside. He very rarely remained indoors during the day, an age-old habit of the farmer he was, but my shoulders fell when I spotted him across the way in the area that was our field last year. He had a hoe and a large, burlap sack with him. I failed to suppress my inward groan and told Kylar to change his course.

As we approached, I could see the moment that Sam sensed me coming. He had been working furiously, his hoe rising and diving deep into the earth at the rapid pace of a woodpecker. His Rounan magic gently lifted each seed one by one out of the sack and planted it into his row. Abruptly, when I knew I was in range of his senses, his hoe slowed as it flashed in the light, and his assembly line of seeds halted wiggling themselves into the dirt. A small part of me never grew tired of watching him farm Rounan style, something he'd never been able to do when we lived in the Canyonlands south of Soläna, the capital city. However, I couldn't help the small bite of anger that arose within me.

3

"Sam," I groaned as I set Rayna on the ground and placed my hands on my hips. "I thought we talked about this. We weren't going to plant anything this year because there's no point."

My husband tugged on the tails of the blue, purple, and gold bandana tied tightly around his head, the one that signified him as Kidek, leader of the Rounans. His brown eyes darted to the hoe in his hands before they reached me. He mumbled, "You don't know that for sure. We've been safe for a year, we could still be here in the autumn to harvest it."

"Sam, there's no way-…"

"There's still a chance." Sam cut me off. He let the hoe drop to the ground and crossed the distance between us, placing his hands on my shoulders. "Rhydin could still reveal his true motives and turn the people against him before he finds us. No one can live a lie forever."

I paused as I stared at him. My eyes traced the puckered edges of the white scar that etched Sam's face from his brow to his jaw, the only physical reminder of when Rhydin imprisoned him during the war. I took a deep breath and tried to say, "But, the money for the seed-…"

"I have to do this, Lina," Sam murmured before he glanced at the toddler and the infant sitting at my feet, the former attempting to hold a conversation with the latter. "If he doesn't come and we don't plant something, we won't have any food this winter. I have to provide for us."

I exhaled louder than what was probably necessary. "Fine. After all, we can't really return the seed now." I gestured to the rows he had already planted.

Sam grimaced, but then responded, "I'm sorry I didn't ask. I just have to do this."

"I don't want to leave either, y'know." I crossed my arms over my chest. "If I could wave my hand and cast a spell that would cause the people of Nerahdis to see Rhydin for who he is, I would have done it a year ago. I don't want to abandon our people any more than you do."

"I know," Sam said quietly. His hands dropped from my shoulders, and one of them found one of mine, his tough calluses grated against my own. He whispered, barely audible, "We don't have to go, you know."

My brow furrowed, and my hand clenched his. "What do you mean? If Rhydin finds us, he'll kill us on sight."

"Not if we fight," Sam hissed. "We've got tons of Rounans here. We could stand a chance!"

"Rounan *families*, Sam," I clarified, "Half the people in this compound are just kids who can't protect themselves, not to mention our own! Even then, the rest of Nerahdis would just see it as a Rounan uprising, and whether we succeed or fail, we'd all be hanged. The Gornish people have to come around to our side first."

"And how's that going?" he scoffed.

"They will! I know they will," I cried.

Sam let go of my hand and reached for his hoe. He brushed the loose dirt off the worn, wooden handle, and then he met my gaze once more. "I'm not leaving my people to be hunted down and killed under Rhydin's rule, Lina. I can't."

"I don't want to either," I sighed defeatedly, my glance sliding to my feet where Rayna babbled happily at something Kylar told her. There we were, back to the same conundrum as always. Stay for our people or go for our children.

"I know," Sam conceded before he turned to his hoe and struck it down into the dark, Lunakan soil. Suddenly, nearly microscopic seeds floated out of the burlap sack a few feet

5

away and began digging themselves into the row he created. "We'll figure it out. We've still got time."

"I hope so," I mumbled before scooping both Kylar and Rayna up under each arm and turning on my heel.

I walked briskly back to our shack, narrowly opening the rickety door and getting it closed again with my full arms. I set Kylar and Rayna down on their little spot in the corner of the room where a blanket was laid on the floor with a few meager, wooden blocks, and then I began to search for our other hoe so I could help Sam. It felt like the right thing to do at the moment to help make amends for our argument, and I also loved to help out however and whenever I could.

When I moved our cloaks on their hooks near the door, a gleam of metal caught my eye, and I unearthed our second hoe. The handle was missing a foot or so off the end after it was accidentally crunched under a wagon, and the wood was cracked down the middle, which reminded me that I should find a pair of gloves or my hands would fill with splinters.

As I searched the counter for my moth-eaten pair, Sam's being hopelessly too large, my fingertips brushed something that felt like the rough texture of parchment underneath a pile of clothing waiting to be mended for the hundredth time. Upon dragging it out into the daylight, I recognized my name in Frederick's familiar script. A smile crept to my lips.

Every once in a while, Frederick would write me a letter to keep in touch. Granted, he never told me where he, his sister, Cornflower, and his son, Dominick, were, but it was better than the absolute silence I had heard from Xavier and Mira over the last year. Rachel and her brothers delivered the letters of course, but they had developed a paranoid habit of hiding them somewhere in my house in case someone else came in. Sometimes, if Luke delivered the letter, I never found it until he helped me. On the other hand, James always made sure some portion of it was sticking out so I could find it, while Rachel would hide it in something I would eventually move. I could only guess whether Rachel or Luke hid this one.

I set the hoe against the wall once more and sat on my stool at our wobbly table. Kylar was very diligently stacking blocks, and he laughed hysterically every time Rayna pushed them over. I broke the brilliant gold wax seal, which was imprinted with the Lunakan Royal family crest – a head of wheat framed by twin moons – and slid the letter out of its envelope.

Dear Lina,

Things are rather quiet here, but I thought I would write you anyway. If anything, you know we are still alive and well. Cornflower sends her greetings and well wishes. She may be young, but I think she is finally adapting to this life. It took her a long time to grow accustomed to being even more secluded than we were in the cottage during the war. I am not sure I can say the same, hiding here while my people continue to throw themselves at Rhydin's feet.

Admittedly, Frederick's letters were often boring. I often thought that he put quill to parchment just to ease his own boredom. He wrote three pages' worth in his beautiful, Royal penmanship that had likely been drilled into his brain since he could first hold a writing utensil. He mostly summarized things I knew well enough by now: Cornflower was becoming a young lady and yet had never experienced any of the normal, coming-of-age events for a princess, and Dominick was growing at the same wickedly fast pace as my own children.

Frederick expressed his feelings of regret that his father, King Adam, was one of Rhydin's Followers, which was nearly the entire reason that Frederick, Cornflower, and Dominick had left Lunaka Castle and Royal society. Rarely, he would mention his grief for Cassandra, his wife who had passed of a serious illness during the war. I always tried to write back something supportive, but on even more seldom occasions, Frederick would ask about Rayna. I almost always wished he wouldn't.

After all, how could I forget? My eyes trailed from the last page of parchment to the tiny girl on my floor. She beamed up at Kylar with her Allyen eyes, brown mixed with golden specks, and there was no denying the red strands streaked through her hair, the same as Sam's. I sometimes forgot she wasn't born that way. That she was born to Frederick and Cassandra with hair blacker than coal, and we had to magically change her into the new Allyen to save our magic, and therefore Nerahdis. Sometimes, I wondered if even her blood was Sam and I's now. If anything at all of Frederick or her late mother remained.

Quite honestly, my eyes glossed over the rest of what Frederick had to say. He'd still heard nothing from Mira and Xavier, his sister and the stubborn heir to Mineraltir's throne she married, which still worried him. They had not parted ways well after the death of Archimage Dathian, and he endlessly hoped that Xavier would eventually come to realize that it wasn't Frederick's fault that Xavier's son, Taisyn, had been blinded by one of Rhydin's Followers. That Follower had been Robert, whom I had discovered was my biological father after running into him while freeing Sam from Rhydin's prison tower. I preferred not to ever think about that either.

I was just coming to the end of Frederick's letter, my hand absentmindedly reaching for the battered hoe once again, when some of the final lines caught my eye:

Anyway, please take care of yourself, Lina. I wish you and Sam were not so stubborn about remaining in that compound, and I really don't see why you two keep up the whole farming thing anyhow. You need to get underground before it's too late. You are more than welcome to join us, although I think our Ranguwariian protectors might object to having so many of us in one place. Tell Sam I say hello, and I look forward to hearing from you.

Best,

Prince Frederick Tané

My blood began to boil. I crumpled the parchment pages and flung them at the door. Frederick had never made any sort of commentary on our farming before. Why couldn't he understand that it was our way of life? Our passion? Our entire worlds for our whole lives had revolved around the rhythm of planting in the spring and harvesting in the fall.

My mind churned with angry thoughts. It was probably because he was a Royal. Royals didn't understand commoners' connections to their jobs, to their livelihoods. Everything was given to Royals on silver platters. Never had to work a day in their lives. I growled as I pushed myself from the table, beginning to pace. After that didn't burn off any of my anger, I at least had enough sense to grab Kylar and Rayna before I stomped out the door.

I marched barely a quarter of a mile toward the next shack along the general string that lead toward the heart of the Rounan compound. The slumped building was nearly identical to ours except for the general absence of any sort of barn or fencing for livestock, but I could hear the twinkling song of a violin from within and that was all that mattered.

I rapped on the rotten door with my free hand, daring to release Kylar's hand for the five seconds it took to do so. My heart still beat out an angry rhythm, but the walk had cooled me ever so slightly. By the time my twin brother finally managed to put down his violin and answer the door, he probably only saw a half-blisteringly-angry woman accompanied by two innocent children who were simply thrilled to see their uncle.

Evan took one look at my expression and then immediately stood to the side to allow me entry. "Come on in, Lina."

I stood on my tippy toes to peer over his shoulder. Cayce, his lavender-haired, Auklian, Rounan wife, sat at the meager table with a strange array of knitting and throwing knives spread before her. I cleared my throat. "Actually, you better come out here if you don't want me to wake your kid, as long as Cayce doesn't mind watching mine too."

Evan's brows threaded together, but he knew me well enough by now not to argue.

Cayce nimbly picked up all of her knives and tossed them into a high cupboard, a white smile gracing her rosy cheeks. "Anytime you like, Lina, just make sure to return your brother to me in one piece." She winked as she took Rayna from my arms.

"You have no idea how much I appreciate it," I said through gritted teeth, trying to contain the level of my voice until we were well away from their slumbering newborn.

Evan tracked silently behind me, ever the quiet twin, but as soon as we were maybe halfway between his house and mine, I whirled on him, fuming. I shouted, "Do you ever get letters from Frederick?"

My brother eyed me with those Allyen eyes of his and reached up to stroke his smooth chin. "Every once in a while, but I think he writes you more than me. I'm not very talkative. Is this about something he wrote to you? What's wrong, Lina?"

"Everything!" I screeched, throwing my hands up in the air just like Kylar did whenever he had a tantrum. "I'm just so fed up with this whole situation! I don't want to leave, but we have to, and Sam refuses, and now Frederick is calling me out for continuing to farm! That's like him telling you that playing the violin is stupid and useless!"

Evan's eyes narrowed. "I see your point," he said glumly.

"Ugh!" I groaned loudly, threading my fingers through my hair repeatedly still it stood on its ends. Then, I let my head hang. "Help me find my sanity again, Evan."

"Well, letting you try to pummel me has always helped in the past," my brother chuckled, knowing I would leap at the bait.

I quirked my brow. "*Try* to pummel you? How about knock you flat on your rear?"

"I'd like to see you try."

Smirking, I reached for the bright red sash around my waist, getting ready to ball it up in my hand and grow my sword magically before a flash of light knocked my hand out of the way. I looked up at Evan in confusion.

"Magic only. You rely on that thing too much," Evan stated plainly.

"Fine. Doesn't mean you'll win though."

With that, Evan pulled an orb of almost sparking, white light out of nowhere and fired at me. I leaped into the air, letting it soar past just underneath me, and charged my own weapon to sling back. Evan dodged it, of course, but there was no mistaking the sly smile that spread across his normally stoic face.

At first, my mind actively thought through each of my moves before I did them, but eventually, it fell away into nothingness. My body settled into an automatic rhythm as the sun made its usual journey across the skies. Charge, fire, dodge. Charge, fire, dodge.

Evan knew I needed to blow off steam, so he valiantly kept up the fight, even though I was sure he was tired as we neared the first hour. As time wore on, I came to realize that Frederick probably had no idea that what he wrote was hurtful. He didn't get it. Yet, while I came up with multiple flippant, rude responses that would likely make me feel better and show him how much of an oaf he was, I knew that I wouldn't be sending any of them.

Instead, I knew I would be sending one that compared our farming to his acting as prince for his people. I hoped that would give him the ability to understand.

Stinging pain woke my mind from its thoughts, and I found myself stumbling to the ground. I shook my head to reorient myself, having gone far too deep in my thinking for multi-tasking to really work. One of the knees of my trousers was ragged with singed, scarlet flesh peeping through. I shuddered to think what it would have looked like if Evan and I didn't tone down our power for our little sparring matches.

"You good?" Evan called from his end of our imaginary arena. I could vaguely detect a winning smirk on his face.

I immediately jumped to my feet, ignoring my stinging knee. "Right as rain!"

Just as I began to summon a new ball of light, unwilling to let my brother claim victory, a new voice reached my ears. "Is this what the Allyens do during their time off? Try to kill each other?"

Both Evan and I dropped our hands and turned toward the source. Standing along the beaten path between our shacks was none other than Rachel, my outrageously tall, red-haired friend who also happened to be the next Clariion, leader of the Ranguvariians. She didn't look amused as she measured the two of us up, complete with my scraped and slightly burned knee. That bossy, demanding voice came too quickly, even if I did know it was only out of concern. "What on Nerahdis are you two doing?"

"Uh… Just keeping ourselves limber, that's all," I lied as I shrugged. Evan walked toward me as I continued, "So, what are you doing here? I normally don't see you on letter drops."

Rachel sighed, her blue eyes sad, "I just got back from my grandfather. I'm sure you know what I'm going to say."

I shook my head, willing it to not be true. "No, Rhydin hasn't come yet, we still have ti-…!"

"It's time to go, Lina. No ifs, ands, or buts."

CHAPTER TWO

M y hands clenched into fists as I roared obstinately, "No! We still have a chance! We shouldn't have to leave if Rhydin doesn't know we're here!"

Rachel reached up to pinch the bridge of her nose, her blue eyes fluttering shut. "I don't think you understand…"

"I know what's at risk-…"

"No, you don't, quite frankly!" Rachel cut me off, her face flushing red. I could tell she was about to launch into a speech when a couple of Rounans caught her attention as they walked the nonexistent path back to the heart of the compound. She eyed them warily, and then turned back to my brother and I. "Let's speak somewhere more private."

When neither Evan or I moved, Rachel groaned, stomped forward, and latched onto each of our wrists, hauling us back toward my house. The thawing prairie grass squished underneath our feet as a cool breeze signified the coming of evening, but my mind barely registered it as it raced to come up with any sort of excuse to stay in the compound longer.

As Rachel tugged open the door and released Evan and I, she finally spoke, "I don't think you two realize the gravity of how disastrous it is that Rhydin is emperor."

"You think we don't?" I groaned. "We're having to possibly abandon our people to save our children, and you think we don't understand the gravity of the situation?"

"Sit," Rachel murmured darkly. As soon as we did, she continued, "What you're having to do, I will admit, is *inconvenient*, yes. But, you both seem to forget that there is another people group on this continent that will literally die if Rhydin's magic even touches them."

I crossed my arms stubbornly. With Sam's worry over the Rounans, and mine over the Gornish, I had slightly forgotten about the Ranguvariians. An image of the finger-width burns on Jaspen's face and Bartholomiiu's marred throat flashed in my memory. All simply because Rhydin touched them skin on skin.

Rachel lowered herself into a chair, her fierce resolve slowly melting. "This is the second time my grandfather, Clariion Arii, has seen Rhydin become emperor…and things are playing out exactly the same as they did last time. And I mean *exactly*. When Rhydin came to power the first time three hundred years ago, he started off small like this, doing all the little things that people wanted. But, it wasn't long before he began targeting his enemies. He created the first Duunzer within a year of becoming emperor, and he nearly exterminated my people with it. When you destroyed Rhydin's second incarnation of the Einanhi dragon, Lina, you avenged thousands upon thousands of Ranguvariians."

"He's not going to create Duunzer a third time, is he?" Evan asked hesitantly, fear clouding his eyes. I remembered how Evan was taken by Duunzer's Darkness while he was in Auklia, and I wondered what he was remembering.

"My grandfather doubts it," Rachel conceded, "The people have seen Duunzer, and it would ruin their trust in Rhydin if he used it now. However, my people are still terrified, and rightly so, that their extermination is forthcoming" – she turned to me, her eyes wide and sad – "There's mass hysteria in our camps, Lina. I've never seen it like this. Everyone is leaving and getting as far into the mountains as physically possible, hoping the magic-less zone will protect them. They know it's imminent, Lina. I need to get you all to safety, too."

I sighed loudly, considering my options. "I hear what you're saying, but-..."

"Lina, I told you. I need to get you all out now!" Rachel said firmly. "I know you have this fantasy in your head that Rhydin will somehow reveal himself to the whole continent as evil, but let's face it. That's not going to happen anytime soon! Even if it does, it's not going to be before Rhydin or his forces discover this compound! You cannot convince an entire continent that they need to change their minds!"

My brow furrowed, but I swallowed my angry, hateful words. "Just give us one more month."

"Not a chance. Start packing."

"Two weeks?" I gambled.

Rachel looked like she was going to pull her eyes out of their sockets. "One week."

"Done." I grinned at Rachel, but it quickly vanished.

A week to pack up our meager possessions and explain to Sam that our time had run out. That we wouldn't be here for harvest. That there wouldn't even be a harvest.

Evan cleared his throat. "Where will we go?"

I hadn't even considered that. All this time I had battled so hard to stay as long as possible or figure out what we were going to do that I hadn't even thought about where Rachel and the rest of our Ranguvariian protectors, the *Alyen nou Clarii*, planned on taking us.

Rachel's eyes darted downward. "It's confidential, for now. We'll tell you when we're en route. To maximize safety."

Evan huffed, scratching the back of his neck, "It's like the war all over again."

Rachel muttered indignantly, "Contrary to popular belief, the war never ended."

"Don't. Say. It."

Sam was sitting on his stool at the rickety table. He had been inhaling his supper, consisting of stew that was really more of a broth considering our low reserves, until I finally told him what Rachel had told me. It had festered in my mind for around three days as I tried to find the best way to tell Sam. Tell him early, to help him get used to the idea? Or tell him late, so he didn't have time to argue his way out of it? I made it three days before I caved.

Now, Sam gripped his spoon so hard I could see it begin to bend, and his other hand came up to cover his eyes. I could only assume he didn't want me to mention that I had been right about wasting the money on the crop seed.

I worked my fingers awkwardly, as if rubbing all my knuckles would somehow make this easier. I mumbled, "We still have a few days to figure things out before we have to-…"

"I'm not going."

My fingers dropped, loose as noodles. "What?"

Sam met my gaze sadly. "I told you, Lina. I can't leave my people."

"We don't have a choice," I responded, and then hesitated. I grew quiet. "Even if Rachel allowed it, would you really stay with your people over staying with me?"

My husband's eyes widened considerably, their gleaming brown flashing in the firelight. "N-No! That's not what I meant!"

I nodded slowly. A couple of seconds of silence went by before I lifted my bowl to my lips and drained the rest of my broth-like stew.

"Lina, you know that's not what I meant," Sam pleaded, nearly dropping his spoon as he reached out and held onto my hand tightly.

I sighed heavily, "I know."

Sam looked down at the table, studying the knots and gnarls in the aged wood. After a moment or two, he spoke firmly, "I will go with you. But we hide my people first."

My brow furrowed, "What do you mean?"

"You said the Ranguvariians are headed to the mountains because magic doesn't work there. That maybe they'll be safe there from Rhydin. A lot of Rounans have been heading to Caark and other discreet locations across Nerahdis, but the mountains are a lot closer," Sam said rapidly as the ideas formed in his mind. His eyes met mine with solidarity. "It's time to disband this compound. And we have four days to do it."

"What about other Rounans across Lunaka? Across Nerahdis?" I asked.

Sam's expression fell a little. "We'll have to hope that news of the mountains travels verbally or that others have already thought of it. It's too dangerous to send letters this time. One of Rhydin's Followers could easily intercept it, and then the mountains wouldn't be safe anymore."

"True," I murmured, trying not to act too bewildered that we finally had a plan. "Will four days be enough time to evacuate the entire compound?"

"It's gonna have to be," Sam declared, the tiniest of hints of frustration in his voice that immediately filled me with guilt as he stood from the table and dumped his bowl in the wash basin. He quickly threw on his cloak and headed toward the door. "No time to lose!"

I watched him disappear into the dark evening, wondering how many households he would go to before he came back to sleep. My eyes wandered to the blanket partition between this room and the bedroom as I rose and washed our bowls. It wouldn't take long to pull together our few belongings. Most of what each of us owned that was worth taking was a set or two of clothing and a handful of mementos, documents, or toys.

My heart ached when I realized we wouldn't have the capacity to take all our farming tools that we had acquired over our years of starting over in the compound. Farming as I knew it likely wouldn't even be possible on the rocky slopes of the mountains or the beaches of Caark.

For the first time, I found myself afraid of leaving.

It was late in the night by the time I settled Kylar and Rayna to sleep, packed our possessions into an old rucksack, and gave up on waiting for Sam before going to bed myself. Even though my eyelids screamed for sleep and my mind felt foggy, sleep evaded me. I must have fallen asleep at one point because the moons had shifted westward when I jolted forward, the hairs on the back of my neck standing rigid.

I breathed rapidly, my senses overloaded and confused by all the magic in the air. My hand fumbled in the dark to find empty space next to me on the hard, straw tick. Sam had never come in.

Without daring to light a lantern, I leaped out of bed, pulled my trousers on up over my night shirt, and shoved my feet into my boots. A red glow was now seeping through the window which only sent more chills down my spine.

I tripped over something in the dark as I hurled myself toward the window and slid the threadbare curtain aside a fraction of an inch. Tall, menacing flames were licking their way through the compound. Yet, a simple fire wouldn't be coupled with so many presences that my mind couldn't sort them out.

Where was Sam?

Someone barged through our door loudly just as I summoned my sword from my sash, but it was Rachel who found her throat at my blade when she pulled the blanket partition down completely. Her blue eyes turned icy as she halted. "Really, Lina? It's me!"

"Sorry! Just…what's going on out there?" I lowered my blade guiltily. The stench of ash and something else was beginning to reach my nostrils. "I can't sense anything for certain. Have you seen Sam?"

"Rhydin's Followers are attacking. I didn't see Sam, but I came straight here from my camp over the hill to get you and your children out of here before it's too late." Rachel strode forward quickly and didn't so much as hesitate before she scooped Rayna out of her bed. I waited for the chiding about how we could have left days ago, but it never came. For once, Rachel appeared frazzled. "Jaspen and my brothers are on their way, but I need to get these two out first. Stay *right* here, I'll transport Kylar next, and then you!"

I opened my mouth to object, but Rachel hurriedly brought forth her great, Ranguvariian wings, made up of brilliant feathers that looked more like suspended glass shards, and wrapped them around her and my slumbering daughter. With a flash of light, the two were gone. I gazed at Kylar, still asleep, but I had no intention of staying put. Five agonizing minutes ticked by before Rachel reappeared just long enough to lift Kylar from his blankets. Then, I slung the rucksack of all our worldly goods across my shoulders, hefted my sword, and rushed out the doorway without looking back.

In the other directions, the Lunakan prairie was dark and silent as a tomb, but the direction of the compound was another story. Fire turned the shacks into black silhouettes and flames danced in the windows and among the grasses outside. Black ash fell from the sky, and my ears registered the cacophony of screams just before I began to sprint in that direction.

Evan exited his shack just as I reached it, Cayce and their month-old newborn Aron not far behind. He appeared just as bewildered as I felt with my magic unable to discern anything in the chaos of presences.

"They're here, aren't they?" he asked quietly.

I nodded shudderingly as I tried to suppress my panic. "Rachel took my kids to safety. She said Jaspen, Luke, and James will be here soon. I have to go find Sam."

"He's not with you?" Evan questioned worriedly.

"No, he went to tell the Rounans to evacuate last night, but I-… I need to go find him. He might be in trouble," I said so fast I tripped over my words.

"I'll come with you." Evan drew his sword from his scabbard. I thanked him, and after telling Cayce to head to my house to find Rachel and be transported to safety, the two of us took off.

I tried to match my breaths to my footfalls as my twin and I raced toward the burning heart of the Rounan compound. The few shacks left strung along the way were completely abandoned, and I could only hope that Sam was able to give them a decent head start. But, judging by the screams I heard in the distance, he didn't make it to all the houses in time. I inwardly chided myself for not helping him spread the word while we had a chance. Who could have known that we had four hours instead of four days?

A dark figure sprinted out from around the next Rounan shanty, and my magical compass focused in enough that I could discern a portion of Rhydin's ancient, cruel presence. Einanhi. One of Rhydin's magically-created humanoids.

Drawing upon my magic and the strength of my Allyen locket, I chucked an orb of light and hit the creation square in the chest. With another shot by Evan, the Einanhi dissolved into sand mid-motion, the particles streaming out in the direction it had been running.

Evan and I never broke our pace until we reached the nearest wall of the shanty where we skidded to a halt and pressed our backs against it. The shouting, the wails, and the sounds of burning wood and breaking glass were just around the corner. With so many mages here, we didn't need to be throwing ourselves into the middle of it before we knew the lay of the land. Of the battlefield that used to be our home.

Rachel was right. The war never ended.

I peeked beyond the corner of the shanty to see Rhydin's Followers rushing everywhere. Many of the Einanhis, and perhaps a few Mineraltins with pyromage magic in their blood, were unleashing vortexes of fire upon everything in sight. The center of the compound had already been reduced to charred remains, their faces blank as if they were doing nothing more than balancing their ledgers. I squeezed my eyes shut when a few Rounans darted out of a burning building for their lives and were caught in the mages' fires just the same. But then, I looked toward where they were running.

On the opposite end of the main road was such a strange-looking object that I had to look twice to figure out what it was. Floating in mid-air, as well as blocking a near steady stream of fire, was a hodge-podge of what seemed to be every metal object in the entire compound. Pots, tools, wagon wheels, all held and being soldered together by the fire it blocked. I squinted beyond the levitating mass to barely make out a few Rounans that I recognized from town with several more behind them. If Sam was anywhere in this nightmare, he'd be holding up that barricade.

I was just about to pull Evan that way when he suddenly pushed me to the side, his magic giving off a golden flare as he headed off another Einanhi coming at us from behind. It was only a few seconds before Evan dispatched it, but my fall caught the attention of one of the few real people out doing Rhydin's bidding. A black-cloaked man turned his head toward us, and I knew it was too late to find Sam behind the barricade. It looked like we would be waltzing into the center of the scene anyway.

I jumped to my feet and swept my leg in a wide arc, spreading a blast of white light toward the Follower who saw us and anybody else who happened to be nearby. A couple Einanhis were knocked off their feet, but the human Follower jumped over it and unleashed a gale of fire upon us. The force of it threw his hood off to reveal Terran, a Mineraltin Follower that had been watching me for years, even before I knew I was an Allyen.

Evan and I dove forward and cast a double-charged spell that sliced Terran's fire in two, routing it around us, although the heat still took my breath away. Terran tried to launch another quick blast to catch us off guard, but he abruptly stopped, his fire colliding with the shanty behind us.

Breathing hard, I instantly went to angle myself between the majority of the Followers and the makeshift, metal shield that protected the Rounans who remained, but Evan didn't react. By the time I took up my position, my sword ready for anything, I noticed Evan staring wide-eyed at the Followers across from us. I followed his gaze, and my heart fell into the pit of my stomach.

Standing in the center of the turmoil as if they hadn't bothered to lift a finger the whole time were two men about the same age, but vastly different. One was tall with dark, peppered curly hair underneath a silver crown, no longer gold. Te other was quite short with hair and eyes that matched my own, the very picture of Evan except with the addition of far too many age lines and an unshaven jaw.

King Adam of Lunaka and Robert, our father.

Bile rose in the back of my throat, and anger threatened to choke me. I called across the burning void, "I should have known this was your handiwork, Adam! You should leave while you still can!"

Adam's dark brow twitched in anger at the lack of his title. He turned to the silent man next to him, who could only stare at my brother and I, before sneering loud enough for me to hear, "I say, Robert, I don't see why you want your children to join Rhydin. They're nothing but arrogant, disrespectful scum!"

"You're not the king anymore! I only wish I could have been the one to dethrone you myself," I glowered, a grin tilting my lips upward for the briefest of moments. It was like pure ecstasy to see Adam's skin flush with anger.

He growled before he could help himself, "Lunaka will be mine to oversee forever, just as Master Rhydin promised! I will never lose my power to my traitorous son thanks to him!"

I rolled my eyes. He may have been governor now instead of king, but he was still underneath Rhydin and a fool at that. I turned to eye Robert and Evan, who had been staring at each other unceasingly. I realized this was the first time Evan had seen Robert face to face, but then Evan abruptly broke the trance and jogged over to join me. As he took up his stance, I took stock of what I could sense now that we were in the middle of the battle.

Rhydin's Followers were mostly congregated before us, with a few out still burning buildings. Since the Rounans were behind us, I had no way of sensing how many of them were still in the compound, but I could hear brisk whispering. I hoped they were taking advantage of this diversion and putting as much space between them and here as possible.

"One last warning, Adam. Leave, now, or you'll die at my hand," I shouted across the distance that separated us.

A few beads of sweat seemed to appear on Robert's brow while Adam chuckled darkly, "Do your worst. Attack!"

All of the Followers and Einanhis in Adam's vicinity turned from their former targets and unleashed their fires upon us. My stomach flip-flopped. We were no match for a dozen pyromages at once. I bared my teeth in anger that Adam wouldn't fight his own fights, and my eyes unwillingly closed.

Another call broke the roar of the flames behind us, "*Duck!*"

CHAPTER THREE

With nothing to lose, Evan and I hit the ground hard, kicking up a cloud of ash. The massive jet of fire was just beginning to heat my scalp when something gigantic flew over our heads, pushing the jet back from where it had come.

I dared look up, my hands covering the top of my head to shield it from the fire. The gigantic metal barricade had been thrust forward with Rounan magic to not only stop the fire from roasting us alive but also to crush maybe a third of the Followers who had stood in front of Adam and Robert. I couldn't believe my eyes at how narrowly we had avoided death.

A few Rounans rushed forward to aid us, and a familiar hand alighted on my back. Sam's eyes bored into mine as I stood, worry creasing his brow. A lop-sided grin broke his face when he saw that I was okay, but then I glanced back toward where the remaining Rounans had come from. There was no one there. The rest of the Rounans had run as I had hoped, but that left only Sam, Evan, and I along with three of our neighbors. Against Rhydin's Followers.

Adam grew enraged at the scene in front of him as the rest of his Einanhi troop made their way back to join him in the center of town, their fiery assignment accomplished. His deep-set eyes shined in the blaze, his jovial mood gone. "You will all be hanged at dawn like the criminals you are! Surrender, you're outnumbered!"

I took a deep breath, forcing the air into the farthest reaches of my lungs, centering myself. Sam reached out to grab my hand and give it a squeeze, eyeing me once more. I nodded at him once more and looked to Evan, who gave me a curt nod in return.

We would stand our ground. We'd give as much time to the running Rounans as possible. It was a worthy end.

In only a second, all of us acted. Sam used his Rounan powers to lift two of the dozen Followers into the air and catapulted them into the burning buildings that lined the road like a flaming hallway. The other three Rounans engaged with Followers nearest to them, pointing their weapons back at them with the magic they could muster. Evan leaped into the air and angled charge after charge at the other Followers to drive them backwards, to concentrate them together.

I spun my sword in my hands, its weight more familiar to me than anything else by now, and then sped forward, my blade catching the back of an Einanhi's knee. The creation crumpled to the ground, unable to stand but not dead. Since it wasn't human, I didn't feel too bad about the second blow to end it.

When I faced the battle again, Adam had me in his sights. I stalked toward him, letting the firelight gleam against my sword. I'd been waiting for this ever since he tried to kill

Frederick before Duunzer attacked by throwing him off the balcony at the Winter Ball.

I didn't wait until I was closer. I began charging and slinging attack spells as hard and rapidly as I could, capable of so much more than I had been three years ago. Adam blocked each of them with his wind magic, being an aeromage like much of Lunaka's mages, but they kept him occupied as I grew closer. My fingers itched on my sword handle, aching to avenge countless innocent Rounan deaths and Gornish war casualties. Maybe, out of all the deaths I had inflicted over the last three years, this one would actually feel good.

As I continued my magical onslaught upon Adam, walking ever so slowly through the chaos around me as Sam and the Rounans handled the rest of the Followers, my ears were dragged away from Adam toward the flank of the battle.

"I will not fight you, Son. Please, let me explain everything. I want you to join me," Robert said softly, his hands stretched outward to Evan.

My brother shook his head violently, appearing more emotionally unhinged than I'd ever known him to be before. He shouted, "You abandoned us! Rhydin only wants us all dead!"

"No… That's not the case at all," Robert responded soothingly.

It was when Evan's defenses dipped that I knew I wouldn't be getting my revenge today.

I chucked another couple of attacks at Adam and then veered off my course, sprinting toward my brother and my father. The point of Evan's sword was nearly in the dirt when I skidded between the two of them, knocking Evan back as I threw my blade in Robert's direction.

Robert's sword clanged against mine, and frustration seethed from him. He raged, "Why won't either of you listen to *reason*?"

His sudden, blistering anger seemed to wake Evan, who thrust a magical charge at Robert while he was entangled with me, blasting him off his feet. Evan spoke gravely, "We don't reason with those who use Rhydin's dark magic!"

Evan and I both raised our hands, ready to begin again, when Adam abruptly yelled, "It's over!"

We turned to face him, and the blood drained from my face. Sam's neck was in danger of being crushed in Adam's grip, the former king's dagger pointed at his throat. Maybe five Followers remained, including Terran, who all leveled their hands at us, ready to unleash their fire once more. The Rounans who had stayed to help fight all lay on the ground unmoving.

"Any last words?" Adam sneered, his grip tightening on Sam. My husband gagged.

"Yeah," Evan answered, grinning so largely as his gaze shifted to the sky I thought he was crazy, "don't look up."

I tore my eyes away from Sam long enough to follow Evan's eyes, and hurtling towards us were four of my favorite Ranguvariians. Jaspen, Rachel, Luke, and James all flew in formation with their swords drawn, and relief flooded my system. The *Alyen nou Clarii*, the soldiers of the Allyen, were here to save the day yet again.

While everybody else's eyes darted to the sky, I concentrated a quick but potent magical orb into my hand and chucked it at Adam's head, well away from where it could possibly hurt Sam. It scraped right by his head, scalding the length of his skull on the right side. Adam bellowed with rage, but when his hand reached for his wound, Sam dropped to the ground and rolled away from him.

The Ranguvariians took out half of the remaining Followers with unhuman, deadly speed before they broke their formation and one of them headed for each of us. I lifted my hands to the sky just before Luke's rock-hard hands locked around my wrists, sweeping me into the air as his beautiful, shard wings flapped powerfully. James connected with Evan, and Jaspen snatched Sam off the ground before Adam could retaliate.

As Luke pulled me up by the wrists into a better carrying position, I caught both Adam and Robert's gazes before they vanished from sight. One full of fury and the other hard to read.

I only looked back once more before the Ranguvariians wrapped us within their glowing wings, ready to transport. The Rounan compound was entirely engulfed in flames that stretched high into the night, the smoke billowing upward to block out the stars and twin moons. Just beyond it was another, separate burning, and I knew in my gut that it was our house. A lump rose in my throat, unbidden. Another home destroyed by Rhydin and his Followers, just like my childhood home in Soläna had been. There was no choice of whether to go or stay now.

The blinding white light of transportation magic blazed, and the air changed. The humidity from the fire and the coming spring vanished, leaving behind thin, cool air, which was a shock to my lungs. I held onto Luke's armor tighter as my head adjusted, unable to see much of anything. Luke and the other Ranguvariians flew upward with their passengers, visible like colorful, glowing stars, and suddenly the rocky face of a mountain came into view.

The Ranguvariians neatly flew around it and a couple other peaks before my nose was assaulted by brine, my ears the crashing of waves. I realized where we were just as we rounded the last peak, a dim window appearing out of the darkness. Ice crept down my spine as the Archimage Palace loomed. If I'd had my way, I would have never laid eyes on this place ever again. Not after what happened last time.

To my relief, the Ranguvariians headed toward the light of an upper balcony rather than the front gate. I didn't need to see the ruin and devastation of the throne room again. I saw it plenty in nightmares. Where Archimage Dathian's throat was slit, Rhydin's cheek cracked like stone, and countless lives were lost. Where we failed.

No sooner did Luke set me down on the balcony than a figure rushed forward from the lit room within. Adrenaline still pumping, I reached for my blade before Luke touched a rocky finger to my shoulder. The figure collided with my brother in a fierce bear hug. My eyes finally made out the lavender curls in the dark, and I realized it was Cayce, Evan's wife. He whispered to her inaudibly before Rachel spread her arms, trying to corral us toward the doorway.

She spoke quietly, her eyes darting above us as if we were in danger of being seen on the palace's ocean side, "Inside, people. We got all the way here without incident, don't ruin it now."

Sam placed a heavy hand on my shoulder as we walked inside a rather bare entryway, and my arm automatically moved around his waist, short as I was. He smelled like fire, and his clothes were singed and sticky with sweat. I was probably the same, but I wasn't about to let go of him. I wondered if other couples worried about losing each other nearly as much as we did.

"It's been a long night," Rachel announced, and I gawked at her for reducing all the events that had transpired as nothing more before she continued. "The others will be arriving first thing in the morning, so you'd all best get some sleep while you can."

"The others?" I asked, my brow furrowing.

"Frederick and Cornflower are on their way. Hopefully Xavier and Mira will be as well, but we don't know yet. With the destruction of your Rounan compound, we need to decide as a group what comes next," Rachel answered dryly. "Your children are sleeping in the bedroom at the end of the hall. Bartholomiiu is watching them."

I waited for some sort of backhanded remark about how I'd disobeyed her by disappearing when she transported my children to safety, but it never came. Rachel appeared lost in her own mind, exhausted after all her frantic energy before.

It was unsettling.

The door on the opposite side of the sparsely-furnished entryway opened into a hallway, and Rachel, Jaspen, and her brothers turned in the opposite direction than Cayce did. Sam and I entered the hallway last, and I found myself surprised that, while I didn't think I had been in this hallway before during previous visits, it seemed as if it was utterly untouched.

Part of me had expected the Archimage Palace to be looted and trashed by either impoverished people or Rhydin's Followers. Instead, the only difference seemed to be a fine layer of dust and grime that had accumulated in the year since Dathian's death. Perhaps, Rhydin didn't care for relics reminding him of his status as First Archimage, or the general populace still didn't know where the palace was. Both were probable.

Evan and Cayce turned into a doorway just past an ancient set of armor that looked like it dated back at least a century if not more. Mineraltir's flaming tree crest still glinted upon it. Down the hall, another door opened to reveal a long, lanky Ranguvariian whom I'd know anywhere. He was dressed in brilliant yellow, orange, and purple robes, but it was his white eyes that gave me pause. They hadn't changed color since the incident.

I swallowed hard, my heart aching. "Hello, Bartholomiiu. Thank you for watching Kylar and Rayna."

To my surprise, instead of staring at me blankly like the last time I'd spoken to him, Bartholomiiu actually gave half a grin and nodded twice, the scar tissue along his neck crinkling where Rhydin choked and burned him. Even his snowy eyes turned the lightest shade possible of pea green, probably imperceptible to anyone who wasn't familiar with Ranguvariian eyes. Then, he walked away, and Sam and I gaped after him.

"That was the same Ranguvariian that couldn't respond to you at all last year, right?" Sam whispered, his eyes following the thin Ranguvariian until he disappeared.

"Uh-huh," I breathed, threads of hope weaving into my heart. "They weren't sure if he'd improve at all after Rhydin choked and burned him for so long. I'm glad they were wrong."

"Me too." Sam gave my hand a squeeze and then guided me through the door.

Sure enough, Kylar and Rayna lay snug and sound asleep in a couple bassinets fit for the children of Royals, so Sam and I didn't waste any time. Sam kicked off his boots and stripped his burned clothing and tossed it into a corner, likely irreparable, before he performed the quickest rinse of his arms and face ever in a wash basin in the corner.

While he did so, I finally removed the heavy rucksack that had miraculously remained on my back, burned though it was, and searched for a roll of bandages. When I turned around, Sam had already flopped forward onto the bed, sound asleep. I could only vaguely remember now that I had gotten a few hours asleep while he had gotten none, spending the night warning as many Rounans as he could.

I removed my own blackened and crusty clothing, and then set about bandaging the cuts and burns that decorated Sam's body, his arms bearing most of them. Then, I wrapped a couple strips around my fingers, which were a little singed and raw from shielding my head from the giant vortex of fire, tucked my back into Sam's chest, and allowed myself to unwind and sleep.

Sheer exhaustion allowed me to sleep for what I could only guess to be a couple hours, but it felt like I had only blinked when dawn's light started filtering through the lightweight, gauzy curtains that appeared to float in the ocean breeze. Sam was still a solid lump behind me, so deep in sleep that his breaths were hardly detectable.

I rose slowly, stretching my arms carefully as throbbing aches rumbled down them. It had been some time since I had fought so hard. My bare feet made slapping noises against the cold flagstones of the floor regardless of how quiet I tried to be as I made my way to check on Kylar and Rayna. The latter stared up at me with her bright, Allyen eyes, so I scooped her up and began a search for clothes so I could take her out and let Sam sleep.

A short rummage through the various dressers in our room revealed nothing but clothes suited for nobility. Long, colorful dresses made of fragile fabric. Elaborate suitcoats and fine trousers that looked like a knee would bust open the first time the wearer knelt to the ground. All of the shoes that were small enough to fit me looked like pajama slippers.

I wrinkled my nose. I wouldn't be me in this type of clothing. My desperate eyes glanced to the pile of crumbled, burned clothes in the corner that Sam and I had worn last night before landing on my blackened rucksack. I gave a sigh of relief and gave the dresser drawer a nice shove to reject what it had to offer.

After dressing in my only other set of normal clothes, a plain, brown tunic, tough, woolen trousers of the same color with a threadbare, black shawl for the drafty palace, I took Rayna and headed out the bedroom door. I was just thinking to myself that the cold, stone building was as silent as a tomb when I remembered that, quite frankly, it was one.

I made my way back down the ancient armor-lined hallway, intending to find the door to the ocean-side balcony we had entered upon last night. All of the armor was Mineraltin in style, each of them seeming to mark different decades as they evolved from crude, ill-fitting iron pieces to refined stuff that shined. We must have been on the Mineraltin floor, judging by the armor and the emerald banners every few feet. The Archimage Palace had floors and suites dedicated to all the Royal families of Nerahdis, even a suite for the Allyen where I'd stayed last time.

My hand was on the latch for the balcony door when a shiver tingled my senses. It was like I had almost felt another presence, but it disappeared before my magic could recognize it. I froze as Rayna babbled a little louder, wondering if I had imagined it. After a second or two went by, I gripped the latch tighter and raised it, beginning to pull the door open when I felt it again. Just a tremble of a presence coming from further down the hallway.

"Hello?" I called as loudly as I dared, seeing as people were still sleeping.

My word echoed through the dusty hall, and while there was no verbal response, I felt another ping of a presence. My mind raced with memories of the strange, distraught presence I had felt before I left the palace after Dathian's death as well as Arii's stories of Dathian's "ghost."

I shook my head and turned to Rayna in my arms, trying to calm myself. "Perhaps, Frederick or one of the other Royals is getting close. Let's go meet them, hmm?"

Rayna gurgled, her tiny mouth hanging open in a smile simply because I was talking to her, but I took it as agreement. I closed the door to the balcony and walked to the other end of the hallway where the main staircase of the palace appeared.

Again, it appeared utterly unchanged from the time I had lived here for a few weeks while Archimage Dathian conducted his experiments to discover why an Allyen would not be born naturally after Evan and I. The spiral, marble behemoth stretched from darkest black on the main floor to the whitest of whites at the very top, and it appeared the Mineraltin floor resided at about the slate gray portion of the spectrum.

I moved to go down the stairs, steeling myself for whatever remnants of that horrific battle still existed, when I felt another tug on my senses. The pull made me glance behind me at the stairs leading up, instead of the ones going down. I swallowed a little hard. If it was a Royal, they'd surely be arriving downstairs. Not up.

Well. I'd faced far more dangerous situations in the past, right?

Taking a deep breath and holding Rayna tight, I magically summoned my sword with my other hand, just in case. Out of habit or paranoia, I wasn't too sure. Regardless, I began the climb up the stairs. Past the third floor, the Auklian floor on which Evan had roomed during our stay since there was only one Allyen suite. Past another floor that appeared Lunakan in style, and then the floor I had stayed on. I kept waiting for some sort of nudge to give me some sort inclination as to whether to exit the staircase or keep climbing, but none came.

As the staircase reached its height, turning snowy white from an ash gray for the Allyen floor, I reached uncharted territory. The top floor was reserved for the Archimage, and I had never stepped foot upon it the times I had been here before. It was Dathian's personal space away from the rest of the Palace. Had been. I grieved more for our failure than the arrogant, pompous man himself.

Sure enough, at the landing for the Archimage's floor, the faint presence gave me a push, a little stronger now, but still so small and weak that I likely would have never felt it if I hadn't been all alone.

This hallway was just like the rest of the palace; black onyx flooring and white marble ceiling with all the shades in between stretching up and down the columns. However, while the rest of what I had seen of the palace had been mostly untouched aside from a layer of dirt and dust, this floor had been trashed. Tapestries had been ripped down from their hangings, and the navy carpet that lined every hallway had been removed entirely. Suits of armor and other decor had been pushed over or ripped to shreds. Portraits lined the walls on both sides, all of people, but those, strangely enough, looked like they hadn't been moved.

On my left, Dathian stared back at me, in painting form. The deep blue of his eyes was unmistakable, although it seemed the artist had been very forgiving of the natural flaws in any human being's appearance. I was beginning to hear noises downstairs, but my curiosity was too piqued to stop.

I walked slowly forward, carefully stepping over the strewn-about paraphernalia. Even Rayna somehow sensed the strange situation we were in and no longer made her constant babbling noises. As we passed more and more portraits of stately-looking people, it hit me that these were all the Archimages Nerahdis had ever had. Men, women, all nationalities, all ages, all Royals who likely weren't in line for the throne. We passed doorways that appeared to lead to bedrooms and living spaces and a majestic library, but no gentle push toward any of them.

At the very end of the hall, I realized that one portrait had been set on the floor between two others, the only one in the whole area that was not still on its nail. The portrait on the floor was of a thin, unremarkable Mineraltin woman, but my breath hitched in my throat at the sight of a much younger Rhydin residing within the final portrait. Or, I guess I should say the first portrait.

A shiver rolled down my spine with the reminder that Rhydin had been the First Archimage, especially with this proof. His likeness commanded my attention; I stared at him, nose to nose, and almost couldn't believe what I saw.

It was definitely him, but he was so unlike the Rhydin that I knew. The Rhydin who had halted his aging in the mid to upper twenties, who had unleashed Duunzer, who had sparked the corrupt, Nerahdian war, who was now emperor in the evilest way possible, who was never to be seen without his death glare or huge, midnight cloak.

The Rhydin in the portrait was so young. Eighteen at most, if that. He was swamped in the regalia of an Archimage, which displayed subtle hints at each of the Three Kingdoms' couture. His dark hair was shorter, tidier, and his familiar, amethyst eyes appeared huge on his slightly less pale face, emphasizing both his youth and…dare I say it, innocence. I couldn't stop gawking. Time had frozen.

How did such a young boy become Archimage of Nerahdis? He looked so *small*. What in the world happened to him to make him the Rhydin I knew now?

An unintelligible call floated up the staircase from down below just as I finally felt a vague pull in the direction of the final door in the hallway, just to the side of Rhydin's young portrait. I walked in hesitantly, only to find a small study that had similarly been upended. Ancient papers, books, crumbling tools that I could only recognize enough to having something to do with astronomy, and various writing utensils were littered about the floor. Bookcases lined the room, their shelves sagging or fallen, and one of them had been tipped over entirely. A bulky desk sat mostly undisturbed in the middle of the room.

My skin crawled. The strange presence that had weakly beckoned me here was at its strongest in this room. Yet, my sword pointed to the floor. I couldn't sense any malice in this presence now. Only sadness and loneliness. A breath of wind pulled me further into the room to where I could see a small trapdoor in the corner sitting open.

Another call sounded from the staircase, louder this time. The presence reacted in a tizzy, pulling on me as hard as it could manage toward the trapdoor. The sad desperation of it made me move faster, so I walked around the desk and began to descend the cold, misshapen steps beneath the trapdoor. I didn't get to the bottom before my chin was forced to the left, right in line with a stone shallowly etched with the seal of the Archimage. Nobody would see it in the hazy light of the trapdoor unless they knew it was there.

I withdrew my sword and dug out a dagger from my boot. Then, one-handedly, I dug it into the paste between the stones, which crumbled from centuries of existence, freeing the marked stone. I put my dagger away, pulled the brick out and set it on the floor, and reached inside up to my elbow, hoping there weren't any creepy-crawlies back there.

"Lina, where are you?" I heard Rachel call from much closer, probably this floor, at the same moment my fingers touched leather.

CHAPTER FOUR

I yanked the book out of the stone wall like it had bit me and rapidly fitted the stone I'd removed back into its spot. I didn't know why, but for some reason, I didn't want Rachel to know what I was doing. I shoved the book into my big cloak pocket, then tripped up the steps and back out into the hallway.

The guiding presence had faded away now that I could sense Rachel nearing the top of the staircase. I jogged down the hallway as far as I could before Rachel's willowy form appeared on the marble landing, and I slowed to a walk.

Apprehension melted into relief before screwing up into suspicion on her freckled face. "Lina, what on Nerahdis are you doing all the way up here? Didn't you hear me calling?"

"Uh, yeah, sorry," I replied, trying not to breathe too hard. "I was just exploring to keep Rayna from waking the whole floor, and I didn't hear you until you got closer. What's going on?"

"The Royals are here, we've been waiting for you downstairs," Rachel chided, gesturing back toward the staircase, "Come on, we don't have all day! It's dangerous to be all together like this."

I nodded, quickening my stride, and then we descended the staircase together. The heavy, leather volume thudded against my thigh with every step I took, and I searched the back of my mind for that pitiful, forlorn presence to no avail. I could sense no one beyond Rachel's warrior-mother-hen air, as well as the other Royals downstairs as Rachel ushered us closer.

To my relief, when we reached the ground floor, Rachel pulled us in the opposite direction of the massive throne room. I never wanted to see that place again. Instead, she guided Rayna and I down a hallway that ended with another balcony overlooking the sea. About halfway down, she turned through a reinforced wooden door into what appeared to have once been a small conference room complete with the same table that Dathian, Arii, and I first met around so long ago.

Gathered around the table now were Frederick, Mira, and Cornflower. It gave me pause to see the three siblings together again. So much had changed since my childhood of growing up terrified of these three Lunakan Royals' mysterious wind magic. The years had not been kind.

Frederick was my age, twenty-three, yet he was beginning to look a full ten years older. His hair was no longer the goldenrod of our late teen years. Instead, it was a dull straw color that was coming away at his temples. His wiry frame was thinner than when I'd last seen him the day Dathian died, and his ice-blue eyes seemed sunken into his skull. Cassandra's death had altered him forever. Dominick, their toddler son, was the image of the young Frederick I remembered, and he sat in his lap as still and silent as stone, which unnerved me.

Mira was dressed in bright, Mineraltin green, although her outfit was more in line with someone in hiding rather than the queen she should be. She looked older than her years as well, but not quite to the extent of her older brother. Cornflower, identical to the dark-haired Mira in every way except for her wavy blonde tresses, appeared too young to be sitting at this table.

"Where's Xavier?" I asked, the words spilling out of my mouth. At Frederick and Mira's pained expressions, I realized I probably should have known better.

"He didn't want to come. He is home with Taisyn," Mira mumbled, her violet eyes downcast.

I eyed Frederick carefully. Was their feud really still ongoing after so many months?

The future king of Lunaka cleared his throat, his eyes hard. "Has Xavier still not accepted that it is not my fault Taisyn was blinded by Robert, Rhydin's Follower?"

"I know, Frederick," Mira sighed, her hands gripping the knees of her skirt. "In my husband's mind, he still thinks you should have been home with your family rather than away in Auklia."

"I was just trying to help Daniel!" Frederick's voice rose. "And to show the people of Lunaka that I was working to end the war! Daniel refused to fight and was trying to reveal the truth about Rhydin."

Mira remained silent, unwilling to engage in an argument that had likely been fought hundreds of times wherever she and Xavier currently called home. I wilted inwardly. I had hoped by now that their feud was over. In the corner, Sam, Evan, and Jaspen stood silently with similar expressions on their faces. I assumed Sam must have left Kylar with Bartholomiiu again.

Frederick pinched the bridge of his nose, a movement I had witnessed too many times to count, until he took a deep breath and turned to me. "Sam was telling me of the destruction of your compound. I am sorry to hear you have lost your home," he said quietly, and then turned to Rachel, "I also understand that this is why you have called us all here?"

Rachel, my best friend and future Clariion, leader of the Ranguvariians, took her place at the head of the table as I grabbed a seat next to Frederick, settling Rayna in my lap. Sam and Evan came to sit on my other side as Rachel began to speak. "There are a couple of matters we need to discuss this morning, all of which are of the utmost secrecy and importance. This is why I asked everyone to come rather than depending on messengers, Ranguvariian though they may be."

I looked to Sam at the sound of that, but his eyes remained on the marble veins of the table in front of us. I wondered if he was still grieving the loss of the compound, our failure to protect the people there.

"The first matter concerns the destruction of the Rounan compound. Tomorrow morning, Jaspen, Bartholomiiu, and I will be escorting the Allyens and their families off the continent," Rachel stated, matter-of-factly, avoiding eye contact with both Evan and I. "With the Lunakan Royals in the mountains and the Mineraltin Royals in the Great Desert, my grandfather feels that we should move the Allyens to an entirely different location to keep Rhydin from wiping us out one blow. This will be in an area of Caark we have chosen."

Sam went rigid beside me, but he didn't say a word. I bit my lip in an attempt to keep my anger to myself. I still wasn't on board with this. How was leaving the continent going to get the population to realize Rhydin was evil? But the thought of my children's safety kept my teeth locked together.

"That's probably wise," Frederick responded stiffly.

I angled daggers in his direction with my eyes. Unfortunately, both he and Rachel noticed.

"The other matter," Rachel announced anyway, "is the status of the Kingdom of Auklia."

Mira piped up, "Were you able to discover the identity of the green-haired woman in Dathian's portrait miniature?"

"No," Rachel admitted, her energy faltering. "My grandfather and I have scoured the known parts of the Auklian Royal family tree with no results. Dathian may have been Daniel's uncle, but when a Royal becomes the Archimage, they are struck from the tree to keep them from favoring their kingdom of origin in continental affairs. We haven't even been able to discover a living relative who knows of Dathian's personal life, even if they happen to remember he was originally Auklian."

"Did Daniel have any other cousins whatsoever?" I asked, "Surely he must have some sort of long-lost aunt or uncle of a grandparent or something!"

"I doubt it," Frederick murmured, shaking his head. "The Auklian Royals have always historically had small families. It's been a belief of theirs for centuries to keep the Royal bloodline small and exclusive to stop any remote chance of a challenge to the throne. They often only produce one heir unless it is Auklia's turn to supply an Archimage, in which they allow two. Dathian was an extremely rare second-born."

"Then what would they do when this happened in the past? When the king dies, his father is gone, and he has no heir?" I grumbled, wondering how the Auklians could be so foolish.

Frederick shrugged. "I don't know. If Duunzer hadn't disrupted the order of things, we would have Daniel's son at least."

"The point is," Rachel interjected, regaining control of the room, "Auklia is a hotbed for Rhydin's supporters with their lack of a ruler. To them, the only possible future is Rhydin. We cannot allow this to continue, and the Ranguvariians have...failed in their investigation. We need help."

I gaped at Rachel. I had never heard her admit that the Ranguvariians had at failed anything before.

Frederick's next words flowed soothingly over the room. "Well, anyone who knows they are remotely related to the Auklian Royals will be in hiding as well. Cornflower and I will start moving around the mountains and foothills to see if there are others who could possibly be connected to Auklia in any way."

"Xavier and I will do the same in the Great Desert," Mira's voice chimed. "Both locations share a border with Auklia. It may be our only hope."

"If any of you come across others in hiding, you should start talking to them about Rhydin," I spoke tersely, allowing my teeth to unlock. Rayna stared up at me with her Allyen eyes, unused to my hard tone. "We're not going to kick Rhydin out of power by hiding from the world. We need to grow the number of people who realize Rhydin is evil and needs to be stopped if we have any hope of succeeding."

In the silence that followed, Frederick and Mira glanced at each other, perhaps realizing for the first time that we couldn't wait for the people to come to that conclusion by themselves anymore. Cornflower eyed them both, appearing confused.

Rachel took a deep breath, and then sighed, facing me for the first time during the whole conversation, "It's not that I don't agree with you, Lina. We just need to get you and your children to safety and find an Auklian heir, or we're doomed regardless."

I gritted my teeth and crossed my arms. She had a point about the Auklian heir, but I couldn't stand by and do nothing!

"If that is all," Rachel said, scanning the room briefly for anyone else to speak, "then we will plan on beginning our journey to Caark in the morning while the Royals search their respective locations for someone who could be a distant Auklian Royal. Meeting adjourned."

Sam was up from the table in a heartbeat while most everyone else filtered out like gravy. I rose to follow him, wondering if I needed to make sure he was okay, and I made it to the hallway before I heard a call behind me.

Frederick entered the hallway as the others dispersed, his expression weary as he balanced Dominick on his hip. The shadow of a smile crept at the edges of his lips, but the effort seemed exhausting. He mumbled, "You never responded to my last letter."

Heat flooded my face. Ah. His last letter where he had flippantly disregarded my life's work as a farmer. I stammered, "Uh…sorry. I got busy."

The Lunakan prince paused, his eyes measuring my expression carefully. He had always been the most observant of the Royals, which played well with his usual role as mediator. While I tried my best to make my face slack, I knew it wasn't good enough. Frederick looked down as he whispered, "You know, I always appreciated being able to write to you. You can imagine that I do not have many friends, and having someone to write to while isolated in the mountains with no one but Dominick and my little sister…it's kept me more sane than I might be otherwise."

"Frederick," I groaned, dashing my fingers through my bangs, "I truly meant to write you back, I promise. I just…needed time to decide how I wanted to write back, that's all."

Frederick's lightening brow quirked. "What do you mean?"

"Let's just say that sometimes I think you forget that you and I come from *very* different spheres of life, Frederick," I grumbled, letting my frustration vent. I began to turn to go find my husband, who was probably just as mad as I was about being forced to leave the continent, but a hand snagged my sleeve.

"Wait, Lina," Frederick said softly, his eyes begging. He eyed Rayna in my arms uncomfortably. "I apologize if something I said was callous to you. It certainly was not intentional. May I still write to you?"

Suddenly, it felt like my anger was bubbling over. I yanked my sleeve out of his hand and responded bitterly, "Yes, Frederick, you can always write to me, but you shouldn't be sitting around, living in isolation, and twiddling your thumbs! I know Evan and I are the Allyens, but we can't do everything in the fight against Rhydin if we want to succeed."

The prince tilted his head, and I felt so angry I could have slapped him.

Peasant girl slap a crown prince. That would have landed me in the gallows once upon a time.

"Think about it, Frederick. The Three Kings have never gotten along or worked together in nearly all of history. Just look at your father and the other rulers, and realize how easy it was for Rhydin to split them apart," I said, my words turning from anger to pleading, "The new kings need to get it together, Frederick, not just go into hiding and stay separated and isolated from their people. You and Xavier need to put this stupid feud behind you and search for an heir to Auklia or that kingdom will be lost forever."

"But, Rachel-..." Frederick tried to interrupt.

"I know, I know, by all means, we have to keep our children safe or there really is no future," I conceded slightly as my eyes dropped to little Dominick. "If anything happens to your son, then Lunaka will be in the same position as Auklia is now. Trust me, I get it. But, don't sit on your hands either. Search the mountains for an heir as you promised, but talk to people about Rhydin too. Sow the seeds of discontent, and hope they spread like dandelion seeds on the wind. People talk, Frederick. You don't have to travel the whole world to reach them all."

Frederick gaped at me for a few seconds, my words visibly washing over him slowly like the ocean's tide. After those moments of silence, he nodded and said, "You're right. I will. Are you going to do the same in Caark when you get there?"

"Yes," I answered slowly, pausing. I'd never been to Caark. I didn't know how much it chose to associate itself with the rest of Nerahdis. Of course, I would try, but there was no escaping the burgeoning thought in my mind that it was the people of the mainland that could help us the most. If I couldn't help from Caark...that wasn't the place for me. I would have to think on that a little more. As I turned to finally follow Sam, I looked back and added, "Yes, I will do the same in Caark. I have to try. I need to find Sam, so I'll see you at lunch."

Frederick nodded a few times, looking like he was still absorbing everything I was saying, and I broke into a brisk walk down the hall back toward the staircase. The brick-like book in my cloak pocket bounced awkwardly, so I put my hand against it to stop it from moving and being noticeable. For whatever reason, I still felt like a kid who had swiped some candy from the mercantile for taking the book. I was anxious to look through it and discover its importance, but now wasn't the time.

I took two steps at a time up the gargantuan, marble staircase back to the second floor, the Mineraltin one we had slept on last night, and trotted down the hallway once more. Sam's presence, smelling of Lunakan earth, wafted down the hall, undetectable to anyone but me because he was a Rounan and I was his wife, so I knew I was in the right place.

The door to our room was standing open, and when I entered, I found Sam silently staring out the window at the great expanse of water, Kylar in his arms. He seemed strangely still, and he didn't turn when I entered. I neared him slowly, in an effort not to scare him. "Hey."

Sam barely turned his head enough to see me through the corner of his eye, and then he turned back to the ocean. "Hey," he repeated, his voice gravelly.

"You okay?" I asked cautiously, my fingers reaching the rough threads of his sleeve as I set Rayna on the floor.

My husband took a deep breath and then placed Kylar by his sister where the two began to play with some wooden blocks that Bartholomiiu must have brought them. Sam levelled his gaze at me finally. "I'm not going to Caark."

My heart sank, wondering if I was really hearing him correctly. "What? You said you were coming with me just yesterday!"

"I know." Sam grimaced, his hand reaching out for mine and gripping it tightly. "That was before the compound was destroyed and my people were scattered. I *need* to know how many of them made it to safety. I can't leave not knowing and without establishing some sort of communication-...."

"No," I interrupted. Sam stared at me. No matter how often we disagreed about things, I didn't often cut him off entirely. "I can't leave without you. I need you to be safe too."

"Lina-..." he tried to begin again, frustration mounting.

"The Ranguvariians can establish a communication line. The mountains are their expertise anyway. But if I leave you here and you're killed... I would never forgive myself." My hands turned into fists. "You're going. Even if it's just to get the kids to safety and regroup. We can make a new plan when we get there."

Before Sam could respond with that temper of his, I spun on my heel and stormed out of the room. He couldn't say no if I didn't give him the chance. I managed to get halfway down the hallway before I whirled and kicked one of the ancient suits of Mineraltin armor. It clamored to the floor with the sound of a hundred pots and pans, but it didn't make me feel any better. How could Sam insist on staying behind? Why couldn't he just come with me without arguing? Was he Kidek first or my husband?

I groaned loudly and sunk to the floor against the cold, stone wall, partially hidden by the pile of armor I likely ruined. Everything seemed hopeless. What if we couldn't kick Rhydin out of power? What if we'd already failed and just didn't know it yet?

Suddenly, what felt like a hand brushed along my shoulder. My head bobbed up from where it had fallen against my knees, hoping it was Sam, but I was still alone in the drafty hallway. I reached out with my magic, trying in vain to sense any presences until I stumbled across the same, vague presence from before. I could hardly feel it behind Sam's much louder presence just a few rooms down. If I hadn't sensed it before, I probably wouldn't have even noticed it. My fingers trembled a bit, but the scarce presence didn't seem threatening. Instead, it reminded me of the book in my pocket.

I glanced up and down the hallway to ensure no one was coming before I slid the fragile volume from my cloak pocket. The cover was so worn, I wasn't sure whether it was leather, like Lunakan books, or some other material. It looked like the corners used to be gilded in gold, but they had long lost their shine and color, instead appearing a greenish black. Some characters used to be inscribed on the front, but they were long gone. This book had to be a hundred years old, if not older.

The pages were in surprisingly good condition once I gingerly opened the cover, trying to support the broken spine. I expected them to be faded or fall apart between my fingers, but instead, the pages were crisp and their print was like new. Magic was the only answer.

I lifted the book to my nose and breathed its scent down into the lowest recesses of my lungs. It definitely smelled like a moldy castle wall, but underneath that was a similar magic to the strange presence I kept sensing. It had preserved this book over the centuries. It led me to find it. It seemed only right that I try to uncover its secrets. Maybe, it would help me understand this strange presence locked away in the Archimage Palace.

I thumbed over to the first page, and my heart plummeted. This book was not written for the average commoner whose reading ability was characteristic of the only education a village school could provide between work shifts, which was leagues behind any Royal's education. I could make out maybe half of the words on the first page, the much smaller ones, but not enough to fully comprehend it without some serious study and likely some help from Frederick.

As I settled for flipping through the pages to see if there were any pictures, I tried to reassure myself. Years ago, it may have taken me a few weeks, but I was able to slowly teach myself to read the old myths and legends book that included Duunzer during my time hidden away in the Owenses' livery basement. Therefore, I could definitely learn how to navigate this book, even if it was the last thing I did.

Just as I was beginning to think that this book didn't contain illustrations, a full page of colors popped into view. My heart nearly stopped. It was a portrait of two people, and the one on the right was none other than a much younger version of Rhydin, about the same age as his First Archimage portrait upstairs. Again, he looked no more than eighteen, and the expression on his pale face puzzled me. His brow was drawn, and he stood very straight like he was trying to appear older than his years. Ultimately, I could detect a tinge of fear in his amethyst eyes, a feeling I had never remotely seen anywhere near the Rhydin I knew now.

The person on the left was a much older man dressed in the richest regalia of gold and purple I had ever seen. His long face was heavily lined above a neat, slate gray beard with white streaks through it, and he was far taller than Rhydin even in his old age. He looked like he had seen worlds take their first breath and breathe their last. I glanced at the caption underneath, pausing to sound out the names I hadn't seen before.

"Emperor Caden and the new Archimage, Rhydin Caldwell."

Rhydin knew Emperor Caden. For some reason, I thought the Archimage position wasn't created until after Emperor

Caden's death. Not only that, but...Rhydin *Caldwell*. A family name humanized him in a way that I never once considered. I wondered if this book could give me any sort of hint of how Rhydin Caldwell became the Rhydin I knew. Was he just a twisted, power-hungry kid? Or did something else happen?

I stood to go find Sam again and tell him of my discovery when the mysterious trickle of a presence suddenly washed over me with the feelings of panic and warning. The overwhelming sensation rocked me, causing me to fall forward onto my knees. I looked around frantically, trying to figure out what could have caused such a reaction from a presence that had been nothing but quiet and weak before.

It was less than a minute before I figured out what the warning was for. My friendly presence dissipated in the wake of a far more powerful one, one that encompassed my magical senses entirely. An ancient, cruel darkness. Rhydin.

Rhydin was at the Archimage Palace. He was here.

I stuffed the book back into my pocket and stumbled to my feet once more, throwing myself inside the nearest room facing the south, toward Lunaka instead of the ocean. Below, a huge army had amassed. They were all dressed in black and purple, waving the flag of the new emperor, which combined Rhydin's old gold and red flame symbol with the purple color of the emperor that hadn't been seen in centuries. Hundreds of people stood at the foot of the mountain ready to charge the palace, and more were marching forward with every second that passed.

We were surrounded.

Fighting the urge to back away, I scanned the regiments closely. I recognized a few of Rhydin's loyal Followers as commanders, but all of the legions were new faces. People who had pledged their loyalty to Rhydin after he "freed" them from Archimage Dathian's control as the Liberator. Heat raced through my veins. They were so painfully clueless, and it was my job to get them to see the truth.

But how?

I finally noticed Rhydin himself standing near the front of his army. I couldn't make out his face from this distance, but he looked larger than the others because of all the fancy robes he was wearing. Crossing my arms, I waited for him to make the first move. To fire some sort of magical charge to begin bombarding the palace, or to send up some sort of purple flare to tell his legions to attack.

But, it never came. Instead, Rhydin signaled with his hand, and his Followers began to lead their respective troops forward, all equipped with plain swords and shields, bows and arrows. I couldn't sense any magic down there at all.

It hit me all at once. Rhydin had won the people over by claiming Dathian had abused his magic to control the Royals and create Duunzer. Every soul on Nerahdis was terrified of magic, just as I had been before I was told I was an Allyen.

Rhydin was hiding his magic so his loyalists would continue to trust him.

That was how I could expose him as a fraud. Reveal to the masses his magic. And what better timing than to do it right now in front of hundreds of common soldiers who were fresh from the War of the Three Kingdoms? The war they all thought put an end to their oppression by mages.

I was just about to bound up on top of the balcony railing, my mind brimming forth with different ideas for spells that I could use to force Rhydin to reveal his hand, when the bedroom door banged open behind me. Mere seconds passed between my looking over my shoulder to see Rachel barreling toward me and her long, rock-hard arms colliding with my back.

Screaming and writhing were no use for her Ranguvariian strength, and my world filled with white as I glanced back at Rhydin in vain. I could have sworn he saw the flash and smirked.

The instant we landed hard on solid rock, I threw myself from her loosened grip and exploded, "*Rachel*! What's *wrong* with you?"

Rachel's red brow furrowed, and she crossed her arms as I realized we had an audience. The others from the Archimage Palace; it appeared I was the last to arrive. She answered firmly, "Uh, I just saved your neck, and *you* were the one off hiding instead of finding us to evacuate. You're welcome."

I growled in my fury, "*I* was *just* about to solve all our problems!! Rhydin is hiding his magic from all his new supporters! I didn't realize it until today, but it makes total sense! The people of Nerahdis think that Rhydin liberated them all from magical leaders, if we expose him, he's ruined! I was just about to do that when you took me away without even listening to me!"

Sam and Evan stared at me in awe, both of them beginning to nod slowly as the idea seeped in. We had always figured that what happened at the Archimage Palace last year was common knowledge. How Rhydin invaded and slew Dathian by magical means. Apparently, it was not.

"I'll give you a hand, Lina, you have a point. But, do you really think Rhydin's stupid enough to fall for that? He had the element of surprise and his backup numbered in the hundreds. Even if magic was necessary to defend himself, I guarantee you, he'd have had one of his old Followers take the fall for him," Rachel chided, her blue eyes narrowing and turning to ice. "I promise to take your idea under consideration, but that was not the time nor the place for it."

I wilted, childishly refusing to believe her. I could have done it. Just one, well-aimed spell from that balcony directed at Rhydin, and all this would have been over. A balcony that was...hundreds of yards away. Where anyone could have seen it coming and raised a shield. Or Eli, Terran, or any of the other old Followers with magic could have countered it, and faced the consequences later.

Rhydin was nearly three hundred years old and had been planning out everything for centuries. Trying to kidnap Evan and I as children, orchestrating Duunzer and the war, and pinning the blame on Dathian. He surely had measures in place to keep his magical abilities hidden.

Rachel may have been right this time, but I would outsmart those measures if it was the last thing I did. I sighed heavily, "Fine."

My red-haired friend nodded, albeit grudgingly. I hoped she was telling the truth when she said she'd consider trying to make my plan happen. She turned to the others and announced, "We make camp here. The Royals have already been transported back to their respective hiding places. Tomorrow, we move out."

CHAPTER FIVE

W e spent the night in what appeared to be an abandoned rock quarry that had once gnawed an entire chunk out of one of the mountains, like a giant had taken a bite out of it. Aside from that, and the fact I could still vaguely smell the ocean on the other side of the range, we were never told where in Lunaka the Ranguvariians had transported us when Rhydin threatened the Archimage Palace.

Sam and I remained wordless throughout the evening and into the morning, when we all awoke to find ourselves covered in leftover white powder from the old excavation site. I could sense his temper radiating from him, and I wondered, as we went about our usual routine of readying our children for the day in a strange place, if he had willingly gone with the Ranguvariian who evacuated him from the palace, or kicking and screaming as I had. I decided not to ask since he was here and wasn't currently threatening to leave to go find the Rounans.

When we set off the next morning, I was surprised to discover that we would be traveling the old-fashioned way on horseback instead of Ranguvariian transportation. Rachel and Jaspen were both convinced that Rhydin had somehow tracked our transportation from the burning Rounan compound to the Archimage Palace using some sort of magical residue, a theory that flew right over my head.

Therefore, several Ranguvariians brought us horses in the night, and the sight of them made my shoulders slump. This journey was going to take far longer than I ever imagined. Especially once I realized that with our young children, the horses would have to walk instead of gallop or even trot. It was going to take at least two weeks to reach Canis, the port town in southeastern Lunaka where I would take my feet from Nerahdian soil for the first time in my entire life.

The first day passed in silence, most of us still absorbing the shock of Rhydin's numbers and ability to find us so quickly, so I spent my time looking at the scenery and making sure my gelding remained on the hardened path ahead of us to avoid leaving tracks. At the end of the third day, I stiffly slid from my saddle, my muscles roaring with pain. I was iffy on when the last time I'd ridden a horse was, but I knew that I'd never done it three days in a row.

Bow-legged, I set Rayna on the ground. She squealed in delight after being stuck in the saddle with me all day besides a few breaks, and I turned to unpack my horse. As I did, my eyes caught the sight of something familiar on the horizon, barely visible with the setting sun. It looked like nothing more than a deep wrinkle in Lunaka's face from this distance, but the meager firelights scattered around it and the vague silhouette of Lunaka Castle confirmed my suspicions.

The canyon that housed Soläna. The city of my childhood that I had not laid eyes on since the day Duunzer covered it in darkness.

My heart ached. I stared at it for as long as I could. The sun was dropping rapidly beyond my city, making the canyon and the land around it appear the most brilliant of crimsons. The constant Lunakan wind was subsiding slightly, and I knew Lunaka's twin moons were rising behind me as I faced west.

Sam came to stand next to me just as the last vestiges of light disappeared behind the western mountains, and the shape of the canyon and its castle sank into darkness. It had been his childhood home as well. Sam rested a heavy hand lined with blisters from the leather reins, identical to the ones on my own hands, on my shoulder.

I looked to him slowly, and our eyes met. Things still hadn't quite gone back to normal after our argument just before Rhydin's armies arrived, but when he leaned forward and planted a kiss on my forehead, I put my faith in the hope that everything would be okay. He silently walked away to help Cayce collect some firewood, leaving me wishing for more and wondering if I should have broken the silence first.

Once Luke and James got the campfire going, I gingerly lowered my tired, aching body to the ground close enough to its heat and far enough that I could watch Kylar and Rayna to keep them away from it. I pushed my rucksack under my head and pulled out the history book to which the strange presence had guided me. I'd stopped hiding it after leaving the palace, and all of my companions seemed to think it was a book from home.

I stared at its worn cover for a few moments, wondering when I would get a response from Frederick to my last letter.

At least half of it was a list of words I was trying to define so that I could read this book, although the other half did try to strike up some new conversations as well as ask if he'd spoken to anyone yet about Rhydin's true nature. I was just about to crack the book open for another go when Evan sat down next to me.

My brother closed his eyes and leveled his chin in concentration, just as he had started doing every evening since our journey had begun. I watched him discreetly, fascinated by this process but too afraid to admit that I didn't understand it at all.

At such close proximity, I could feel Evan's magic swell within him, like the first light of a sunrise. My own power responded within me at such a surge, the twin of Evan's, which was what always made it impossible for me to ignore Evan's spell. Even Rayna would sometimes look to her uncle suddenly in confusion, even though I knew well enough that her magic hadn't awakened yet.

In front of Evan, a small, golden orb materialized, about the size of a cherry before growing to roughly the size of a crabapple. Then, the orb became oblong with an offshoot as Evan reopened his eyes and muttered, "*Anadlu.*"

Instantaneously, the yellow blob burst like a bubble, and in its place was the usual adorable squirrel, its fuzzy fur black as midnight just like the rest of Lunaka's squirrels. Evan watched it for a few moments, as he always did although I didn't know why. Then, he whispered, "Keep an eye on the camp. Alert me if you see anyone."

The squirrel bobbed its tiny head and then scampered off into the small patch of woods we had stopped in for the night to do its master's bidding. Evan had created an Einanhi. That much, I could understand.

I tucked tonight's creation into the back of my mind as I had done the other two evenings I had witnessed this, ready to turn my attention back to my book. It didn't do to dwell on a cute, tiny creature who was destined to dissolve into sand in the morning when Evan's purpose for it was fulfilled. I was thumbing to the first page when Evan caught my eye before I could keep my watching from his notice.

He measured my slightly fear-filled expression at having been discovered, and then he cracked a rare grin. "You don't know how to make one. Do you?"

Heat flushed my cheeks. "Maybe I do, maybe I don't."

Evan chuckled, "Do you want to learn?"

Alas, my brother had discovered my weakness.

I slapped my book shut and returned it to its home in my rucksack, carefully wrapped in a swatch of leather to protect it from my journey. As I scooted closer to my brother, Evan eyed my movements suspiciously with those Allyen eyes of his. "What is that book you read every evening anyway?"

"Uh…" I stuttered, freezing slightly as I thought. "Nothing really. I haven't entirely found out to be honest. It's a…project I'm working on with Frederick."

"Oh. Interesting. You'll have to tell me about it when you're finished." Evan gave a small grin before his face relaxed into his usual somber mask. "Daniel was the one who taught me how to really use my magic" – Evan paused, but he didn't allow any emotion to cross his face at the mention of the deceased Auklian king – "While he could never create an Einanhi himself, he was able to supply me books with which I could teach myself. Creating an Einanhi requires very complicated and rather powerful magic. It is not a feat that any mage can accomplish, especially the larger and more complex the creature becomes. I can't create anything much larger than a small dog myself, but I haven't really tried to make anything bigger."

My ears soaked up every word like a sponge. I had encountered so many Einanhis in the last several years, yet I still didn't fully understand how they worked. I knew they were shells of magic and not truly living from my time receiving magic lessons from Frederick in the Owenses' basement. And, I knew that Rhydin had created all of the Einanhis I'd met so far: Duunzer, the dragon that covered Nerahdis in darkness, Birdie, the little bird that lived next to my childhood home that had been spying on me, and the countless, bland-featured humanoids that Rhydin had among his ranks.

But as to what went into creating them? How they actually worked? No idea.

"First, you have to really concentrate on your magic, focusing it out in front of you. You'll need to make sure you have your half of the locket too, because doing this is downright impossible without it," Evan stated, his hands moving absentmindedly. "I don't have enough power to make another Einanhi tonight. Since I gave my power to my squirrel willingly, I'll be back to tip top shape in the morning, even if I don't reabsorb it like I usually do. That's why Rhydin has so many Einanhis running around without it affecting his power. His magic just regenerates after making them since he did it on purpose."

I thought for a moment. "Is there ever a time where your magic wouldn't regenerate after making an Einanhi?"

"The only time your magic would ever not come back is if someone steals it from you, but that's pretty rare," Evan admitted. "There's a lot of science involved in that like your magic and the thief's magic being *perfectly* compatible and a bunch of other complicated circumstances. Plus, you'd *really* have to screw up making your Einanhi. It's really only possible in prime conditions, so you really don't have to worry about it, I promise."

I nodded slowly, waiting for him to continue as Sam and Cayce returned to the camp, their arms laden with firewood.

"I'll try to talk you through this the best I can. You'll want to decide in your mind what kind of creature you want to create, and then picture it the best you can. How big is it? What sounds does it make? What does it smell like, and what kind of texture does it have? How does it move? All that is why I usually make a squirrel," Evan chuckled, "They're pretty straight forward. The hard part is pushing your magic out of yourself and into that form. It's a precarious process, and if one thing goes wrong, you're in trouble."

"Trouble?" I asked, my brow furrowing. "What kind of trouble?"

"Well, if you don't give the Einanhi enough magic, then it'll die or be deficient physically or mentally when you create it," my brother answered as he grimaced. "Then again, if you give it too much magic, it'll disconnect from your will entirely and be uncontrollable."

"Is that a bad thing?" I murmured and turned to stare at the fire, thinking of how mindless it must be to only exist to fulfill another's will.

"Very," he said firmly. "Even when given too much power, it's not like an Einanhi is given all the same instincts as a real animal or reasoning abilities and emotions as a real human. An uncontrollable squirrel is one thing...an uncontrollable dragon or humanoid like what Rhydin makes? It could be absolutely devastating for not only the creator, but all of Nerahdis. That's also the kind of situation where you could suddenly find all your power stolen if the conditions are absolutely perfect."

The blood drained from my face. I imagined Duunzer not under any sort of control. Rhydin may have created it to destroy, but he had mostly been focused on finding me and taking my locket. As hard as it was to believe, Duunzer had its limits, albeit destructive ones. If it had been left to its own devices... I shuddered at the thought of how much *more* pain, devastation, and death it would have likely wrought.

"You have a point," I responded quietly. "How do I know whether I've given the Einanhi too much or too little of my magic?

Evan's eyes glazed over as he peered off into the distance. "To be honest, it's one of those things that just comes with time. You have no idea how many squirrels I've made that couldn't move their limbs or almost bit my fingers off. With practice, you'll find the thin line down the middle."

A shiver ran down my spine.

"Once you've given your Einanhi the exact right amount of power, the only thing left is to speak the incantation. While we normally don't have to speak a word to cast our magic, creating Einanhis requires such a massive amount of power that it's necessary to finish the spell," Evan said seriously as his eyes drifted to the fire. "Rhydin is so ridiculously powerful that he doesn't have to speak the incantation. He can just think it, and the Einanhi is. I've seen him do it once."

Fear crept into my heart. Yet another reminder of how much power Rhydin wielded. How could one man be so powerful? I turned to Evan slowly. "The word you said. *Anadlu.* What does it mean?"

Evan met my gaze. "It means 'breathe.' In Old Gornish. Just like 'Einanhi' means 'puppet,' though that word made the transition into our modern Gornish language that developed when our ancestors moved from Gornan to Nerahdis."

That information washed over me, definitely the kind of history they didn't teach in the village schools. I let myself sit in it and absorb it, along with all the steps of creating an Einanhi, trying to commit them to memory. I would have been content to sit like that for the rest of the evening until we went to sleep if Evan hadn't interrupted me.

"Try to make an Einanhi."

"What? Now?" I asked panickily, my fingers digging into the dirt around me. "You literally just gave me a verbal lesson, and you want me to try and make one right now?"

"Why not?" Evan shrugged. "It's not like we're busy doing anything else."

I anxiously looked around the fire. Sam had Kylar in his lap and was feeding him hardtack and beans from the blackened kettle over the fire. Rayna looked like she had already been fed and was passed out on a blanket next to her father. Cayce had come to curl up next Evan, resting their tiny son against her chest. I couldn't tell if she was awake or not, there were such circles under her closed eyelids.

After building the campfire, Luke and James had disappeared, likely on guard duty with Evan's Einanhi squirrel, and Jaspen and Bartholomiiu snoozed next to the fire, probably readying for the next shift. Rachel sat quietly next to her slumbering mate, looking lost in thought. I hoped they all stayed that way so I wouldn't have much of an audience.

My heart began to hammer out of my chest. I didn't feel prepared for this at all!

"You can do it," Evan reassured me. "It definitely won't be perfect, but you won't learn without trying."

I pushed air into my cheeks, probably appearing much like Evan's squirrel, and then blew it out slowly, biding my time as I ran through all of the steps again. My hand left the dirt and reached for my locket, which hung around my neck just as it did every hour of every day for as long as I could remember. It still helped to hold its warm metal when I really needed to focus on the magic in my body.

Instead of a squirrel, I imagined a bird. Small, easy to think of, right? A bird no bigger than the palm of my hand, one with the bright red plumage of a Lunakan wren. I played its song in my head: a high-pitched squeal accompanied by light coos and rattles. Once I had the image of the bird firmly in my mind, I pushed my magic outward, and a gold orb appeared just like with Evan's Einanhi. I tried not to let myself get too excited, and instead focused on how much magic I needed to give this little bird. I could feel my magic siphoning from me already, and I panicked. What if I had already given it too much?

As the orb grew to the size of a lemon with a few golden sprigs growing from it, I hurriedly whispered the incantation, "*Anadlu!*"

The bubble of magic popped, revealing a beautiful Lunakan wren, but only seconds passed before the little Einanhi collapsed into a pile of feathers. I gasped and leaned forward on my knees over it, and the poor bird stared up at me with its beady eyes, chirping weakly. It reminded me of a baby bird I'd found as a child after it had fallen out of its nest. I couldn't hardly look at it. The sight of such a tiny animal in such a state stabbed my heart, and I immediately turned to Evan, warbling, "What's wrong with it? How do I fix it?"

Evan's expression was grim as he pressed his lips into a thin line. "You didn't give it enough magic. It's too weak to stand. All you can do now is reabsorb it."

"How do I do that?" I asked frantically.

"You're still connected to it magically. Find that connection and break the bird back down the way you created it," Evan answered stoically.

Rapidly, I found the tether in my mind that linked the bird with me and drew upon my magic. The wren evaporated back into tiny glowing spheres that quickly disappeared, and I breathed a sigh of relief.

A few moments of silence went by as Evan measured my expression. He spoke slowly and carefully as he said, "Remember, Lina. It's just an Einanhi. They're not real."

My shoulders slumped as I stared at the little patch of dirt where my failed bird had lain. I could barely see it now that the sun was beyond the western mountains where Mineraltir lay. Evan shrugged a half-witted, nonverbal apology, and turned to his wife. Apparently, our lesson was over.

Glumly, I stood and shook my rucksack and blanket of any dirt they had collected, and tiptoed my way around the silent, exhausted camp to where Sam sat beside our slumbering children. He gazed at the fire forlornly, still upset about being forced to leave Lunaka. I squeezed his shoulder, just enough so he could feel my love but not so much that necessitated a response, and then I laid out my blanket and rucksack again. I plopped down, stretched my weary muscles, and peered up at the darkened sky. No stars were visible tonight, and it made me feel that much more isolated from the rest of the world as I fell asleep.

The next morning, we all fell back into our routine of feeding the three children breakfast, packing everything up,

Evan's absorbing of his Einanhi squirrel, and mounting our horses yet again. I tried very hard to put the image of my weak little wren out of my mind, but it wasn't working. As I climbed my tawny gelding and the Ranguvariians at the front of our party began our walk, I looked over my shoulder.

Soläna still lay there in the distance, nothing more than a long, dark hole since the town itself was buried so far below. Wisps of black smoke lilted from the canyon as the churning heart of Lunaka's capital, the mines, pumped into existence for the day ahead. Morning light reflected from the castle windows as servants opened them to air the Royal chambers. Homesickness flooded me so hard that I could smell the earthy, coal dust and hear the whisper of the wheat heads rubbing against each other in the Lunakan wind.

With every hoof my horse planted into the ground on the path away from Soläna toward Stellan and Canis, the port town, it seemed like miles of distance were materializing between me and the people I was supposed to be helping.

CHAPTER SIX

A s days bled into weeks, I found myself no longer looking at the world around me. It hurt too much. Instead, the days brought letters to and from Frederick via Ranguvariian, which allowed me to spend my endless hours in the saddle decoding the rich language of the Archimage Palace's history book.

Thankfully, Frederick never asked why I spent the vast majority of our letters asking for definitions of words that I painstakingly copied from the book when no one else was looking. While I wasn't anywhere near finished, the first several chapters were transforming from confusing, lofty words to meaningful – and downright surprising – stories.

The first few chapters detailed accounts that I had heard before in school, although in a much less sugar-coated way. While my meager education had glossed over such topics as the enslavement of the Rounans, it had completely left out things like stealing land from the indigenous Ranguvariians and the establishment of the Archimage position. This book gave the real story.

I knew the nostalgic tale of how my ancestors were the few lucky ones to evacuate not only Gornan, their homeland oceans away, but Rounia as well where they stopped and acquired "helpers" before having to leave once again. They then "discovered" Nerahdis and created a new order that would avoid the corruption of Gornan and Rounia under Emperor Caden, the youngest son of the previous Gornish emperor, who promised a different world.

While this book did agree that Emperor Caden had the best of intentions, it painted my ancestors' story in a far darker light. The Rounans were slaves, and even once they were freed, they were kept from being equal in other ways. My limited education also had suggested that Nerahdis was utterly empty when the Gornish arrived, but this book detailed how the Gornish took advantage of the "ignorant" Ranguvariians who believed they could share Nerahdis. Instead, they were pushed back and back until the Gornish had control of everything. Our history apparently wasn't as golden as they taught in the schools.

When Emperor Caden's three sons, Joshuua, Ivann, and Spenser, became of age, he divided Nerahdis into the Three Kingdoms I knew today to keep his sons from starting wars over who would inherit. Joshuua became the first king of Mineraltir, Ivann of Auklia, and Spenser of Lunaka. Even after doing this, Emperor Caden could foresee that his sons would begin to quarrel as soon as he was gone, so he created the Archimage to keep the Three Kings in check. This story mostly matched up with what Dathian had told me last year, but it was the next chapter where things turned mind-blowing.

Emperor Caden sent scouts all around Nerahdis to discover someone who could become the Archimage. The book got confusing here, even though Frederick had sent me definitions for all the words, because it started discussing magical theory that was quite frankly so far over my head it hurt. What I could decipher was that not anyone could become Archimage. Emperor Caden believed it had to be a young man who, while not being born with magic, had the capability of receiving it.

This reminded me of how we had to search for Rayna. A newborn born of mages to whom we could bequeath Allyen magic because otherwise she would have been too old and her birth magic too defined. Emperor Caden's theory was a bit different, but similar, although I didn't fully understand it. It sort of made sense that he needed someone more the same age as his sons instead of a newborn, although I'd have to do more research as to how it could even work on someone so old.

They searched for two years before they found a boy named Rhydin Caldwell. An eighteen-year-old from a town in Lunaka that no longer existed: Diagalo.

I was getting toward the end of what I had managed to translate into common terms, but I couldn't keep my nose out of my book. Rhydin was the only child of a wealthy, Lunakan merchant, and he was described as a "good-natured, young man with a lot of potential and a knack for astronomy." While I gawked at this, the scouts apparently thought him such a good candidate that Emperor Caden met with him within the week.

As I turned the page, I nearly pulled a lock of hair out at my frustration. The narrative pulled back out! It didn't detail how Rhydin became Archimage, or if it was even his choice! It only gave a brief summary about Rhydin being successfully given all the different magics of Nerahdis – fire magic, water magic, *and* wind magic – in order to transform a common boy into someone with dominion over the Three Kings.

This astounded me. I shook my head in sheer disbelief. So much power given to such a young boy. It far exceeded what I'd had to deal with when my Allyen magic awakened. Then, to my dismay, the chapter ended.

I slapped the book shut loudly as I returned to the real world in frustration. I was still waiting on Frederick to supply me with my latest list of definitions before I could decode the next chapter, so I couldn't find out what happened next yet. Groaning, I tucked the book away and resituated Rayna in front of me.

By the looks of the sun and how much our horse had slowed down, I guessed it was nearing evening. We crossed the second river a few days ago, which meant we were very close to Canis now. If I didn't know any better, the regular prairie speckled with trees around me suggested I was just as close to Soläna as I'd ever been.

Sam's mahogany stallion clopped along in front of me, so I squeezed my gelding faster to catch up, unable to stop thinking about my book. I'd yet to share it with anyone, but my mind brimmed with so many questions and observations that I felt like I *needed* to tell someone about what I'd read right now. He still wasn't quite speaking to me, so I hoped that the surprise of this information would pique his interest and open him back up so we could return to normalcy again.

"Sam, I've gotta tell you something!" I said cheerily, although only loud enough for him to hear.

"Oh?" Sam answered quietly, his eyes darting to me quickly before returning to the road ahead of our caravan. Kylar snoozed on the saddle horn in front of him.

"It's about that book. The book I've been reading. It's a history book about when Rhydin became the First Archimage!" I gushed, eager to finally share my secrets with my husband.

That earned more of a glance from Sam, although he still returned his gaze to the road. "I'm surprised that even exists. Where did you get it?"

"Uh," I uttered, gulping. My "helpful presence" story seemed awfully insane at the moment. "That...uh...that doesn't matter! This book is about Rhydin! The Rhydin he was *before* he became the Rhydin we know!"

"Lina, those books were all destroyed centuries ago. Why do you think everyone forgot Rhydin even existed? The First Three Kings were so ashamed of their failures that they wiped him from history, even from the Archimage Palace itself. The Rounans tell of it," Sam grumbled, turning toward me fully, finally giving me the attention I desired but not in the way I ever imagined. "Besides, we all know you're not very good at reading."

Heat flushed my cheeks. I tried to ignore the dagger in my heart, crying out, "I trust who I got the book from! And I may not read very well, but Frederick has been helping me! This book is *real*, Sam. I'm trying to share it with you of all people."

A pained expression flashed across Sam's face. For a split second, it looked as if I had slapped him in the face, but it was rapidly gone, which puzzled me. Once it became apparent that he was not going to respond, I urged my horse faster once again in my pain, leaving him in my wake.

How could Sam be so callous? I knew we'd had a falling out over leaving, but that final silence was so out of character for him that it felt like being rubbed with sandpaper. I peeked over my shoulder once or twice, eyeing Sam's glum expression out of the corner of my eye, but I stayed ahead of him. Childish or not, it was him who needed to apologize and cross the gap between us now. I'd tried.

After several minutes of staring at the veins of copper in my gelding's otherwise nut-brown mane, I noticed that a different horse had slowed its pace to walk aside mine. The thin Bartholomiiu beamed back down at me from the height of his seventeen-hands-tall, midnight-black horse, his eyes again shading the lightest of colors of pea green into the sea of white. He was covered head to toe in a heavy cloak, as always, to prevent other travelers from realizing he wasn't human. My eyes grazed across the horrific scarring that would forever mar his throat and darted back to the copper strands in front of my hands.

"Believe you, I." A raspy, nails-on-a-chalkboard voice said.

I rapidly met Bartholomiiu's gaze, shocked at both that he could speak and that he'd heard my conversation with Sam. "You do?" I asked.

"Yes!" Bartholomiiu nodded like his head was on a spring.

A smile cracked my weary heart. I was just about to share everything else I had learned with Bartholomiiu, anxious to ask for his advice on how to handle this information, when suddenly, one of his long, pointed ears twitched.

As the rest of the caravan came to a halt for whatever reason, Bartholomiiu's eyes were washed pure white again as he stammered incoherently, "Why green are the trees?"

My shoulders slumped like air being let out of a balloon, but I said nothing. It was my fault Bartholomiiu was like this. That in some ways, his mind had been reduced to the capacity of a child's. But he had already improved so much, so I hoped even more that he would continue to do so.

Ahead of us were only Rachel, James, and Evan, sitting still in their saddles as their horses pranced and kicked their legs. I motioned my gelding forward to see why we had stopped, seeing as we probably still had an hour or two of daylight left of the day. Bartholomiiu followed me automatically, his personality gone for the time being.

There were three people dressed in clothes littered with holes standing next to a wagon that was stacked to the heavens with every material possession a person could own. Rickety chairs, barrels of supplies, and clinking iron pots and pans were roped to the sides and tops. Their wagon was hitched to a couple starving-looking mules pointed southwest, the same direction we were going.

Although Rachel had slowly become quieter with each day that passed, she had apparently already quizzed the three tired travelers with the usual questions disguised as niceties: why they were headed to Canis and so on and so forth. I wasn't quite prepared for the turn their conversation had taken when I reached earshot.

"Emperor Rhydin is the best of men!" declared the youngest of the three travelers, a man who appeared to be in his upper teens or lower twenties. "He's cut taxes on the common folk and raised them on the rich!"

"Yes!" An older woman added, coils of black hair sneaking out from under the kerchief on her head. "If it weren't for him, we could never've afforded food after the crop failed. Those Royals and nobles have far too much money anyhow!"

The eldest of the travelers, an aging man, piped up, "I ne'er thought I'd live to see the day the Royals were struck down. Things're finally looking up!"

My brow furrowed. I cut Rachel off before she could respond, "What do you mean the crop failed? Planting season just finished and Lunaka has had plenty of rain. What part of Lunaka are you from?"

Rachel eyed me with icy daggers, a silent warning not to reveal who I was.

"The Canyonlands 'round Soläna, ma'am," the young man answered as he fingered his threadbare hat gingerly. "We got just the right amount of rain, you're right. But the seedlin's never came up. Plumb died right there in the ground despite all the sunshine and rain. Pa's never seen anything like it!"

The color drained from my face. How could this be? The Canyonlands contained some of the most fertile ground in the kingdom. I should know, I grew up there. Spilled my blood, sweat, and tears there to reap a living from the ground as an adult and alongside the man I called father as a child. Some years were rough, of course, but this had been a good year. There was no logical reason why the crop would have failed so early.

Unless it had nothing to do with the weather or the land or the seeds, nature in general, at all.

With Rachel's eyes boring into me, I shook my head, pushed my horse back into a walk, and said softly, "I'm sorry to hear it. Perhaps Emperor Rhydin isn't all he's cracked up to be."

The three travelers stared at me in confusion, but I left them in the dust. I had to say something to even remotely shake their confidence in Rhydin, even if it was subtle. Regardless of whether the blooming, possibly far-fetched theory in my mind was true or not. I'd need more evidence first.

We traveled the rest of the day before making camp at the last tree line. After weeks of patchy prairie and forests, the horizon was beginning to level out, and I could vaguely detect the sting of salt in my nostrils. We were so close to Canis, my aching back, legs, and rear sang their song of exhaustion even louder. Maybe tomorrow, Rachel had said. Tomorrow. For the first time, I was actually looking forward to reaching Canis since it meant not having to sit in a saddle day after day after day anymore.

Seconds before I could drop to the hard earth after feeding Rayna her supper, a hand tapped my shoulder. Evan's gaze was level with mine when I turned. "It's time to try again, Lina. It's been weeks."

I grimaced, the image of my poor little wren twitching on the ground too much to bear. "No, thanks. You can be the Einanhi-creator of the family."

"Lina, they're not real! Their pain isn't real."

"It sure looked real!"

"You killed Duunzer without batting an eye," Evan muttered, crossing his arms over his chest. "How is this any different? Besides, once you get familiar with the process, that'll never happen again. This is a skill you *need* to know."

I groaned, "Duunzer was an evil dragon trying to kill everybody, there's a difference!"

"Even so," my brother answered quietly, "your ability to make an Einanhi could make the difference between your life and death."

My jaw clenched tight. "Fine."

I slid to the ground quickly and set Rayna onto her wobbly feet to allow her to run around for a little while before bed. In hopes of getting this over with as soon as possible, I instantly shut my eyes and recalled all the details of my little Lunakan wren that I had painstakingly conjured up the first time. Then, I took a deep breath and focused on the warm spot in my chest until I could push my magic outwards.

Once again, an oblong, golden orb slightly smaller than my fist materialized in front of us, and my anxiety heightened as it began to draw magic from me. I felt its drain clearly, yet I waited, wanting to make sure that it got enough this time. I didn't want to see another floppy bird on the ground when the bubble of magic burst. After a few more moments, I cut it off and said, "*Anadlu.*"

The orb of magic vanished, and in its place stood a slightly larger than normal Lunakan wren, its red breast puffed out. A flood of relief washed over me when the bird continued to stand strong, tilting its head from side to side, instead of collapsing into a ball of feathers again. I smiled, and I noticed Luke and James stationed on the opposite side of the campfire nodding at my little creation.

"Alright," Evan broke the silence as he stared at my Einanhi warily, "give it an order."

"Uh, okay," I answered breathily, excitement still pumping through my veins. Turning back to the bird, I said, "Go keep watch."

Instead of ushering itself off obediently as Evan's squirrel did night after night, the bird remained stock-still for perhaps five seconds. Then, it went utterly berserk.

The wren squalled and darted around the campsite as nothing more than a red, feathery blur. James cried out and was suddenly holding his elbow, Jaspen dove to the ground as it soared above his head, and Sam crouched down over our kids even as the bird delivered a hard peck to his scalp. I barely saw the bird before I felt a sting of pain in my neck.

"H-How do I stop it?" I cried, searching in vain for the magical cord that I had felt with the first, powerless Einanhi I had made that had allowed me to reabsorb it. It was gone!

"There's only one way now," Evan answered, eerily calm even in the midst of the insanity.

He stood, angling his finger at the lightning-fast bird, waiting and watching as it scurried around from person to person. I wondered what he was doing until the wren dashed toward Rachel, who had been cooking our supper over the fire.

With a *clang*, Rachel raised her greasy, iron skillet in the nick of time to smack the Einanhi bird before it could injure her as well, all without dropping a single piece of browning meat. The thing gave a shudder before it slid off the skillet, dissolving into that familiar sand that all dead Einanhis turned into before it could reach the ground.

Five pairs of Ranguvariian eyes and two human pairs turned to level their gazes at me. Only Evan spared me from his as my teacher not wanting to embarrass his student.

Heat flooded my face and neck. "I'm so sorry, everybody…"

Bartholomiiu began to laugh as Jaspen tapped Luke on the shoulder, and the two walked away from the fire to take first watch. James rubbed his elbow and then delivered it into Bartholomiiu's ribs along with a jab in Ranguvariian. Sam just stared at me sadly, still in his strange little world separate from me that I just couldn't wrap my mind around, until Rachel came around with bowls of her finished stew. Kylar seemed to be the only one he showed any attention all these weeks, but he diligently kept the boy safe and fed him before himself.

I couldn't argue with that, no matter how strange things had turned.

Evan returned to my side as Cayce accepted her own bowl of stew while cradling their son, and he seemed content to tuck in as if nothing had ever happened. Rachel handed me a bowl quietly. I let it warm my hands for several moments even though they didn't really need it in the warming springtime, staring at the bobbing chunks of rabbit and carrots in their brown bath. My throat closed upon sight of it, so I focused on shredding all the chunks as it cooled before feeding my bouncing toddler who had raced back to me with a goofy grin and a shiny rock in her pudgy hands.

After I finished feeding Rayna her dinner, I guided her over to where Sam and Kylar were curled up in a blanket made up of some sort of animal hide that I didn't recognize. I knelt and stretched my weary body before gathering Rayna into a warm little ball and scooting backwards until my shoulder blades met Sam's. Even though I couldn't understand Sam's behavior, my heart was still his, and it craved being near him even through it all. While Sam didn't so much as twitch in response, I fell asleep quickly.

It was mid-morning when the horizon suddenly stopped expanding out in front of our caravan. It appeared like an optical illusion in my mind's eye, the road just continuing into the sky even as we were rapidly approaching the edge of Nerahdis itself. The stench of salt was overpowering now, and the moisture in the air was palpable even though beyond the road's end was simply gray sky. As Rachel continued to lead us forward, I actually began to wonder if her horse would either sprout wings and fly or plummet to an unknown death. Where was the ocean?

My horse was a few feet behind Rachel's when hers reached what I thought was the end of the road and pivoted to the left a full ninety degrees before beginning to descend. Confusion skittered through my veins as my horse also reached "the end" and turned to follow. There was a very narrow, zigzag path carved out of what was actually a cliff wall, and I had to look straight down to see what was beneath us.

Hundreds of feet below this sheer drop-off and terrifying path was the town of Canis nestled between the towering edge of Lunaka and the lapping waves of an ocean far lower than I'd ever imagined. I gaped at it the entire way down after using a long, leather cord to tie both Rayna and Kylar to me, Sam having given me the latter for once surprisingly. Even then, I kept my hands firmly planted on both of them.

As we grew closer, it appeared that Canis possessed its own kind of culture just as Soläna and Lun were both unique for being in the same kingdom. It didn't have the height or wealth of Lun or the distinct social districts of Soläna. Instead, Canis seemed to have a ramshackle layout of taller buildings back toward the cliff wall and shorter shacks closer to the water's edge with all the other heights in between. After an hour or two, I could make out the roofs of the buildings closer to the shoreline. They were constructed of heavy, green tarps and old, blackened fishnets that seemed centuries old. I could only wonder if their colors were original or mold as we finally reached the bottom.

"There it is," Rachel breathed, although her voice was still drenched in apprehension. She gestured beyond the village to the docks. "The *Moon Jumper*. The ship that will deliver us to Caark."

My eyes roamed from the buildings and the stocky frames of their inhabitants to something that I'd only ever seen illustrations of in books or paintings. A rocking wall of wood rose from the frothy waves just beyond the farthest dock, and its hull was blackened from its hundreds of voyages. Tiny, circular holes dotted the upper portions of the ship while rising from its deck were trees of stained, navy linen. These massive sheets billowed in the breeze along with an entire network of ropes that appeared to me as a tangled mess.

As we rode through the town and grew closer, I could see dozens of thick, rugged men hauling ropes and chests to and fro, and the part of me that remains a child wondered if any of them had done any pirating in their days. I turned to Rachel, aiming to elbow her as I voiced this funny thought, but I paused at her stressed, vacant expression. I asked, "What's wrong? We're here, aren't we? Not much longer and we'll be in Caark."

"It's not that," Rachel answered, swallowing hard.

"Then what is it?" I implored. I began slowing my horse to stop and give her my full attention, but she tugged me along toward the docks.

My red-haired friend sighed and lowered her voice so that only I could hear, "I just learned that there are new rumors spreading among my people. That Rhydin has been trying to capture a Ranguvariian. Apparently, he's been spotted close to our camps, and he's been scouring the countryside trying to find our little caravan."

"But why?" I shook my head. "What would he gain by capturing a Ranguvariian?"

By this point, we had reached the docks. We all disembarked from our horses, but I kept Kylar and Rayna aloft on each of my hips away from the waves and the unsteady, wooden walkway. Rachel gave several rapid, short instructions to a sailor who was missing all of his front teeth as Luke and James began unloading our horses of their cargo for the last time. Jaspen and Bartholomiiu had remained at the top of the cliff, and they would join us on the ship after it had departed in order to draw as little attention to their seven-foot frames as possible. Sam met my eyes ever so briefly, his face ashen. I briefly found myself wondering if he was the type to get seasick.

Once the sailor nodded at Rachel and he had stridden away to gather help for loading our miniscule amount of luggage, she turned to me once again and whispered, "My grandfather thinks Rhydin may be trying to study Ranguvariians. To figure out how our magic works. After all, if he can somehow remove us from the equation, you Allyens wouldn't have nearly as much help."

My heart sank, and my eyes widened. "But there's no way he could succeed in capturing a Ranguvariian, right? I mean, you guys are like warrior extraordinaires! You even scare *me* sometimes."

The corner of Rachel's mouth twitched upward and back so quickly I nearly missed it. "I know. But Rhydin is Rhydin. I'm the next Clariion, and I *must* protect my people. We have certainly learned by now never to underestimate him."

"True," I conceded. A new worry entered my heart, and I wondered how many I could bear.

The lot of us followed our belongings in the hands of the sailors along the crowded docks, and I found myself needing to firmly focus on each step I took. I had never walked on something that wasn't solidly rooted in the earth before, and each step made me feel like I was falling one way or another. Of course, Rachel walked surefootedly as if she was flying, and I jealously wondered if it was more Ranguvariian magic at work. The number of people bustling around to and from other ships didn't help.

When we reached the gangplank, a homely little thing that had absolutely no spare inches to give, Rachel took Kylar and Rayna from me without even asking so that I could focus on my balance. I shimmied my way up without daring to look back, although I was somewhat sure that Evan, with his years of living in watery Auklia, was braced to catch me from behind if necessary.

I gave a big sigh of relief when I reached the main deck, which was also bustling with activity. The ship rocked slightly less than the docks below, so I stared at my feet a couple of seconds, trying to acclimate myself to this new feeling that wasn't going away anytime soon. The salty wind ripped through my hair relentlessly up here in the open, and I peeled the strands away from my face as I turned back toward the gangplank.

Both Evan and Cayce had reached the dock now with Luke's head and shoulders close behind. When James's head appeared, I began to wonder if Sam would be okay without anybody behind him, seeing as he was just as unused to being on the water as I was. I took a few careful steps to the battered railing that seemed awfully short to keep anyone from falling overboard, and to my confusion, there was no one behind James on the gangplank.

My brow furrowed as I shot a glance around the deck, thinking that perhaps Sam came up without my noticing. Plenty of people, but no six-foot, bandana-wearing farmer types.

Panic took hold as I leaned over the railing, desperately scanning the crowd below for some sort of ruckus, some sort of evidence that Sam had been detained by one of Rhydin's people or something.

A woman tugging along a squalling child. A man yelling out his prices for his catches of the day. A girl running up and down the dock with a messenger bag.

A man pulling a hood over his bandana as he carefully disappeared among the crowd heading back into the town, no confrontation in sight.

CHAPTER SEVEN

My heart shattered. But I wasn't about to stand around and do nothing.

I flung myself back over the railing and slid down the gangplank, knocking into a woman in a large, lacy dress in the process. She shouted at me, but I sidestepped her and trotted as fast as I dared up the perilous dock. Rachel's confused calls were drowned out by the creaking wood and deafening chatter of those around me.

I'd lost my visual of Sam as soon as I left the ship, but I continued running and diving through people and cargo, fishnets and their slimy inhabitants. The crowd spread out significantly as soon as I reached shore, and the steady ground beneath my feet shot me forward faster. I ran back the way we had come, reaching out with my magic frantically and becoming frustrated when my senses returned with nothing.

Sam was a Rounan. Most of the time, you could only sense Rounans by being within eyesight, but I could usually sense Sam within probably a quarter mile regardless of whether I could see him or not due to our bond. Of course, we discovered last year that Evan and I's combined power could sense him anywhere in the world, but that wasn't at my disposal right now.

People stared at me like I was a lunatic, but I kept going. Lightning struck my system once I was maybe halfway between the docks and the treacherous path up the cliff. Sam's earthy presence resonated in my mind, but it wasn't straight ahead. Instead, I jetted off onto a sideroad, which was dim because of the amount of fishy laundry stretched out above my head. Yet, there was no mistaking the tall, cloaked figure that loomed ahead of me.

"Sam!" I yelled, gasping for breath through the stitch in my side. When he didn't turn around, I shouted again as I slowed to a stomp, "*Sam*!"

My husband silently turned and simply stared at me, his brown eyes blank.

I swallowed hard, trying to contain my ragged breathing as I reached for him. "Sam…what are you doing? Why…didn't you board…the ship?"

"You know why, Lina," Sam answered tersely, his voice gravelly. "Now, go back, and get on that ship."

I looked at him like he'd gone mad. I grabbed onto his wrist as tight as a shackle. "No! Not without you!"

Sam shook his head and made to continue moving in the opposite direction, trying to pull his wrist from my grip. "You don't understand."

"*I* don't understand? Seriously? You are *not* the only person feeling like they're abandoning their duty here!" I argued, my voice pitched high with anger. "How many times do we have to have this fight, Sam?"

He stopped moving, but he didn't look back at me, his wrist suspended behind him.

"Do I think hiding in Caark is a good idea? Of course not! But I know we at least have to get our children to safety before trying to reevaluate and return!" I said firmly, my voice falling slightly. A knife pricked my heart as my next words tumbled out. "Even then, I would *never* walk away from you."

Sam whirled around, his face red. "Lina, this was the only solution I could come up with! How many times do I have to tell you that I. Can't. Leave? Not during my people's biggest crisis in three hundred years!"

"So, what, you were just going to vanish? Thinking none of us would notice that you simply weren't on the ship with us?" I started screaming at him, my arms crossing over my chest as I released him.

"Do you think this was *easy* for me? To push you away from me to get used to the idea of you not being in my life?" Sam's temper exploded.

"Then why didn't you tell me?" I cried.

"Because you would have done exactly what you're doing right now!" he yelled. "Lina, I need you and our kids to be safe!"

"There you two are! You're about to miss our ship, what's going on?"

Both of us froze briefly at the sound of Rachel's call from the end of the sideroad. She stood there expectantly, her pale hands in fists on her hips. She shouted again, "Come on! This is the last ship to Caark for the whole week!"

I turned back to Sam and snipped out of Rachel's earshot, "I'm not going without you. And if you think I'm some sort of damsel in distress who needs protection and can't fight alongside you, then I don't know who I married anymore."

Pain entered Sam's eyes, and his voice turned quiet and frightened. "Lina, please…"

"We go to Caark. We see what good we can do from there. We reevaluate our plans when we can. Got it?" I stated matter-of-factly, my emotions shutting down completely.

Sam slowly nodded, his temper dissolving completely into sadness and hurt, which only fueled my anger. He reached for me cautiously, threading his fingers through mine and going for some sort of hug, but I began walking briskly back toward Rachel before that could happen.

I kept holding his hand tightly, a link I wasn't willing to break until we were safely out into the open ocean where he couldn't simply disappear. I swallowed the tears that threatened to spill forth as we passed Rachel, and she said nothing as she ushered us back toward the docks and onto the ship that was getting ready to pull away.

Evan, Cayce, Luke, and James all stared at us as we reached the deck, but mercifully, none of them said anything. I maintained my hold on Sam's hand until the gangplank was hauled away and the sails were repositioned into the wind. The ship moaned underneath us as she caught the powerful western wind and propelled forward. Just as I was getting ready to drop Sam's hand, Rachel elbowed me and gestured discreetly back toward the gray, soggy town of Canis and its menacing cliff.

At the very top was a figure I'd recognize anywhere, although at this distance he looked more like a very tall, orange smudge. Clariion Arii, leader of the Ranguvariians, was seeing us off from the mainland of Nerahdis.

He could likely see me a lot better than I could see him, so I placed my hand over my heart, where my locket lay, and gave a respectful bow to acknowledge him.

To my surprise, he bowed much deeper in return, the orange smudge doubling over.

I stared at Arii a few more moments before he and the rest of the cliff, the town, and the docks melted away into grayness. Until it all was just gone. Struck from existence by a painter's brush, yet I knew it was still there underneath. Waiting for us to rescue it.

People wandered about around us, chattering to their companions or staring wistfully at the foaming waves beneath us. Nearly all of them appeared Lunakan by their clothing, although there were a handful of Auklians mixed in. They stood out like sore thumbs with their rainbow-colored silks and bright hair colors. I hoped maybe they would keep our large, ragtag group out of the spotlight.

It was only seconds before Rachel approached an elderly Auklian couple standing at the railing, him in a set of scarlet red robes and her draped in ornate, sapphire sashes. The Ranguvariians were still doing their best to discover the identity of the woman in Archimage Dathian's miniature and if she was the rightful heir to the throne.

As the ship really got underway, the sailors minding their jobs and the passengers dispersing to find either their rooms or their dinner, I finally dropped Sam's hand like it had burned me. Evan continued to stare at me, his arms laden with my two children as Cayce held their own child, and I felt in my bones that he could probably guess what had transpired.

My brother nodded at me, and I took that as permission to spin on my heel and head to the ladder that led belowdecks. I had no idea where I was going or where our compartments were, but I had no desire to see Sam now that we were where he couldn't disappear again.

After several minutes of wobbling up and down the narrowest hallways I'd ever seen in my life with no success of discerning which rooms belonged to any of us, I planted myself on a three-legged stool in a large area that appeared to be some sort of mess hall. A few others milled about trying to obtain their sea legs, but for the most part, the room was dim and empty. I was just beginning to entertain the thought that I might get a few precious minutes to myself when a heavy hand fell on my shoulder.

I startled hard, my hand reflexively darting for my sash that magically contained my sword, but another hand stopped me before my magic could spring forth in full view of other passengers. I blinked at the person behind me, studying him closely. "...Jaspen?"

"Are very perceptive, you," the creature chuckled, but for all intents and purposes, I could have sworn a human man sat before me. He had come to sit at my little table undetected, his head only an average amount above mine now versus what it would be like if he were standing. A thick, worn bandage wove around his head, masking his colorful eyes and Ranguvariian ears. He appeared to anyone else on the ship as nothing more than a poor, blind man in ragged, traveling clothes headed for Caark just like the rest of the passengers.

"I'm impressed. I didn't know Ranguvariians had such skill in the art of disguise," I remarked, a smile threatening to crack my melancholy.

"Is a lot still don't know about us, you." Jaspen grinned, the edges of the bandage around his eyes wrinkling upward. "Received this before snuck aboard, I."

Jaspen revealed a thick envelope from underneath his ratty cloak and tunic and slipped it to me with his long, leathery fingers. Frederick's beautiful script leapt up at me from the parchment, and I jumped up, snatching it out of his hands. More definitions! I could decipher the next chapter of my history book and find out what happened to Rhydin Caldwell!

But, I couldn't do that in front of Jaspen. For whatever reason, I just *knew* that if the Ranguvariians realized what was within my book, it would be taken from me before I could say a single word. Looking at it in front of them was one thing, intently cross-referencing it with a letter was another. The strange presence of the Archimage Palace had given this book to me. Therefore, its secrets were only mine to discover.

"Jaspen, where are our quarters? I'd like to read Frederick's letter in private," I said as calmly as possible, trying to make it appear like no big deal.

The disguised Ranguvariian tilted his head to the side like he was thinking, and I realized in a moment how much I had come to depend on the Ranguvariians' changing eye colors for a guess at what they were feeling. He stated matter-of-factly, "Go down a level, you. Is yours and Sam's, third cabin on the left."

I grimaced and was suddenly glad for the bandage that hid Jaspen's sight. Sam's name dredged up my feelings of hurt and isolation all over again. I muttered a brief thank you and scurried away in hopes that I could have more alone time before Sam managed to find his way to our cabin.

The word "cabin" was a gross overstatement when I arrived. It was more like a rotting, mildew-smelling cubby hole that was hardly wide enough for the two, slim cots it possessed, which scraped slightly back and forth along the floor with the movement of the ship. I swallowed my disgust and fear of finding a rat later, and plopped onto the nearest cot after lighting the stubby, moldy candle beside the door.

The only other light filtered through a porthole maybe the size of my fists from the setting sun outside. While part of me wanted to go up to the deck and view the sunset along the open ocean, the other part nimbly ripped Frederick's letter open, bypassed the first two pages of actual communication, and buried my nose in his list of definitions.

Time faded away. It had no meaning for me as I struggled to sound out the words of the history book and matched them Frederick's definitions. To my frustration, the next chapter was only halfway useful. The narrative remained aloof and detached, again not detailing how a boy named Rhydin Caldwell was given enough magic to become Archimage or anything about his time in the position.

I was ready to throw the book into the ocean as a total waste of time when I reached the last paragraph of the section:

"Toward the conclusion of Caldwell's brief tenure as Archimage, it became transparent that too much responsibility had been laid on the shoulders on too young of a boy. Seemingly overnight, his most intimate colleagues detected a radical shift in Caldwell's nature. His goals, ambitions, and personality soon no longer aligned with the description of the Archimage duties. Therefore, the council diagnosed their miscalculations in granting magical powers to a commoner, and Caldwell was unanimously eradicated from office. In his stead, Princess Minndosia of Mineraltir, an endowed pyromage, was elected Archimage and divested of her Mineraltin liaisons. This culminated in an era of peace and prosperity where Archimages were then on elected from second-born Royals to advise the Three Kings."

I held the book numbly. This wasn't true. Rhydin used his position as Archimage to boost himself into the role of emperor and reigned for at least a few years before my ancestor, Nora Soreta, created the Allyen magic and kicked him out of power. I had been told before how all the history books were burned and how even the dating of our years was reorganized in order to cover up the fact that Rhydin ever existed, but I had never seen it so plainly in front of my own face before.

This book acknowledged Rhydin's existence at least, but it still put forth a false history to make the world forget their mistake in placing Rhydin on a throne. Or at least the Gornish, since the Ranguvariians and the Rounans each passed the story down. It made me sick. If the people at the time had owned their mistakes, none of what was happening now would be possible. I glanced at the tiny porthole, which had long grown dark now that the sun was gone, and found myself wondering if I could fit the book of lies through it.

Suddenly, the door to our little compartment creaked open, and I wasn't quick enough to hide the book and letter under the threadbare, moth-eaten blanket on my cot. Sam sidled through the door sideways, a slumbering child in each arm, and his eyes grazed across the book in my lap as he used the toe of his boot to shove the door closed behind him. I leaned forward so perhaps my arms would somewhat hide my studies, but I couldn't look him in the eye which caused feelings of guilt to bubble up in my throat.

Sam gently eased Kylar and Rayna onto the measly cot next to me, the cabin barely big enough for him to even turn around between the two cots, and then he sat a few inches away from me, his fingers threaded together. I didn't have time to wonder how long we would sit in silence before he lightly cleared his throat, glancing at me every couple of seconds. "I've been talking to a bunch of the other passengers. Turns out a lot of them are Rounans."

My curiosity betrayed me. I looked over at him slowly, his mud-colored eyes clearer than they'd been in weeks. I asked quietly, "Really?"

Sam nodded slowly. "They're escaping from Rhydin. They know he's not who he says he is, but they couldn't come forward in their hometowns without being hanged for being Rounans. So, they're going to Caark in hopes that Rhydin will turn a blind eye to the island since it's tiny with no kingdom or magic."

"Just like we are," I mumbled, my shoulders dipping as I turned to stare at Kylar and Rayna's dreaming faces.

"Yeah," Sam admitted softly. A few seconds of silence enveloped us before he spoke again. "Maybe we're not completely abandoning our people by leaving."

I nodded slowly, hoping this wasn't his version of an apology. I bit my lip, and my fingers had minds of their own as they rubbed the worn corners of the history book that lay half-hidden in my lap.

Sam judged the ancient cover. "That's the book you were trying to tell me about. Isn't it?" He reached for it, like I might give it to him to inspect and make up for lost time, but my fingers tightened like cement. He withdrew his hand sluggishly and whispered, "Would you like to tell me about it now?"

"Apparently, I'm not a good enough reader to understand it," I answered spitefully.

"Lina, I... I didn't mean that. I'm proud of you for trying to be a better reader. If I hadn't been raised as the next Kidek, I'm sure my reading and writing skills would be far worse than yours, although they still don't compare to a Royal's." Sam eyed the letter from Frederick that still lay next to me on the cot.

"Then why did you say it?" I asked, finally meeting his gaze again.

Sam's eyes turned a bit glassy, and he cleared his throat before staring at his folded hands again. "To push you away. To somehow make you think that it would be alright to go to Caark without me if you thought I didn't want to be around you."

"Even if you'd told me you hated me, I wouldn't have gone to Caark without you." I shook my head, pondering how he could have ever thought such a thing.

"Why?" Sam turned his body more toward me, swinging a long leg up onto the cot as he did, and I recognized my own pain and neediness in his expression. He needed reassurance just as much as I did.

"Because even if you stopped loving me, I could never stop loving you." I reached for one of his hands and gripped it tight. "You're my husband, my childhood friend, the father of my children, my partner both in the crop field and the battlefield. That doesn't just go away."

Sam hooked his arm around my neck and pulled me across the inches that separated us, planting a kiss on my temple. "I'll never stop loving you either."

I smiled and relaxed into him, finally feeling at ease.

"Now," Sam said as he pulled back and grinned at me, "tell me about your book."

Excitement brewing, I uncovered the book and began flipping pages. Sam's eyes widened at the sight of the tattered exterior in comparison to the pristine pages on the inside. I was just about to the first chapter that detailed Rhydin when abruptly the whole ship lurched forward, throwing us both on the floor before it catapulted backward and stayed there.

In the seconds that followed, I threw a hand in either kid's direction, keeping them from tumbling off their cot, and then rubbed my aching head where it had bashed into the leg of the cot. Both children began to bawl as Sam helped me off the ground. I was trying to get the words out to ask what had happened when I realized that the endless rocking of the ship had stopped completely.

"The ship isn't moving," Sam breathed, his hand still firm on my arm like we could be tossed again any second. "Let's go up-..."

The presence I feared the most suddenly busted through the pain in my head, and ice slid down my spine.

The ship had not stopped. Rhydin stopped the ship.

CHAPTER EIGHT

With our crying children in our arms, Sam and I threw the door of our compartment open to find a current of water trickling down the hallway and passengers running against the flow. Strange lights flickered into the narrow hall from the other ajar doors, and as the pungent odor of smoke stung my nose, I realized that some of the candles must have fallen and caught something on fire. Which was worse, death by fire or water?

"We've run aground!" one passenger yelled as he splashed toward the exit and pushed others out of the way.

"Or hit an underwater shoal or shipwreck!" a woman squealed as she followed after him, clutching her tattered skirts.

A third person came rushing up the hallway before we could manage to get out of our doorway, a thin man without any shoes, but to my surprise, he stopped abruptly upon the sight of Sam. The other passengers we had seen had a sort of panicked fear in their eyes, but this third man... It was absolute, wild terror in his as he stared at Sam.

Sam's eyes darted to a ragged bandage on the man's wrist, and mine followed suit to see what could only be the mark of a Rounan peeking through. He knew this was no natural occurrence, that Rhydin was making it look like the ship was crashing rather than stopping it like the dictator he was, and it made my heart race faster.

Sam immediately barked orders, "Get up to the main deck and hide your mark. Stay as far away from you-know-who as you can. We need to get off this ship."

The Rounan man snapped his head up and down, and took off toward the exit, but while I turned to follow, Sam darted in the direction of the flooding water. I called after him, bracing myself against the subtle tilt the ship was beginning to acquire, "Sam! Sam, what are you doing?"

Sam poked his head into each of the doorways, his trousers now wet up to his knees as he sloshed around, and then kicked one of the last doors open. I heard the screech of one of the cots against the floor as the door opened, and a young, Auklian woman suddenly dove out of her room with a silk scarf plastered to her nose and mouth. She coughed and sputtered as Sam pushed her in my direction, and that was all she needed to get herself past me and up the ladder down the hall.

"Sam, come on!" I coughed as smoke began to really fill the hall and the water reached my shins.

"One more!" he called back as he looked in the last room on our level. Then, he hustled back up the hallway the best he could, slowed by the higher water at the bottom and the worsening tilt of the ship.

At the sight of him heading back toward me, I turned and worked my way toward the ladder leading through the upper levels to the main deck. My worn, leather boots slid on the wet wood underneath, the gurgling water threatening to pull each of my steps back out from under me. As I hurried, I shouted back over my shoulder, "Where are Evan and Cayce?"

"They were up on the deck when I came down to find you," Sam responded as he finally caught up with me. He put a hand in the center of my back to brace against the strengthening water flow and urged me forward faster. All the while, the cold blackness of Rhydin's presence was building in the back of my mind.

After what felt like an eternity, but in reality was only a few minutes, we reached the ladder and hoisted ourselves up, each of us balancing a child in one arm. We met with quite a bit of traffic on the upper levels before we were able to slowly reach the top deck.

Just as the cold, ocean breeze caught my hair, I came nose to nose with Rachel, the dark sky clouding over beyond her. She hauled me up and out of the ladder hole like as if I weighed nothing more than a sack of potatoes, and then she scowled in my face, "Where have you been? I was about to start shoving people back down so I could come find you!"

"Sorry, we-…!" I tried to say before Rachel locked her hand around my wrist and dragged me toward the wall of the captain's quarters.

"Quiet!" she hissed even as the rest of the passengers scurried and screamed around us. "He's here."

Initially, I folded myself closer into the damp, moldy wall. Then, I peered around the ship, taking in all the terrified passengers in various stages of undress from the lateness of the hour as well as the frazzled crewmembers attempting to give directions. They were scrambling for the two very meager lifeboats that looked more like they were constructed of matchsticks. The tilt of the ship now was undeniable; this thing was going down, so I certainly didn't blame them. I couldn't deny the innate urge to board one myself considering I couldn't swim well and I had my children to think of. But what I did not see was Rhydin or any of his Followers, even though my senses were screaming the opposite.

"Where?" I breathed, scared of being overheard even in the ruckus.

Rachel subtly pointed a finger to the sky. "From Jaspen and Bartholomiiu's reconnaissance, it appears to be Rhydin with only an Einanhi or two. They're just watching from beyond the cloud cover. We think they're waiting for the ship to sink before doing anything else."

"Why?" I whispered, "Do they know we're here?"

"They shouldn't, since you all are wearing our feathers and we can't be sensed. But anything is possible, and we're not taking any chances," Rachel stated solemnly as Luke subtly rounded the bend behind her. His face was paler than usual, and his eyes had shifted to a molten copper color. I could only guess from the set of his brow that he was tense for more reasons than one.

"So, what's the plan?" I asked, knowing that there seemed to always be one. "Board a lifeboat? Where're Evan and Cayce?"

Rachel shook her head, and Luke's entire body suddenly shuddered as if something had chilled him. "The lifeboats will be packed full of all the passengers and crew, exactly where Rhydin's Einanhis will start searching for any of his enemies. With where we are in the ocean, I'm sure they'll head back to

Lunaka too which is the last place we want to go. We're going to wait until the ship is nearly submerged, when the life boats are as far from us as possible, and then fly the rest of the way to Caark."

Luke gulped, hard. I could only stare at him in bewilderment. Of all the Ranguvariians, he had always seemed the most unshakable. Sam became jittery behind me.

"Evan and Cayce are just on the other side of this building with Jaspen and James," Rachel continued. "We had them at the bow of the ship, but…"

My head swiveled to my left, and I couldn't stop my heart from sinking to my stomach. The bow of the ship was underwater, and the eerily calm waves continued to lap at the main deck, as if slowly ingesting it. That's when I heard it. The creaking moan of the ship as the bow sunk lower and lower, which in turn caused the slant of the main deck to worsen. The cry echoed onto the empty ocean.

I stammered, "So, we're just going to stand here and do absolutely nothing until the ship is pretty much sunk?"

"To keep Rhydin from discovering that we're here? Yes," Rachel said firmly, her blue eyes like ice.

"But-…!" I tried to cry.

"Not gonna happen," Sam interrupted, thrusting Kylar into my other arm and beginning to pace away before any of us could stop him. "If Rhydin's going to check the lifeboats, all of the Rounans on this ship are going to be killed. We're going to make a stand right now because Rhydin can't reveal himself without losing the support of the people."

Rachel yelled after him, but it was no use. Sam trotted and slid down the deck toward the nearest lifeboat, starting to bellow something to the extent of getting off the lifeboats, his Kidek bandana clearly visible even in the night. Even though he never used the word "Rounan," it was obvious who was and who wasn't. Those who weren't gawked at him like he was insane from their perches in their lifeboat, while those who were began to begrudgingly obey. Rachel took off after him after a quick look to Jaspen.

I was in the middle of wondering how on Nerahdis we would get these people out of here without the lifeboats even if we somehow did manage to fight Rhydin off when the clouds above suddenly began to churn angrily and glow purple. The hair on the back of my neck stood on end as my senses overpowered me with Rhydin's darkness.

I screamed, *"Sam!"*

Amethyst lightning cracked open the sky with both light and the sound of a hundred trees exploding. My ears rang too loud to hear the subsequent groan of the ship beneath our feet as it snapped in half. The back end of the ship, which had been slowly rising out of the ocean due to the sinking front, suddenly fell backwards back into the ocean as its innards crumbled and burned.

Luke leapt toward me as the gaping holes of every floor beneath us rapidly filled with water, which sent the deck tilting in the opposite direction. I tried to turn my head to find Sam or Rachel, but it was no use. What was left of the ship blocked my vision. Soon, the angle was so drastic that our feet slipped out from under us, and Luke and I were sent sliding feet first along what was left of the deck straight into the dark, watery depths below.

I started kicking fiercely as the warm, tropical water enveloped us, trying to keep mine and my children's two heads above water without the use of my arms, and Luke began to wail, his head disappearing several times before I realized why he'd been so nervous. He couldn't swim at all.

Luke panickily thrust himself out of the water with an appearance from his beautiful, shard wings, but their glow rippled off the water around us like a beacon. We only had seconds before the rest of the ship, which was currently hiding us from sight, sank beneath the surface of the water. My legs burned like fire trying to keep us afloat. My children screamed. I couldn't reach for anything. For the first time, the possibility of my drowning crossed my mind.

My flailing Ranguvariian companion used his flying spell for the briefest of moments longer to push himself toward a large scrap of wood from the wreckage, which looked to be the remains of part of the roof of the captain's quarters judging by the mildew-stained shingles. His wings disappeared just as the rest of the ship went under, and he managed to kick the wood back toward me even as he clung to it for dear life.

I rapidly pushed Kylar and Rayna out of the water and on top of the shingles, which in turn shoved my own head under the water. I surfaced and gasped for breath as I threw my arms over the wood, allowing my exhausted legs to go limp as I tucked each of my arms around my crying children, urging them to settle so we wouldn't be found.

Luke seemed to be even more terrified now, even though he wasn't actively drowning anymore. His eyes darted back and forth along the water's edge, the color of a lemon. He stuttered over and over, "In the water, in the water... We are going to be killed! They'll kill us from below!"

I breathed slowly now, trying to steady my anxious nerves, and hushed him, "Luke, everything's fine. There's nothing in the water but us and some fish. Just relax. As soon as Rhydin leaves, you can fly us to Caark just like planned."

Luke shuddered and squeezed his eyes shut. Despite my speech, I couldn't help but glance to the warm water again myself. Were there sharks in the eastern ocean? Or were there other creatures in this world I didn't know about?

Rhydin studied the foaming waters several hundred feet below him fiercely. The Einanhi upon which he rode, a strange mix of a black stallion and a majestic eagle, snorted angrily as it hovered in place just beyond the cloud cover. Rhydin had come to stop this ship and its passengers from leaving Nerahdis and his empire, as he had done with quite a few before it. Anyone trying to leave was highly likely to be a Rounan after all, which necessitated swift attention. Although, he certainly hadn't expected to come across Kidek Samton Greene of all people.

Rhydin's pale fingers itched along his black leather reins. He studied every swell and piece of debris, looking for any inkling that a person was hiding there instead of in one of the lifeboats. It was taking all of his willpower to remain where he was, out of sight of people whose support he still required, instead of down among the waves combing the wreckage for a certain pair of Allyen twins. He had no proof they were here of course, but if the Kidek was present, Allyen Linaria couldn't be too far behind.

A light broke out upon the water below Rhydin, and he didn't have to turn to know what it was. It was a much larger ship filled with his imperial forces, arriving just in time to save the day. Of course, only the Gornish on those lifeboats would be allowed to return to Nerahdis. The Rounans on the other hand... Rhydin chuckled. At least the people's absolute terror of magic still supported the extermination of those troublesome folk.

Cheers rippled forth from the two lifeboats as the imperial ship reached them and let down a ladder. Rhydin smirked as praises for his name drifted upward to where he flew, but he forcibly moved himself into a position to transport away from the scene of the crime, no matter how much of every fiber of his being urged him downward to find the Allyens.

All in due time, he thought to himself. If they happened to survive the sinking, he could have forces to Caark in a matter of weeks. The Chancellor of Caark had been left undisturbed for far too long anyway, even if Rhydin didn't much care to give any attention to Caark in the long run. Once the Allyens were in his grasp, he could rest easy that his reign was ensured for the rest of time.

"You idiot! You've ruined everything!" Rachel yelled as she sputtered water and grasped the remnants of a door with all the strength she had.

Sam rolled his eyes. *Here we go again*, he thought as he treaded water. "I couldn't just let them die! I wouldn't be able to live with myself."

Rachel groaned loudly, "I know, I know! Trust me, I wish it was different. Contrary to popular belief, I don't particularly *like* having to be the bad guy all the time…" She tapered off, staring sadly at her door. "I would have saved them too if I could have. But now, we're just worse off than we were before."

Sam turned in the water toward something behind him that Rachel had nodded at. Rapidly approaching was an even larger ship than the one they had embarked on, and this one looked like it was made of sheet metal instead of rickety wood. Rhydin's imperial banners waved from every mast, and hatred bubbled up in Sam's throat.

The Rounans who had gotten off the lifeboats had scattered in the wreckage, and Sam wasn't sure where they all ended up. But if any were still in those lifeboats, their death sentences would be signed as soon as Rhydin's ship picked them up. And there was really nothing he could do this time as a sitting duck in the water. Sam had to turn away when the people in the lifeboats began to cheer. It hurt too much.

After a few moments of blocking out any sounds around him, Sam noticed that Rhydin's presence disappeared from his senses. Rachel announced the same and gracefully sprouted the wings of her flying spell. She linked her arms under Sam's and around his shoulders, and scooped him out of the water like he weighed half of what he did. She mumbled in his ear, "If I see any Rounans in the water, we'll pick them up and take them with us."

Sam nodded quietly, feeling deflated now. His spirits arose a little at the sight of Lina, Kylar, and Rayna in the arms of Luke, as well as Evan, Cayce, and their child safe and sound with Jaspen and James. The Ranguvariians hovered low, close to the waves, for several minutes as they searched the wreckage for survivors.

They did ultimately pluck three Rounans from the water, the man Sam had given orders to as well as a young woman with a small boy. There was no one else. Sam tried to keep the three Rounans calm and answered the fewest required questions of whom the Ranguvariians were and that they were against Rhydin as well, but the weary group of castaways quickly fell silent as the Ranguvariians broke off their search and began flying east toward Caark.

More so than ever, Sam felt like a failure.

Hours ticked by as slow as molasses. Numbness had started in my fingers and slowly trickled up my wrists and forearms to the point where I really had no feeling left in my arms at all, which kept my almost-dried-out children safe and warm even as we flew. I was rather sure Luke had lost all feeling in his arms as well, between me and the small, Rounan boy in his other arm. Now I understood why the Ranguvariians had wanted us to get to Caark by ship.

The five Ranguvariians took turns flying in a formation that reminded me of the geese that soared over our heads to the south every winter. It appeared like the tip of an arrow, where the person at the point was exerting the most effort while those behind him or her could glide more and conserve their energy. They would swap out leaders from one of the back people maybe every thirty minutes. At first, this helped me to keep track of the time, but instead, I quickly lost sense of how many times everyone had served as leader.

At some point, the eastern horizon began to glow pink as a rose. It burned against my bleary eyes, and I realized how much I'd been walking the line between sleep and wakefulness. I shook my head in a sad attempt to rouse myself, but all around us was still nothing but empty ocean. The black waters sluggishly took on the hues from the sky, a light pink before a soft, golden yellow took its place. It was beginning to feel like the entire world had vanished beneath the rolling swells.

I looked around at my companions. Evan's head was bobbing as he struggled to stay awake in Jaspen's arms, his tiny son curled into him, almost invisible from this distance.

Cayce diligently sat as upright as possible in James's grasp, her lavender curls springing in every direction with the salt and humidity of the ocean just below.

Sam appeared the most awake of anyone as he stared down at the ocean broodily from his perch with Rachel, and from him, I looked to the other two Rounans we had managed to save in the lanky Bartholomiiu's grip. They both still looked absolutely terrified, but they were alive and that's what mattered. While I wished for Sam's sake we could have saved more, even I knew that our Ranguvariians probably couldn't have carried any more.

"There," I heard Luke breathe in relief, "finally."

A dark smudge had appeared on the line that divided the sky and sea, right underneath where the brilliant, white sun was starting its day. The tension in my shoulders suddenly lifted. It could only be Caark. The island republic that was part of Nerahdis, and yet not, due to some weird exception that dated back hundreds of years before my birth.

As we grew closer, my eyes widened at the sight of tall, thin trees that only had leaves at the very tippy tops and coasts of pristine, gilded sand that put Auklia's shorelines to shame. My curiosity mounted with every passing minute as more of Caark became visible, and I found myself wondering what the people would be like and how they compared to the Three Kingdoms.

I also wondered how long we had before Rhydin sent his troops after us now that he had seen Sam.

Frederick paused on his trek to wipe his brow. Summer was coming along rapidly in Lunaka, a season which was truly defined by its humidity more than anything else, although the thin mountain air did assuage that a mite. The former prince looked over his shoulder at the small cottage nestled into the rocky face of the mountain, almost completely camouflaged now. Cornflower, his teenage sister, was home caring for his son, Dominick, while he did his daily walk.

It was slightly ironic now. Totally inconvenient at first. Frederick had once written Lina how he didn't understand her desire to work, and now he had found himself in the very strange position of having to.

As a Royal, money had never held any meaning for Frederick. It was all the same. If he wanted food, he went downstairs to the dining room and a four-course meal awaited him. If he wanted to go somewhere, he simply took his horse from the royal stables or borrowed his father's carriage. If he required new clothes, a master tailor would visit him in his chambers, collect his measurements, and send a new wardrobe to him within the week. It didn't occur to Frederick until he was much older than these things cost money for everyone else on Nerahdis. Yet, someone in the Royal household ensured that the cooks, stable boys, and tailors were paid accordingly from the bountiful Royal vault.

It was an entirely new experience to leave Lunaka Castle with only what was in his pocket and to learn how much it cost to live. This first happened when he left after Duunzer's attack and lived in the cottage between Lun and the Rounan Compound, although their one servant was typically the one who took Frederick's money to Lun and acquired what they needed.

Again, when Frederick traveled to Auklia to assist King Daniel with the running of his kingdom, he got by on Daniel's good will for longer than he cared to admit. It wasn't until now that Frederick, alone with his son and sister, actually had to take care of these things himself, and his reserves were becoming dry.

Therefore, every day, he had taken to walking different mountain paths in search of anything he could sell or hunt. As a Royal, Frederick had been dutifully trained in the art of the hunt, although it had never really been his thing. Just another thing about him that angered his father. But, as the old adage said, desperate times called for desperate measures.

While Frederick didn't necessarily consider their situation desperate, he and Cornflower simply couldn't turn their noses up to squirrel or hare, even if those had never been on their menus before. A Ranguvariian checked in with them every other day, and Frederick wasn't too proud to admit that that Ranguvariian was often the person that skinned the meat and took the pelts and whatever else he happened to scavenge to town. This ensured that Frederick never needed to step foot anywhere he could be recognized.

Frederick paused, checking one of his traps. Empty, again. He sighed and tried not to think about his rumbling stomach.

In an effort to make it up to Lina for his rude comments, Frederick asked any person he happened to see on his walks about the Auklian Royal family and their opinion of Rhydin. He saw maybe two or three people in a week's time, so it wasn't the greatest source of information. They were normally Rounans trying to find a safe place to live, so the opinions of Rhydin he had received were negative across the board.

However, only a few of them expressed interest in fighting back while most did not. It confused Frederick truly. One man's reign causes you to have to leave the life you know and find safety and anonymity in the mountains. Why wouldn't one want that to change?

As for the Auklian Royal family, so far none of them could even name Daniel's father due to Queen Maria's long, solitary reign after his death decades ago. Frederick tried not to let his mind wander too much on this…but were Royals so hated that they were, in fact, forgettable? Would any of his people remember him, whether he ever got to be king or not?

A twig snapped. The prince rapidly drew his sword, scanning in all directions before his eyes landed on a tanned, young Auklian woman. She appeared utterly out of her element. Her clothing was fine indeed, and she had managed to snag her silk cloak on a piece of mountain brush.

Frederick sheathed his sword and stepped toward her slowly, trying not to frighten her. "Hello there. Do you need help?"

The woman jumped, her brilliant teal eyes going wide underneath a hood that obscured most of her face. She stuttered in a nasal, Auklian accent, "F-Frederick?"

The prince hesitated in his approach. It wasn't uncommon for the people he ran into to recognize him. But none of them had ever referred to him by only his name with no title tacked on to either end. He studied her a little closer. Why did she sound familiar? He asked cautiously, "Do I know you?"

The teal eyes were magnetized to the ground, anger flashing in them. After a couple of seconds, the woman angrily tore off her hood, revealing a head of tousled hair that was bright orange. Like tiger lilies.

Queen Lily of Auklia. Daniel's wife who had simply disappeared during the fray at the Archimage Palace. He, and everyone else, had assumed she died when she never turned up.

"Lily," Frederick gasped before he rubbed his eyes, wondering if he was seeing things. She was still there when he stopped. "How is this possible? Where have you been?"

Lily's hands clenched into fists. "None of your business! My son and my husband are dead. Leave me be, Frederick." She ripped her cloak from the limb that had dared snag it and moved to walk away.

"Wait!" Frederick shouted before he closed the distance between them. "You're still the queen of Auklia! Your people need a leader-…"

"No, Frederick," Lily responded harshly, glaring at him with her nose in the air. "I am the queen who abandoned her people not just once, but twice. I have received death threats of all things, why do you think I am here and not home with what family I have left in Auklia?"

A rare sense of ire entered Frederick, and he felt the back of his neck grow hot. "So now you will do it a third time, is that it? You will simply disappear like you don't exist?"

"Rhydin has won, Frederick. Even if Auklia wanted me, it's too late," Lily chastised him. "We were foolish to believe we could stop him."

"I can't believe that," Frederick responded adamantly. "There's always hope."

The orange-haired woman merely shook her head and began to walk away once more, mumbling something disparaging about their odds.

The prince almost let her leave, but then called after her from where he stood, "If you won't help us, then fine. But did Daniel ever say anything about Archimage Dathian's family? A green-haired woman, perhaps?"

Lily paused and turned, saying slyly, "Maybe. What's it worth to you?"

CHAPTER NINE

"I told ya, your Lunakan pieces are no good here! Don't bother coming back until you trade that junk for Caarkian pounds!" a thick-waisted man with chocolate-colored skin spat at me for the third time in three days.

I groaned, "And I told you that we just arrived and don't have any Caarkian pounds yet! I have children to feed!"

"I'm sorry, lass, but there's nothin' I can do! None of the Three Kingdoms' money is worth anything here," the shopkeeper shrugged, the dimmest of sparks of sympathy in his eyes. "You immigrants are flooding our economy. If you can't find a job, you better find someone heading back to the Continent to trade with."

I heaved a heavy sigh and thrust my useless Lunakan money back into my pocket, releasing the small crate of what I had considered bare necessities and abandoning it on the counter. The small store was jam-packed with people of every culture. The Caarkians were nearly outnumbered by the plethora of Mineraltins, Auklians, and Lunakans that rubbed shoulders with each other fighting for the last bag of coffee or the meager stack of canned beans.

Of course, all the Caarkian fares were mostly untouched; fresh, sweet-smelling fruit I'd never seen before, tiny sea creatures that looked more like insects in a big tank of water, and a green, creamy liquid that I wasn't sure I wanted to know its origin. We were not the only ones haggling with the shopkeeper or his assistants to accept Lunakan pieces, Mineraltin dollars, or Auklian bars.

"It'll be okay, Lina," Cayce called into my ear over the ruckus of the store. "Sam found a job this morning, and I started mine yesterday. We'll just ration out what we have left from our journey a little longer."

"All we have left is half a bag of deer jerky and a handful of hardtack that I'm not sure is even edible anymore," I whined as we exited the claustrophobic shop.

Outdoors wasn't much better, and I found myself wavering between clinging to the walls of the various shops while weaving through thick foot traffic and taking my chances in the middle of the sandy road where small buggies threatened to run over anything in their way. I usually heard at least one person get hit every time we entered the swollen, port city of Calitia. I'd never realized how much I was used to the tiny Rounan Compound, where you could shop sometimes without ever seeing another soul aside from the shopkeeper, until we entered Calitia for the first time three days ago.

"All we can do is the best we can," my sister-in-law retorted before she took hold of my hand and yanked me down the nearest alleyway rather than trying to do battle with either the boardwalk or the road. "Now, let's get out of this disaster zone."

The two of us walked quietly for a few moments, waiting for the roar of the city's heart to die down, our arms painfully empty. Just as we were reaching the end of the alleyway, which resulted in the horizon opening up before us between crystalline blue sky and thick greenery that knotted the sand together beneath our feet, I mumbled, "Y'know, when I started hearing the rumors of people considering leaving Nerahdis for Caark, I imagined Caark a lot bigger."

Cayce shrugged, "Perhaps, there are more people out there unhappy with having an emperor than you thought. Not just the Rounans. That's good for us, isn't it?"

"I don't know," I responded just as my foot got caught by a strand of sticky ivy. "The few people I've managed to question about their opinions of Rhydin since arriving seem to have written off the Three Kingdoms entirely and aren't interested in going back. Or, they're Rounans terrified of returning after the effort it took to get here. Apparently, our shipwreck hasn't been the only one Rhydin has caused."

"I see the problem," Cayce mused as we finally reached the path through the island vegetation that led north. "Well, then. I guess it's a good thing we'll be headed back to the Continent soon since Rhydin knows we're here. We need supporters who care about the Three Kingdoms. Ones that live there and are invested in their futures."

I scowled, "Yeah, tell that to Rachel. All she can think about is trying to get a house built, and I just can't figure out why when the rest of what comes out of her mouth is about how we need to be ready to leave at a moment's notice."

"I do often wonder if my sister is crazy," a light-hearted voice came out of nowhere, "but she usually reveals a method to her madness eventually!"

Cayce and I jumped, both of us reaching out with our hands to be ready to blast a spell in any direction, but it was only James who peeped out of the overgrown brush ahead of us, his round face amused.

"James, for heaven's sake, I could have snapped you like a twig!" Cayce chastised as she tossed a lavender curl over her shoulder, her Rounan mark flashing from under her silk sleeve.

Rachel's youngest brother tossed his shaggy, brown head and laughed, "I'd like to see you try! But then again, maybe I don't. Anyway, it's about time you two got here! Any luck?"

"What's it look like?" I grumbled as I flashed my empty hands. James's expression drooped.

Cayce started walking again before James could declare his disappointment. "Come along, you two. Sam may have been lucky enough to find a job in Calitia, but mine is in Aemita and I'm going to be fired if we don't get going! We can't take that risk since the rest of you couldn't find one."

"What can I say? My only skill is farming and Evan's is playing his violin. Neither of those are particularly in demand here," I replied as I began a steady pace. "At least Sam can put his handyman skills to work."

"He's trying, Lina. He's been working all hours of the day to make up for blowing our cover." Cayce smiled at me sadly, and then our small group melted into silence.

We walked along at a pretty good clip for close to an hour before the greenery thinned out and a few trees – and by trees, I mean more like oversized plants compared to the beautiful branches I was used to at home – popped up. Our small caravan had set up camp in what could probably be described as a dead zone between the cities of Calitia and Aemita.

Caark was so small that people didn't seem to really travel back and forth between the towns at all; each town already possessed everything that people needed so there was no point in traveling to a different one, especially since horses seemed to be a luxury item. This resulted in an area of little traffic for us, which was what we all thought was best for keeping a low profile. There was one small shack maybe half a mile to the east of our chosen spot. It appeared to be inhabited, but none of us had seen who lived there. They seemed to be recluses.

As we approached our campsite, the usual fire roaring in the center, Cayce took off at a faster pace, greeted Evan and Aron, their baby, briefly, and then trotted away to the south for her job with promises of bringing food back if she happened to be paid today. Evan watched her go wistfully before pushing himself back up to the frame of Rachel's house that was slowly taking shape from the available, free materials around us, namely tree trunks, until we had money.

Bartholomiiu, Luke, and, to my surprise, Jaspen all stood in three corners of the skeleton house, and James rushed to join them in the fourth as Evan and Rachel rushed around securing them in place as straight as possible. Jaspen had left Caark shortly after our arrival for some important business back in the Ranguvariian Camp. He must have just returned.

Instead of joining them, I plopped myself down by the fire and my two napping children. If I had to hear Rachel's speech of "hurry up, hurry up, we don't know how much time we have before Rhydin arrives to capture us" in the middle of building what appeared to be a very permanent structure, I would pull my hair out.

Therefore, the hours passed slowly as midmorning melted into noontime as surely as the sun reached its zenith in the clear, cloudless sky. I could feel the burn of my skin under its gaze, regardless of the hours upon hours I'd spent in the saddle this year frying myself, and my clothing began to stick to me as the island humidity soared. A few times, my eyes wandered to the strange little shack within eyesight of our campsite, and I wondered about the people who lived there. I was heating the very last of our stew on the fire while dreading the coming of evening and its thousands of little buzzing things that left itchy, red welts all over me when Rachel finally called for a lunch break.

All the boys hopped down from their various assignments before the words had completely left Rachel's mouth. They urgently grabbed the nearest bowl only to have them be quarter-filled on top of one shred of jerky and one rock-hard lump of something that had no business being related to bread. I cringed as I ladled out the sad excuse for a meal, and there was more than one pair of male eyes that turned away disappointed. Rachel, however, remained stoically standing within the framework, turned away from the rest of us.

I made up a bowl for her and walked the short distance between the campfire and the shack-to-be before offering it to her silently. She reacted like I had broken a deep train of thought and gazed at the bowl as if it was foreign to her. It took a moment or two for her to accept it from me, and yet another moment before she pinched the hardtack between two fingers and tried to use it to mop up some stew to make it edible. I watched her soundlessly before beginning to turn back for a bowl of my own, but she stopped me in my tracks with three little words.

"You were right."

I gaped at her for a second. "What do you mean?"

"About leaving the Three Kingdoms. That we can't discover and grow discontent with Rhydin's empire from

Caark," Rachel mumbled as she stared at the foot of one of the corner posts.

"Uh…okay. What's bringing this on?" I asked skeptically, crossing my arms over my chest. Although, I wasn't going to lie, I could feel my ego growing now that she had admitted that I'd been right all along.

"It was moronic of me to think that we could all just disappear to Caark without Rhydin finding us. I just wanted you to be safe." Rachel peered down at me, her blue eyes sad. "Also, I've overheard the conversations you've tried to create with the native Caarkians and the other immigrants. That none of them really care about Rhydin or what he's doing, the supposed good he pretends to do and the bad he's capable of. We're not going to find any help here like I'd once hoped."

"So, does that mean we'll return to the Three Kingdoms?" I asked, trying in vain to keep the smile of victory off my face.

Rachel leveled her gaze at me in such a way that immediately struck any joy from my being. "Not all of us."

My brow furrowed. I eyed the frame of the building in which we stood a little harder. "What do you mean?"

"I've been in nearly constant communication with my grandfather for the last three days. That's why Jaspen hasn't been around until now, so I could speak to him through Jaspen and I's *matrii* connection," Rachel responded slowly, her eyes drifting to the foot of the corner post again. "It's been decided that you and Evan should return to the mainland to begin creating some sort of rebellion against Rhydin, as well as to continue the search for the heir to Auklia, the woman in Archimage Dathian's portrait miniature. That's of the utmost importance now that Caark is no longer an option for you."

I stared at her for a moment, waiting for her to continue speaking. When she didn't, I interjected, "But?"

Rachel's eyes were threatening to brim over with tears when she looked at me again. "You have to go. But I have to stay."

"Why?" I demanded, my voice shooting up.

"Because I am no longer your *Alyen nou Clarii*," Rachel blubbered. "My grandfather has reassigned me to be Rayna's protector, and the children are to remain here in Caark."

Abruptly, I felt like a rug had been pulled out from under me, even though my boots remained firmly planted in the grassy sand of Caark. Confusion washed over me like rolling waves. I squeaked, "You have been saying this whole time that Caark is no longer safe since Rhydin saw Sam! Why in Nerahdis would we leave them here?"

"Lina, we have a plan in place to make Rhydin think that the children return to the Three Kingdoms with you. You're facing a life on the road, constantly moving around anywhere from the far east of Caark to the far west of Mineraltir and the Great Desert," Rachel replied soothingly as she composed herself. "Being out in the open for long periods of time and making contact with strangers who could very well support Rhydin is no place for toddlers. Especially not the future Allyen and Kidek. After everything we went through last year to ensure the Allyen lineage's continuation, do I really need to say more?"

I gaped at her angrily, my words stricken from me.

"It's true, Caark is no longer safe for you, Evan, and Sam. But if we play our cards correctly, it can become safe for however long we need it to be for Rayna, Kylar, and Aron," Rachel persuaded.

"F-For how long?" I stuttered numbly.

Rachel placed her long hands on my shoulders. "Only as long as it is necessary. Once you start recruiting people to our cause, you'll have to find some sort of permanent base of operations. Once it's safe, we'll all be together again in no time."

Her calming words had no effect on me. I couldn't look at her anymore. I had never once considered that the safest place for our children wasn't even on the same landmass as Sam and I. My gaze cautiously rotated back toward where Kylar and Rayna were jabbering to one another in a mixed language of words I recognized and some I didn't. I thought I had won at the notion of returning to the Three Kingdoms to gain as many supporters as possible, yet now I felt like I had lost more than I thought I could lose.

Rachel seemed to sense that there were no more words that could be said. She wandered away from me before returning briefly with the last of the stew and hardtack in another bowl. As she handed it to me, I forced one more word out of my mouth, "When?"

"As soon as the house is finished," she answered before leaving me once again.

I stared at the skeleton frame around me with new eyes. There were very simple corner posts in a basic, square design. They were connected at the tops with the beginnings of a roof outlined above. They'd need actual lumber before being able to do much else, which was outrageously expensive since it was imported from Mineraltir, but still. We likely had no more than a week with our kids.

How was I going to tell Sam when he got home?

Time ceased to exist around me. I managed to force myself to eat the now cold stew in my bowl and even choke down the hardtack without breaking any teeth, but aside from that, my mind seeped away into its own recesses. How could this be happening? Was there any possible solution that kept us all together *and* led back to Nerahdis to begin creating a rebellion? My mind racked itself for answers endlessly as my brother and the Ranguvariians returned to their work on the measly shack that would take my children from me.

I kept Kylar and Rayna close to me throughout the afternoon. I soaked up their words and their smells. The feel of Kylar's soft hair that was growing in as muddy brown as my own, and Rayna's firm grasp on my fingers. I may have only given birth to one of them, but there was no difference for me now.

As the sun stretched toward the horizon, I ignored the progress on the house. The humidity began to intensify as I had discovered it often did during these island evenings, and I cleared my mind enough to watch for the little buzzing things that made us itch.

A sense of relief washed over me once it was dark enough that the building crew stopped for the night, but it didn't last long before another wave of anxiety flooded me upon sight of Sam striding in from the north with a bag strapped to his back and some wooden boards stacked and perfectly balanced on his shoulder. Cayce, too, arrived with another small bag from the south.

"*Please* tell me that at least one of those bags has food in it!" chimed James as Sam and Cayce neared the campfire.

"Yes," Cayce answered sweetly as she sat with her bag in her lap, "although I warn you, the exotic, Caarkian stuff is far easier to buy than the stuff we're used to, so you may have to broaden your horizons, James."

The youngest Ranguvariian quirked his eyebrow. "Ranguvariian food has *way* more flavor than the stuff you Lunakans eat. If beef stew or bread and cheese ever went out of style, you all would starve."

Cayce cackled, "You have a point! I'd take my mother's Auklian cooking over Lunakan any day, but for now, Caarkian will have to do."

My attention was dragged away from Sam setting the lumber down near the construction site toward Cayce's bag that she meticulously unpacked. First, she removed half a dozen small, circular rolls that looked far more orange than the bread I was used to, then a handful of purple orbs the size of apples came after those. In the very bottom of her sack was what looked to be a couple pounds of those same gray, insect-like sea creatures we had seen in the shop that morning.

Evan turned up his nose at the sight and smell of those, saying, "Of all the meat options on this island, why did you have to buy the ones that look like bugs?"

"Because fish from Auklia costs an arm and a leg, Evan dear, with beef and goat from Lunaka and venison from Mineraltir being three times that," Cayce chided, defending her purchases like a child might defend his point of view. She bequeathed the creepy crawlies to Rachel to cook for supper. "Better put whatever we don't eat tonight in some sort of net in the ocean! If they die before cooking, they turn to poison."

Evan blanched even further while Sam added a couple of more normal-looking cans of beans to the pile as well as some greens that looked more like seaweed than something edible. Rachel thanked him for the food and lumber, glanced at me briefly, and then turned to the task of turning the hodge-podge of ingredients into a meal.

I stood from the campfire and walked timidly toward the now finished frame of the house, catching Sam's eyes in the process. He didn't need to be told that I needed to talk to him, and I was thankful for the nonverbal connection we still had even after so many weeks of distance. He followed me soundlessly, and he seemed to sense that what I had to share wasn't exactly good news. He tilted his head to the side kind of like a puppy as he asked, "What's wrong?"

I struggled to swallow, trying to compose myself. "I figured out why Rachel is having us build this house. Some of us are returning to the Three Kingdoms, and some of us aren't."

Sam's brow furrowed, but those grooves only deepened as I relayed to him everything Rachel had said. That we were returning, but our children were not. That Rachel was Rayna's protector now, and not mine. That we were leaving as soon as the house was finished with Luke, James, and Bartholomiiu, that there was a plan to make sure Rhydin thinks the children do return with us to keep their location a mystery, and that there was really no telling how much time would pass before our lives on the mainland were stable enough to have them rejoin us.

I pulled my cloak tighter around me as I finished speaking. Whether the island heat was dying away or my chills came from inside, I wasn't entirely sure. Sam could only stare at me for a few moments, the gears of his mind racing to fully comprehend everything I had just unloaded on him.

"No," he said finally, life and fire coming back to him. "No, there's no way! Of all the solutions out there, that can't be the one that's decided upon!"

"What other solutions, Sam?" I croaked as my throat closed. "What other solution allows our children to be safe and for us to save Nerahdis?"

"There has to be another way, I-I-..." Sam stuttered before he threw his hands up into the air and growled, "You don't understand! I *can't* do this to my kids, especially not Kylar!"

A shred of confusion grounded my aching heart for a moment. "What are you saying? Rayna is our child too!"

Sam shook his head, exasperated before looking to me sadly. "No, no, that's not what I meant, Lina… It's difficult for me to explain."

"Try to," I said as I crossed my arms, suddenly feeling defensive. "Why especially Ky-…?"

"Because my father left me, Lina," Sam interrupted, a new kind of pain entering his eyes. "Well before I ever met you, I barely remember him myself. All I remember is him disappearing and me abruptly becoming Kidek without anyone to teach me how it's done. My mother tried for as long as she could, but it wasn't the same. I didn't have mentors filing in left and right to help me like when you figured out you're an Allyen."

I immediately could have run my head into the nearest tree. I met Sam when he was ten years old and remembered perfectly well never seeing any sort of fatherly figure in the picture. It was always just him, his mother, and his older sister, Kelsi.

"I never planned on staying away long when I tried to get you to go to Caark without me. I wanted things to be different for Kylar. I wanted to help him learn his Rounan magic and help him into being Kidek slowly. Not alone," Sam mumbled morosely, losing his temper. "Not like this."

I reached out and touched his arm, curling in close to him. "Sam, you're making it seem like we're never going to see them again. That's not true. No matter how long it takes for us to establish some sort of safe base, we *will* bring them back to us from Caark. We will never allow for this to be a permanent arrangement. You'll be able to teach our son so many things about being Kidek that he'll be overprepared and might actually resent you for it like all kids do their parents at some point!"

I received the tiniest of chuckles from Sam in response, but then his face slackened as he mused, "Hopefully, they don't resent us regardless."

"What do you mean?" I asked.

"We have two toddlers who before they've even turned five have so much riding on their shoulders," Sam elaborated as he stared back at the campfire where the two in question were gleefully playing with Evan. "The future leader of an entire, persecuted people group stretched from one end of Nerahdis to the other and a future sorceress heir to one of the most powerful magical lineages there is, destined to continue the battle with Rhydin if we fail. No pressure," Sam added sarcastically.

My gaze followed his to Kylar and Rayna, my heart aching. "They never asked for any of this."

"And neither did we." Sam's eyes returned to me. He took my hand tightly. "Maybe we can end it all before it ever has to be their turn."

I nodded quietly and hugged him. Suddenly, more than anything else in the world, I so desperately wanted that to be true.

Even as I write this, I ardently hope that we can accomplish that and spare our children from inheriting our problems as well as our magics. Ultimately, only time will tell. But I can't stop the feeling that the odds won't be in our favor.

CHAPTER TEN

A few days went by after that, each of which took Sam and Cayce away empty-handed in the morning and home bearing food and building supplies in the evening, never a spare cent to be seen. Each day also saw significant progress on the house that would shelter Rachel, Jaspen, and our children for an indefinite amount of time, and all the lumber from the previous day was always completely gone by the time we quit building for the day.

I had joined the building crew now. Even though every nail I pounded into every board felt more like a spike to my own heart as I watched Kylar and Rayna nap or play nearby, I knew that I needed to help or I'd never forgive myself.

One day, during our lunch break, we finally met the people who lived in the shack just about a quarter mile away from ours. They were two young women who dressed as though they were Auklian, although they didn't have the usual, nasal Auklian accent that even my brother showed traces of at times. The first, who was short with hair a mint green color,

Chelsea, was nice enough, but Sonya, statuesque with hair the color of blood, pretty much ignored the whole lot of us. They had tried to scrape by our camp on their way home from town unseen, but managed to be caught by the ever-sociable Rachel who pried as much information as she could out of them like the good investigator she was.

"I still don't know about those two! I'm starting to wonder if we should have built this house somewhere else," Rachel abruptly mused aloud as the rest of us worked the next day.

"Wouldn't know, I," Jaspen responded moodily as he lifted a beam into place just a bit above his seven-foot head. "Looked fine from a mile away, they!"

Rachel rolled her eyes at her mate. Jaspen was apparently still peeved at how short of notice he and Bartholomiiu were given to make themselves scarce before Chelsea and Sonya were called over to our camp.

Bartholomiiu began to cackle, his eyes like a fragile, pink petal, "The ocean is happy!"

We all kind of just smiled or agreed in response as we had taken to doing whenever Bartholomiiu had something to say. I still hoped he continued to improve from the brain damage Rhydin had inflicted, but maybe that was impossible.

"Why don't you like them?" Evan asked as he nailed Jaspen's beam into place. "They're probably just more refugees since they're Auklian, although I couldn't sense any magic from them."

"Just a feeling," Rachel harrumphed as she warmed a kettle over the fire. Luke and James glanced at her knowingly, and I couldn't help but wonder what she meant.

Meanwhile, I ran out of nails and hopped down a makeshift ladder to grab more. Evan met me halfway with another bagful, and his eyes met mine sadly as he handed them over.

We'd told him and Cayce about the Ranguvariians' plan last night, and it'd been slow and painful. They had finally come to accept it as we had, but it was at a much steeper price.

Their tiny baby could not be separated from Cayce yet, so she would remain in Caark with him until he was weaned. Therefore, in order for Rhydin to believe our ruse of returning to the mainland with the children, we would have to create Einanhis of not only the three children but of Cayce as well, which only complicated things. Either way, I had been suddenly humbled about my own situation. I, at least, did not have to be separated from Sam.

"Well," I called out to distract my own mind as I returned to my post, "we should at least invite them over for a meal or something before we leave. They are going to our children's neighbors, and it would be best if they don't think we hate their guts."

Rachel grumped, "No way. Jaspen and I are more than capable of guarding three small children by ourselves regardless of whether they like us or not. It's much harder to guard adult twins who seem to have a knack for finding danger."

"Which, I might add, is not entirely our fault," Evan announced as he hammered a window frame into one of the walls.

"Hey, look," I said loudly as my eyes picked up two figures leaving the shack across the way. "There they are now. Go invite them to dinner, Rachel," I laughed.

My friend glared at me, her blue eyes like ice. "No, thanks."

"Fine, I'll do it. I want our kids to be as safe as possible," I responded. Then, I set my tools down on some shingles I had already nailed down and put both arms into the air, yelling, "Hey! Chelsea, Sonya! Come here for a sec'!"

The two people paused for a moment, seeming to deliberate, and then continued on toward town a little bit more in our direction. I was left wondering whether they really were heading our way for several more minutes before they clearly left the main road and truly headed toward us.

Rachel rolled her eyes as both Jaspen and Bartholomiiu disappeared into flashes of bright light, no doubt to go visit Bartholomiiu's "happy ocean" again since they couldn't be seen. Luke and James remained busy with putting up walls, but I could tell they were keenly paying more attention to the world beyond their work than they were before. What was it about Chelsea and Sonya that sprung their gut instincts so much when they seemed perfectly normal to Evan and I?

Chelsea had a political smile on her angelic face when they arrived at our campsite while Sonya wore her usual scowl. The first flicked a strand of mint green hair out of her eyes and then planted a hand on her hip as she said, "Hello there, again. What is it?"

As both Sonya and Rachel grumbled in the background, I climbed back down our homemade ladder and smiled politely. "We were wondering if you two would like to join us for dinner sometime? To get to know each other better."

"Ah," Chelsea responded, hesitation flashing across her face briefly. She looked to Sonya so rapidly I nearly missed it, and then turned back to me. "Sure. Of course. Just name the date."

"Great!" I replied a little too enthusiastically in my effort to cover the awkwardness. "How about…?"

I trailed off, and panic gripped my throat as heat gripped my spine. For just a few seconds, it seemed that I was the only one who could sense it, but when my gaze shot behind me, I could see the realization and fear on Evan's face as well.

Darkness had arrived. Rhydin's darkness.

Immediately, Rachel, Luke, and James stopped what they were doing and jumped up, looking all around them to find the source of Rhydin's magic that we were sensing. I tried not to panic as I looked around and instinctually located Kylar and Rayna sleeping peacefully between the fire and the house. However, a bloodcurdling snarl erupted from behind me and instilled a new kind of fear in my heart.

Where Chelsea and Sonya once stood were now two, beast-looking humanoids. They were only around four feet tall, but my eyes were arrested by the sight of ferocious fangs and long, lethal claws that extended from fingers clad in lavender skin as smooth as an eel's. They glared up at me in fury with golden eyes, one of them capped with mint green hair and one with crimson hair that spiked in every which direction.

I finally got a hold of myself and jumped back just as Jaspen and Bartholomiiu reappeared in a burst of light declaring, "On the beach, they! Headed fast this way! Not sure if Followers or Einanhis, th-…"

The two Ranguvariians stopped dead in their tracks at the sight of what used to be Chelsea and Sonya, and the two dwarf-like beasts hissed maniacally at their appearance. Rachel, Luke, and James leapt forward to separate Evan and I from the two strange beings as a cacophony of voices and magic reached my ears from the direction of the beach. Half a dozen figures in black were racing this direction with all of us squarely in their sights.

Rachel growled in frustration, momentarily torn between whom she needed to take care of first. I snatched my sash, balled it up, and summoned my sword from within, trying to be ready for anything. I turned to the creatures in front of me, but to my surprise, they snarled, hissed, and leapt right over our heads, furiously sprinting toward the oncoming midnight squadron.

While the Owenses stared in shock, Jaspen and Bartholomiiu didn't waste any time gaining on their heels, drawing their blades to engage with Rhydin's scouts. Evan and I hurried after them, and as soon as we grew close, I gained confidence when I saw one of the black-clad invaders dissolve into sand after being impaled by the crimson-haired creature's claws.

They were just Einanhis. We had hope.

"Don't let any of them get away!" I shouted as I reached the fray, charging an attack spell and launching it at the Einanhi that was sparring with Bartholomiiu. The Einanhi dissolved, and I hoped I had gotten to Bartholomiiu fast enough to stop him from getting fatigued.

To my surprise, he turned to me with a wild grin on his face, not weary at all compared to when they normally came into close contact with Rhydin's magic. My mind raced with confusion, but now simply wasn't the time. Bartholomiiu, instead, turned like lightning on his heel and plunged his blade deep into an Einanhi trying to sneak up behind him. It turned to dust.

Evan made quick work of the fourth Einanhi while the two bloodthirsty terrors took care of the fifth. There was only one remaining that had separated itself from the rest, and my jaw dropped when I realized it was about to lay hands on Luke from behind. Images of Jaspen's and Bartholomiiu's horrific wounds and scars from the last time they had been touched by Rhydin's magic, Rhydin himself in that instance, during the war burst in my mind. Before I even knew what I was doing, I drew upon my magic and summoned an attack spell, hurling it over my head as hard as I could.

Before the buzzing ball of golden energy could make it, the last Einanhi grabbed Luke by his bare forearm. While my ears expected a scream of agony, Luke gave a loud grunt before he shoved the Einanhi off, and my spell collided with it, reducing it to sand the same as the rest. As soon as the danger had vanished, Luke rapidly began inspecting his forearm, his eyes widening and turning a deeper topaz with every passing second.

Rachel jogged over to her brother, concern swamping her face. "What's wrong? Are you okay?"

Luke nodded numbly as the rest of approached. His forearm looked nothing like the ugly, melted skin that Jaspen and Bartholomiiu experienced. It was red and blistering a little, like a bad sunburn that would likely peel at some point, but nothing more.

An idea popped into my mind. "The Einanhi, Rhydin's pure magic, touched him," I said slowly, "Is it not as bad because he's part human?"

Rachel shook her head like molasses, incomprehension perfectly visible on her face. "No. We've been touched by Rhydin's magic before and have plenty of scars to prove it." She paused for a moment, still thinking, and then turned to her mate and other brother. She stuttered, "Did either of you feel tired at all around them?"

One by one, Jaspen, James, and even Bartholomiiu shook their heads back and forth, their eyes as wide as saucers.

"Neither did I," Rachel murmured, before she suddenly remembered that the two creatures that were once Chelsea and Sonya were still here.

She whirled on the two of them just as they turned into glowing, soft-blue silhouettes which stretched back up to the average height of a human being and lost the claw outlines. When the glowing faded, they appeared as Chelsea and Sonya again, the former appearing very sheepish while the latter seemed even angrier than she was before.

Rachel crossed her arms furiously. "I knew it. I knew we couldn't trust them."

Before she could move, I threw my hands in her direction. "W-w-wait! Our neighbors randomly transform into terrifying creatures, and that's *all* you have to say about it?" I looked around at all the Ranguvariians surrounding me, who all appeared calm if not a teensy bit miffed. Evan, on the other hand, seemed as panicked as I was. "What's going on here?" – I turned to Chelsea and Sonya now – "What are you?"

Sonya threw a hateful glance at my five Ranguvariian friends. She said still with the hint of a hiss, "I'm not surprised your *special* Ranguvariians didn't tell you about us. They like to think Nerahdis only belonged to them before the humans invaded!"

"And it did!" Rachel's temper flared. "The land was ours and the seas were yours! That was the agreement that dates back a thousand years! I don't see why you're all still so angry considering the humans actually stole our territory while your waters remain untouched!"

"Untouched?" Chelsea scoffed, "The humans have fished our waters so thoroughly that species have gone extinct and our hunters must work night and day to feed us! When we wanted to attack the humans and drive them back to their ships, your great Clariion refused!"

Luke spat in response, "They had nowhere to go! We wanted to live in harmony with them. We Ranguvariians actually want peace unlike you filthy nymphs!"

"Aatarilecs," Chelsea corrected with a sneer. "Address us properly you 'giants'!"

"Alright, alright, enough already!" I shouted as I put myself between Rachel and Chelsea. "Will somebody *please* enlighten my brother and I as to what's going on here?"

James piped up with a surprisingly calm voice even as his eyes never left Chelsea and Sonya. "Ranguvariians are not the only native inhabitants of Nerahdis, or 'mythical creatures' as you humans like to call us. There are also Aatarilecs. Our mortal enemies for as long as our peoples have existed."

"Ah-try-lehks?" I sounded out the strange word and looked Chelsea and Sonya up and down. "Why do you look human?"

"We have a small amount of power that allows us to change form, although anger or fear will often revert us back to our true form," Chelsea answered as Sonya balked at her. "However, now I must ask, who are you? And why have you brought Rhydin to our home?"

Rachel cut in before I had a chance to answer, "These are the Allyens. The ones who will destroy Rhydin. We are helping them, unlike you."

"My apologies," Chelsea replied with a bitter smile, "my tribe was not made aware that the Allyens were in such dire need of our help."

Rachel could have blown steam out of her nostrils. She yelled, "Get out of here! We don't need your help!"

"Ha, we'd never help you anyway," Sonya mocked just as she and Chelsea began to turn back toward town once more.

"But, wait!" I shouted and put my hand on Rachel's steaming shoulder. "You just said so yourself that you've *never* fought Rhydin's power without feeling drained or been touched by that power without nearly dying! Just now, Luke looks like he simply got a sunburn when the last time, Bartholomiiu's neck was absolutely destroyed, and he had brain damage! What if it was Chelsea and Sonya's presence that made the difference? That's the only thing that's different about this fight!"

"It's doesn't matter," Rachel responded. "It would never work. There's too much history between our peoples."

"But you just said that the Ranguvariians want peace. Why don't you want peace with the Aatarilecs too? Maybe then, you'd all know how to swim," I added disdainfully.

Chelsea and Sonya snickered as all five Ranguvariians blushed, and I realized I might have gone too far. Chelsea crossed her arms, and one of her hips jutted out as she spoke, "Even if we did want to help our mortal enemies, what's in it for us?"

"A world free of Rhydin," Evan announced to the group, reminding us all that he was still here. "Plus, two of the future Three Kings are our friends. We could try to fix the overfishing problem that's leaving you hungry."

"And what of the third?" Sonya asked harshly. "Auklia has no leader anymore, and our tribe lives in the Auklian Basin."

"We're working on finding one, and when we do, we'll fix it, I promise," I declared, and then changed my tone. "Please help us. When those Einanhis don't return to Rhydin, he'll know that something is up here. We're running out of time to build a shelter to keep our children safe after we return to the mainland. Even just helping us finish this building would be great."

Chelsea and Sonya glanced at each other, a full, nonverbal conversation unfolding between them before our eyes. After a few moments, Sonya tossed her head and gave a short, strange bow to Chelsea.

The mint-green-haired woman smirked at us. "Sure. We'll see what we can do. On one condition."

Rachel groaned loudly and turned away like she couldn't watch, plucking up hammer to play with absentmindedly. Jaspen glanced at her sadly.

"What is it?" I asked.

"You not only rid us of Rhydin and the human encroachment on our fishing grounds, but you also make us out to be the heroes to the rest of our tribe. They banished us here to Caark, and we want to go home," Chelsea stated stoically.

"Done," I answered before I could think better of it.

Rachel angrily tossed her hammer and began marching away with Jaspen on her heels. Luke and James looked at each other with worried expressions, but said nothing more, while nothing seemed to be able to sway Bartholomiiu's happy mood. Evan nodded at me, and I ardently hoped that we had made the right decision. I stuck my hand out to Chelsea, and after she considered the very human gesture for a few moments, she reached out and accepted it, for better or worse.

With Chelsea and Sonya's help and resources, we finished the house as fast as we could in two days' time. It was small with an earthen floor, but aside from the island materials, it reminded me a lot of the house I had grown up in Soläna. More important, it was solid, and we had chinked and sealed it twice as well as we would have in Lunaka in our best attempt to brace it for the island storms to come. Although, in my mind, I continued to insist that our children wouldn't even be here a year.

The morning of our departure, my feet dragged. My hands were numb as I gathered my things. Sam would waver between sticking to my side like glue and not being able to look at me. Evan and Cayce remained sequestered away from the campfire with Aron for as long as possible. Meanwhile, Jaspen and Rachel stood around the house awkwardly, seeming to study its walls and beams for the first time. They, too, seemed to be having trouble soaking in the fact that Evan and I, people they had looked after for many years, were leaving the island without them.

We made sure both Kylar and Rayna were awake for our departure, and they carried on with their usual morning routine like nothing was different. We served them a breakfast of the sweet, purple, Caarkian fruit along with a couple of duck eggs that Cayce had managed to haggle down to a realistic price yesterday.

I took a deep breath and knelt down next to Kylar as purple juice dribbled down his chin. I rubbed his head and thick hair the color of my own, and I willed myself to keep it together. I warbled, "Mama and Papa have somewhere very important to go, Kylar. But we'll be back soon. We promise. We love you."

Kylar glanced at me with his big, brown eyes and smiled, purple egg squeezing out between his baby teeth. I grinned in spite of myself, and I hoped that he understood most of what I had said if not all of it. I repeated something similar to Rayna, who likely didn't understand all of what I had said, but I think it was more for me than for her. Sam bid his own quiet adieus to the two toddlers. We both planted kisses on their heads before ushering ourselves out the door as quickly as possible before it was too hard to leave.

Cayce was immediately on the other side, running through the open door stone-faced likely in the same goal, little Aron tucked into her side, snoozing. She didn't look at us, but I didn't blame her. Evan stood several feet away with his hands in his pockets, his shoulders slumped. I began to walk toward him as Rachel followed us out the door, her face pink.

"Well," she said breathily, "this is it."

I stopped and turned. "Yeah. I guess it is."

Rachel swallowed hard and then grasped my hand. "I'm sorry. For everything. I know we haven't always seen eye to eye, and I know I can be bossy. But it's because you're not just the Allyen to me. You're my friend. My best friend."

"Easy, Rachel." I tried to crack a smile to keep myself from crying. "You're acting like this is forever. I'm going to do everything in my power to find our new rebellion a safe place, and you'll see me again before you know it. You're my best friend, too."

Rachel nodded and sniffed as Luke, James, and Bartholomiiu appeared behind us to transport us to the port in Calitia. She chuckled to break the tension, "Keep my brothers in line, will ya? They won't know what to do without me bossing them around all the time."

Luke and James glanced at each other and rolled their eyes. I laughed and agreed before I gave her a quick hug. Then, I took one last long look at the tiny house with our children inside before turning on my heel and walking in the opposite direction.

The three Ranguvariians transported the three of us humans as close to Calitia as they dared get without being spotted, maybe a quarter mile away in a brushy clearing. I asked why we couldn't just transport all the way back to the mainland instead of bothering with the ship, but I had forgotten that we needed to create a few Einanhis to travel with us to complete our façade that the children returned with us.

Sweat balled up on my skin regardless of the island humidity. With Sam's being a Rounan and the three Ranguvariians also having an entirely different type of magic, it was up to Evan and I to create these Einanhis. And it was impossible for him to create them by himself. Two failed birds or not, it was crunch time now.

"Alright, so we have these," Luke announced as he pointed to two bundles in James's arms, one tiny like a newborn and the other much larger, "to simulate Aron and Rayna since we can only make two Einanhis and they're small enough that this will work. You two just need to be the ones to carry them so that your presences mask the fact that these bundles don't have any magic. Speaking of which, hand over your feathers."

Evan's eyes went wide, and I gaped. Sam showed no reaction.

"Rhydin has to be able to *sense* that you guys have returned to the mainland, he's watching all these ships like a hawk. That's the whole point, otherwise he'll still come to Caark to search for you," Luke explained. "Now, hand 'em over."

I reached for my neck soundlessly, picking out the leather cord from the metal chain, both of which I had worn for so many years they were like a part of my skin. I threaded the sleek, purple feather shard away from my locket and looped it over my head, dropping it into Luke's hand. It all felt very surreal as Evan and Sam followed suit.

"Good. You'll get those back after we've been in Lunaka for maybe a week so that Rhydin doesn't grow suspicious," Luke said as he pocketed the three feather charms. "Now, we just need to create Einanhis of Cayce and Kylar, and we can go board our boat! Once there, we have some important information to tell you."

I opened my mouth to ask about this information, but Evan put a solid hand on my shoulder and leaned in to say, "You can do this. I'll do Cayce's and you can do Kylar's. That way, just hedge more toward not giving him enough magic if you're worried. If he looks limp, it won't be the end of the world since he's just a kid. We can pretend he's sleeping. So, you can do this. Don't worry about messing up."

My heart began to pound. Evan closed his eyes, took a deep breath, and concentrated. This would be the largest and most complex Einanhi he had ever attempted, I remembered.

Before I knew it, a large, golden orb had appeared. It grew to a couple inches taller than Evan, which I had never realized before, and the glowing ball thinned down and sprouted two limbs on either side, looking more human-like with every passing second. Finally, Evan focused for a moment or two before his eyes opened with a sad gleam, and he whispered, "*Anadlu.*"

The yellow, human-shaped bubble burst, and in its place was Cayce's identical twin. Her lavender curls were spot on, and she wore an outfit that I recognized although hadn't seen since before we'd left the Compound, one that likely burnt up in its destruction but must have been Evan's favorite. The Einanhi Cayce blinked at us slowly and then smiled, and I noticed that Evan had neglected to put Cayce's small scar on her cheek. Actual human beings had to be the hardest Einanhis to create, I decided.

Luke and James nodded in approval, and then turned to me expectantly. My heart rate doubled, and I tried to breathe evenly. I could do this.

I shut my eyes tightly and pictured my son. This was somewhat easy to do since I had just seen him, yet it was hard when I remembered that I wouldn't actually see him again for some time. I familiarized myself with his height, taller than the average two-and-a-half-year-old due to his father's frame, and his coloring. His face that reminded me of Sam's when I'd first met him as a child. It was hard not to get choked up, but I had to focus.

I shifted my magic outwards, and judging by the glow against my eyelids and the sudden siphoning of my energy, I knew my orb had appeared. Anxiously, I cut off the flow a little earlier than I probably should have, but a limp Einanhi was better than one on an uncontrollable rampage. I stammered, "*Anadlu*," and opened my eyes.

Standing before me was not quite Kylar's twin, but Luke and James grinned in response so it must not have been too bad. I was his mother after all. The Einanhi Kylar's eyelids and shoulders drooped. It didn't have quite enough power, and even though I had planned for this, I was still disappointed in myself.

Sam stooped and collected the Einanhi Kylar into his arms, and Evan and I took our respective bundles. We made our way to Calitia in silence where we were enveloped in the noise of an overcrowded city. Bartholomiiu broke away to meet us on the ship, and Luke and James guided us through the sardined alleyways and treacherous streets to the port with the Einanhi Cayce following dutifully. My eyes glazed over and didn't see much of what went on around us. With every step we took, the distance between us and our children became more tangible.

We boarded a Caarkian ship that was sleeker in style than the Lunakan liner we had set out on, and we all walked toward the entrance to the underbelly of the ship, none of us really interested in remaining on the main deck this go around. I reached for Sam's hand, but he didn't respond. His eyes empty and sad as he lugged around a magical shell shaped like our son. I guess I couldn't blame him too much.

When we reached the compartment we would all be sharing on this much smaller ship, Luke gave a sigh of relief as he shut the tiny door behind us. "That was good. If Rhydin is watching this port as closely as we think, he'll have seen us. You can take a break from keeping up the Einanhis for now, but if we ever go up to the main deck, we should have them with us, as well as when we arrive in Canis."

Instantly, the Einanhi of Cayce disappeared, and Evan gasped for breath as if he had just sprinted a mile. It must have been more complicated and draining to keep her up than I'd thought. I let Kylar disappear as well, if only not to have the reminder that he really wasn't here.

I turned to Luke keenly and asked, "So what was this important thing you had to tell us?"

The edges of Luke's mouth twitched upwards as he said, "Frederick figured out who the woman in Archimage Dathian's portrait miniature is."

Chapter Eleven

"Her name is Sabine." Luke's voice trickled back to me from our voyage back across the ocean nearly a month ago. "She's Dathian's daughter and the only heir left to the Auklian throne. She disappeared over a decade ago when her mother left Dathian and the Archimage Palace."

"If she disappeared so long ago, how do you think we could ever find her?" My response echoed in my ears. "She could be dead for all we know."

Luke had simply shrugged. "In my experience, you can't assume someone is dead until you see the light leave their eyes yourself."

A month had passed since that conversation. Once arriving back on the mainland, we spent a few days in Canis before discovering that very few of the people there were remotely interested in joining our cause. Canis's economy was booming between the fish trade gaining customers throughout Nerahdis as Rhydin struck down trade laws and tariffs and the massive influx of travelers paying their ships for passage to Caark.

People couldn't have cared less about anything beyond their city and didn't believe us when we claimed that Rhydin was sinking their ships. He was too much of a "hero" for that. I wondered how long it would take before Rhydin thoroughly made sure they all knew that he was in charge.

When we left Canis, we began cycling back and forth over the border between Lunaka and Auklia. We searched for random settlements and other secret Rounan compounds on our way to Rondeau, a small town in northeastern Auklia. With every stop, we tried to discover any interest in a rebellion against Rhydin as well as any leads on what happened to Lady Sabine. Sometimes there was some interest due to older folks' nostalgia for the old ways. Sometimes there wasn't, due to the "good" things people still believed Rhydin to be doing, but there was never any information on Sabine. I was beginning to wonder if both of our tasks were impossible.

I let myself fade back into the present moment, which I had purposely left to let my thoughts ramble for a reason. The sun was beating down on the top of my head, roasting my scalp. Sam, Evan, and I stood in the middle of a crowd of Rounans at yet another small Rounan settlement at the base of the mountains dividing Lunaka and Auklia. They had listened to our speech intently, as most Rounans did due to their experience with Rhydin, but the conversation afterward had taken a nasty turn from a polite debate of pros and cons for stepping forward against Rhydin.

"If we oppose Rhydin, won't the Royals step back into control?" one portly man bellowed. "Nothing will change for us! Rhydin hunts us down and so do the Gornish!"

"No, things will change!" Sam tried to say. "If we succeed, we will make sure that Prince Frederick and Prince Xavier are placed on their rightful thrones, and both of them have sworn against ever allowing Rounan persecution again!"

"That's what you think!" an old, scrawny woman in a threadbare cap called. "The Gornish have always lied, we can't trust them! Besides, Auklia has no leader anymore!"

Another young man chimed in, "Can we trust you, Kidek? You've married a Gornish witch, how do we know she isn't manipulating you into our destruction?"

Evan instinctively put a hand in front of me, and Sam's jaw tightened. My eyes wandered over to Sam, wondering how he would react. He had shut down after we left Caark, and I could only assume that it was because of how he felt about leaving our children.

Sam responded more politically than I would have preferred, "I assure you, that is not the case. My wife has everyone's best interests at heart, and she lived with me in another Rounan compound in Lunaka for over two years before it was destroyed."

"By the Gornish?" the first man sneered.

"No. By Rhydin and his Followers. And if we don't do something about it, he'll just keep destroying our homes and murdering us!" Sam replied tersely.

A couple people shook their heads and walked away, but the majority of the crowd remained. They looked at each other, and I could see a few nod, even if it was hesitantly.

A young woman shouted, "If we want to join you, what do we do?"

The smallest hints of a smile lingered on Sam's lips. "Right now, we are still searching for a safe, central location to establish a base. We want it to be new so that Rhydin has no knowledge of it. When that day comes, I will send word to this compound to come join us there."

The woman and a few other people nodded again while the rest looked on. Some of them appeared intrigued, and others were utterly unreadable. As per usual, we left that compound with a vague idea that we may have reached more than we could tell, but without any real idea of numbers. Too many people, Gornish and Rounan alike, seemed to have been terrorized by the magic-hungry Royals for far too long.

The Ranguvariians rejoined us shortly outside the compound, and we rode on in silence. Technically, our numbers had evened out to the point where Luke, James, and Bartholomiiu could transport us anywhere in Nerahdis, but traveling the old-fashioned way gave us more of an excuse to search for a safe place to make our new home. A big place to hold lots of people, yet nondescript as to not gain unwanted attention. It had to be the perfect combination, and we needed to see as many options as possible.

As the sun stretched toward the western horizon, its rays lingering just for a few minutes more before disappearing, my mind harkened back to Sam's mention of Frederick and Xavier. It seemed like ages since we'd seen them or spoken to them. Mine and Frederick's letter-writing had ended when we left for Caark, and I hadn't seen Xavier since the battle at the Archimage Palace because he'd refused to show up at our meeting earlier in the year. After being around them for so long, it felt strange to be separated and have no contact. How were they faring? Mira and Taisyn, Cornflower and Dominick, too?

My saddle felt empty without Rayna tucked in with me. I noticed her and Kylar's absence wherever I looked, especially whenever I looked at Sam. It'd been so long since it was just the two of us. My heart ached.

Evan's horse suddenly sped up to match mine's pace. He peered over at me in the fading light. "You okay?"

I looked at him funny, trying to figure out what he was talking about. Then, I remembered the comments from the Rounans. "Yeah," I sighed. "I guess I should be used to it by now. It took a long time for the Rounans at our old compound to not hate me, and some of them never did quite get there."

"Well, I just want you to know that I think they're disillusioned," Evan replied, his voice becoming harder. "They like to play the victims that paint the Gornish as the bad guys, but it seems to be that they're just as judgmental."

"You got that right," I blurted, feeling vindicated. After a few seconds of thought, I added, "Do you think there's truly good and evil? I mean… We *are* the good guys, right?"

To my dismay, Evan screwed up his face a little as he considered his answer. "To be honest, I don't really believe in absolutes like that. Nobody is perfectly good and nobody is perfectly evil," Evan responded. "I mean, Rhydin obviously thinks that he is in the right and that he is doing something good by usurping the Royals and taking Nerahdis. He doesn't see what he's doing as evil."

"Are you *defending* Rhydin?" I demanded, nearly stopping my horse in its tracks.

"Of course not!" Evan replied. "I'm just saying that I don't think there's such a thing as totally good or totally evil. It's more complicated than that. People are more complicated than that. I think good and evil are things that are determined by how it affects others, not the person themselves. Which is why it's so important that we do what we're doing for the right reasons."

"What do you mean?" I asked.

"Well, Frederick and Xavier are our friends. We like them, and we want them to have their thrones back. But we need to be doing that because it's what's best for the people, not just because we like them and don't like Rhydin," Evan explained.

"Which is what we're doing," I answered, starting to feel defensive. "What's best for the people is to not be ruled by a dictator who murders people and lies to them."

"I know," Evan said sheepishly, his shoulders hunching a little. "We just need to make sure to never lose sight of that. Y'know?"

I nodded quietly, turning my attention back to my horse. The Ranguvariians had stopped ahead, likely ready to make camp for the night.

"I think," Evan declared, "that the next Gornish town we come to, we should try a different tactic."

"Like what?" I questioned doubtfully.

"I think instead of just trying to attack Rhydin, whom people really like right now, and advocate for what people see as the old way, we should try putting you forward as a leader," Evan suggested hesitantly.

As my horse came to a halt, I looked at my brother like he had two heads. "*Why?*"

Evan shrugged. "Because you're a commoner. Just like them. They might relate to you more."

"But I have magic. They might not think that," I answered sadly. "Besides, I'll never be a leader of one of the kingdoms. Isn't that lying?"

"Not necessarily," my twin replied as he slid off his saddle to the ground. "You're more of a leader than you think, and this rebellion is going to need as much guidance as it can get."

I let his words soak in as I dismounted. I'd never thought of myself as much of a leader really. I was going to have to think about that one for a little while.

Our life settled back into its new routine, which felt eerily similar to the rituals we had created during our journey to Caark. Even though our numbers had been cut in half. Luke, James, and Bartholomiiu busied themselves with preparing the fire and establishing a perimeter for watch duty while Evan prepared to make our meal. It turned out that he actually somewhat enjoyed cooking even if he preferred fish and destroyed any beef or venison that made it into his unfortunate hands. Since returning to the Three Kingdoms, I had eaten far more fish than I had in my entire life.

I settled myself next to Sam by the fire, trying to ignore the empty ache that always plagued my arms this time of night. Kylar and Rayna were far safer where they were, even if it hurt. Sam, I knew, was quietly struggling with the same thing. He remained close to me, but he never brought up any topics of conversation. At the beginning of our travels to the different towns in Lunaka and Auklia, I used to bury my nose in the history book, but even that had lost my interest now.

There was nothing else about Rhydin. The rest of the book was useless to me, aside from one interesting portrait of my ancestor, Nora Soreta, the first Allyen. She was tall and muscular with a lean face. But I couldn't read anything about her since Frederick and I's correspondence had ended while we were in Caark. I kept meaning to strike it up again, but I felt guilty that the only real reason I wanted to talk to him was to pick his brain for definitions.

When the sun rose the next day, bringing with it the moist heat of summer, I dragged my feet in preparation for the day's ride. Every morning for the last month had been the same, and it was wearing on me. The dew would burn off shortly, and the clothes I'd been wearing for the last month would gather more dust, more sweat, and more dirt. It was rare when we'd come across a stream in which to wash. Life on the road was getting old rapidly.

As Evan willed an Einanhi squirrel into existence to help the Ranguvariians scout our route ahead, an idea occurred to me. Maybe, I could create my own little Einanhi to steer our group more toward a river or inlet from Auklia's basin. The practice certainly wouldn't hurt after my last attempt, which resulted in a very low-power Kylar.

I closed my eyes, and after a few moments, I felt the siphoning of my magic away from me and toward the small bird in my mind. Another Lunakan wren, quite a bit simpler than creating a pint-sized human being. I let the power drain into it a little more than I had with the Einanhi Kylar, but then abruptly shut it off as I suddenly sensed the bird felt…full, in some weird way. Whispering the incantation, I hesitantly opened my eyes, afraid to see if I'd created another uncontrollable monster.

There, in front of me, was a tiny, Lunakan wren, exactly how I'd pictured it. It twitched its head back and forth, eyeing me with one eye before flipping its head to the other side to get a good look at me with the other. Seemed like typical bird behavior. I stared at it for a few more seconds, anxiously ready to end it if I needed to. But the attack never came. Instead, it just stared back.

"Uh…" I uttered, not sure of what to say. "Follow my brother's squirrel and steer it toward some sort of body of water, if it's not too far."

The bird dipped its head and beak as if in a bow, then flew off in the direction Evan's squirrel had scurried. I couldn't help but stare after it. Had I really successfully created an Einanhi? And, of course, when no one else was watching.

I darted to my horse and threw myself up into the burning-hot, leather saddle. I hollered as I kicked its sides to follow, "I made an Einanhi! I made an Einanhi! Hurry up, boys, you've gotta see it!"

Before Sam, Evan, or the three Ranguvariians could even mount their horses, I was gone in a flash. Feeling the wind in my face was like a breath of fresh air now, and I didn't feel the heat bouncing off the top of my head or singeing my bare arms. We were still in a forest in southern Lunaka, having recently crossed the mountains from Auklia for the umpteenth time, but the trees didn't slow me down. My horse expertly maneuvered through them, the joy of a run evident in his perky ears and gleeful trot compared to the boring walks he'd been subjected to for the last month.

All of a sudden, there was a flash of orange out of nowhere. My horse reared up so fast that his neck collided with my nose, and before I knew it, I was tumbling backwards out of the saddle and fell hard to the ground. My horse screamed and snorted, prancing around as he reared a couple more times. I tried to roll and get away from him, but my ribs were screaming with red-hot pain.

I threw my hands up to stop the stomping horse with some sort of magic, lights flashing at my fingertips, but a figure jumped in the way. A woman's voice crooned as she held her hands up toward the spooked beast, "Easy, easy!"

After a few moments, the screeching and snorting horse eased himself back down onto all four hooves. He shook his head and took several gasping breaths, although he never took his eyes off of the woman in front of him, especially the bright, orange turban wrapped around her head.

I coughed and sputtered, "I'm so sorry! I nearly ran you over!"

The woman turned in surprise, her eyes a beautiful crimson color like I'd never seen before. She chuckled deeply as she noticed me holding my ribs, unable to get up. "Somehow, I think we're even," she said melodically, a thick Auklian accent coming out loud and clear. She held her darkly tanned hand out to me, "My name is Anne. Now, who might you be with that fancy light magic of yours?"

I grunted and groaned loudly as she hauled me to my feet, clutching my ribs fiercely. "I'm Lina," I mumbled before looking around the small clearing briefly to make sure it was safe. "I'm one of the Allyens."

"No kiddin'?" Anne huffed before the sounds of bickering reached our ears. The woman, who looked like she could be close to thirty, shouted over her shoulder, "You quit that and come on out here, boys!"

Two young boys, who were the spitting image of each other and looked to be around five, sprinted out of the thick bushes behind Anne and dashed over to Anne, hiding behind her plethora of rainbow sashes and sensible trousers. Both of them had bright red hair and eyes the color of a green, Auklian tree frog.

I struggled to breathe, holding my ribs tighter and trying not to focus on their faces too long lest I be reminded of my own little ones. I asked, "Are these your sons?"

"Good gracious, no. These two are Chretien and Willian, a couple of war orphans I stumbled across about a year ago. I guess I might as well start calling them my own, I suppose. They're as good as such!" Anne snorted a couple times, and then turned a serious, scarlet eye in my direction. "So. An

Allyen, huh? What's one of the Allyens doing all the way out here?"

"Eh, it's a long story," I replied as I scratched the back of my neck. Abruptly, it occurred to me that this woman was a living, breathing soul who didn't seem to hate my guts, so I took a deep breath. "Actually, my brother and I are traveling around to find any opposition against Rhydin. What do you think of him?"

"Ugh, I hate that sorry scoundrel!" Anne seethed as the twin boys huddled behind her.

"Really," I responded, trying not to sound too shocked. It wasn't often I ran into someone who actually disliked him, much less hated him. "Why?"

"Well, why do you hate him?" Anne shrugged, looking at me like I was crazy. "He just swooped in after the war and took control of the whole entire continent. I'm a skeptical person, Miss Allyen. I know when I smell fish, there's usually something fishy."

"Yes! I-I agree with you!" I stammered with excitement. "He shouldn't be in charge, and you don't even know the half of it! Would you be interested in joining my brother and I in creating a rebellion against his reign?"

"Well. That depends," Anne responded as she cocked one of her hips out. For the first time, I noticed a well-shined, well-worn sword at her side. "What will you Allyens do when he's out of power? How do I know you two won't just create your own empire in Rhydin's place?"

I gawked at her, totally taken off guard.

"I don't trust people very easily, Miss Allyen," Anne continued, her eyes falling to the two boys who had slowly come out from behind her to play in the clearing. "I'm just a wanderer. In my experience, I can't trust anyone but myself."

"Please, call me Lina," I pleaded, "and I completely understand where you're coming from. There are very few people in Nerahdis I can trust too. I promise you that Evan and I aren't interested in ruling, only in removing Rhydin from power and putting Prince Frederick and Prince Xavier back on their rightful thrones."

"Great," Anne scoffed, "so we can be abused again?"

"No, no!" I cried urgently. "Frederick and Xavier are different. They're going to end the persecution of Rounans and non-Royals with magic. They're my friends, and I trust them with my life and the lives of my own children!"

"And what about Auklia, hm?" Anne asked testily.

"Well, we're working on that," I said quietly. "We're searching for the heir to the Auklian throne as well as traveling Nerahdis looking for support against Rhydin. A Lady Sabine, actually. Have you heard any stories about where she could be?"

Anne's lips pressed into a line. "I heard that she was dead."

"No." I wilted, deflating.

"Yes, ma'am. I heard that she died just a few years after leaving the Archimage Palace with her mother. My own mother was a maid there," Anne said slowly.

I looked down, distraught. Sabine was our only hope at finding an heir who could lead Auklia alongside Frederick and Xavier. What would we do now?

"But," Anne announced rather loudly as she planted her fists on her hips, "I am interested in seeing what this rebellion of yours is all about. As well as meeting these two princes and seeing if they are who you say they are. I suppose we can quit our aimless wandering for a little while, and come along on your journey." She mused the last part as she turned to look at the two playing boys.

Suddenly, it felt like my shoulders had been strung too tight, and the ache in my ribs worsened. What would the Ranguvariians think when they discovered that a stranger would be traveling with us? Bartholomiiu would have to keep his distance for sure. Not to mention the two young boys. We had just left our own children behind because of the danger we were constantly in, yet we had just gained two more young people to have to worry about. But, we were in such need of support, could I really tell her no?

"That sounds great," I replied through my teeth, trying to sound as genuine as possible. "We're headed to Stellan right now, as well as any settlements we happen upon in between. You're welcome to participate, although not all of our debates have been pretty to watch."

Anne shrugged. "That's alright. With how ridiculously skewed Rhydin's reign has made everything appear to most people, I couldn't imagine anything less than chaotic!"

CHAPTER TWELVE

———⟨⟨✦⟩⟩———

A rare, summer rain rolled into the mountains above the small cottage that Frederick and the fractured remains of his family called home. The much-needed water soaked into the rocky ground and trickled down the slope, re-carving a myriad of paths down the mountain's face that had been there for centuries. For far longer than any Gornish person had set foot on Nerahdis, much less Rhydin or Frederick's ancestors for that matter.

Frederick sat quietly at the table in the center of the home. Instead of the gold-lined, mahogany table that had occupied the Royals' former cottage between Lun and the Rounan Compound, this one was hand-hewn from rough wood. Its place was in the home of a peasant, most certainly not that of a Royal.

But, quite frankly, the former table had been sold so long ago to pay for food that Frederick no longer noticed its plain replacement. Nearly all of their fine items were gone at this point, especially after Frederick was forced to give the former

Queen Lily all the gold he'd had on hand in exchange for the identity of Archimage Dathian's daughter, her husband's cousin, Lady Sabine.

Cornflower, however, tried to retain any remote resemblance to her previous life as she could. While Frederick journeyed from the cottage each day to hunt and forage, to provide for them, the fifteen-year-old girl would remain indoors doing what princesses typically did on their days off: stitching a tapestry, reading the last few books Frederick hadn't managed to sell yet, or continuing her education from the last textbook her tutor had given her before she left Lunaka Castle at the beginning of the war. She also provided care for the almost three-year-old Dominick, which Frederick appreciated immensely. Oh, how things would be different if Cassandra, his beloved wife, was still alive.

Frederick was just thinking to himself how their Ranguvariian messenger, whom he'd yet to learn the name of, had just checked in with them yesterday as Cornflower embroidered a red rayna flower to her tapestry, much like the pin Cassandra used to wear in her midnight hair, when a dark cloud crossed his senses. Everything went eerily quiet aside from the sound of the rain pattering outside. The Lunakan prince rapidly glanced down at the glass shard charm around his neck, a Ranguvariian feather that could hide his presence from being sensed by another mage. Surely, his senses had to be mistaken.

"Cornie," he breathed as his blue gaze met hers.

She was the picture of their mother, Gloria, as she sat on a mediocre, cushioned seat in the corner of the cottage, her golden curls spread behind her. Frederick watched as the darkness dawned on her senses as well, hers being slightly less trained at her age, and she mirrored his movement of looking for the shining, amethyst feather around her neck. Dominick was curled up on her lap underneath her tapestry, and Frederick could see the orange feather hanging from him.

How could he be sensing Rhydin's cruel, dark magic? There should have been no possible way for them to be found.

The prince jumped from his seat, accidentally knocking his stool over backwards. He drew upon his magic, summoning every air molecule in the general vicinity toward the cottage to make a defensive barrier of wind. Cornflower tossed her tapestry to the side and rapidly gathered Dominick into her arms. Then, she reached out with one hand and tried to aid her brother with what little magic she possessed.

They weren't quick enough.

Frederick was attempting to close the gaps in their barrier when somewhere out in the rain, a sharp slice of dark magic pierced their wind. He felt as if a dagger had truly nicked his heart. He grunted, his sister gasping in pain. Clutching his chest, Frederick pushed Cornflower away from the door toward the one, tiny window in the back and thrust a blast of wind at it. The window shattered into a million pieces, and the damp smell of the rain seeped into the cottage. Cornflower was hoisted halfway through the window, her blond hair darkening and plastering to her head in the wet, when the door to the cottage was blasted off its hinges.

Framed within the smoldering threshold was none other than Rhydin himself, and Frederick's heart nearly stopped beating. He dropped his sister and immediately fired two gusts of hurricane-force winds at the man who had tricked the rest of the world into calling him Emperor.

To Frederick's surprise, Rhydin didn't simply hold a hand up and catch his spells as he had in the past. Instead, the black-haired man threw his body sideways between the two charges, one of which happened to rip one of his regal sashes off, and then fired a blast of purple energy at Frederick's legs. The prince found this odd as well, but he was too busy dodging the surge to really think about it at the moment.

Rhydin's eyes narrowed. He was still unnervingly silent.

Frederick shouted, "How did you find us? What do you want?"

The hint of a smirk played at one of the edges of Rhydin's mouth. All of a sudden, he crossed his arms like a frustrated parent, and figures in black armor filtered through the hole in the wall. Frederick's heart sank lower than ever before when he realized that these people weren't Einanhis but actual, human soldiers of Nerahdis. His people.

Rhydin tried to keep his face slack for the sake of the soldiers around him, but for Frederick, there was no mistaking the dark joy in his violet eyes. "Prince Frederick and Princess Cornflower Tané of Lunaka, you are both under arrest for attacking your emperor with witchcraft."

Close to a week after we met Anne and added her and her two boys to our strange little caravan, Stellan appeared on the horizon. It started as nothing more than a tiny, black smudge, being the smallest town in Lunaka by far and one of the few that was built above ground. As we grew closer and the smudge grew larger, my eyes were arrested by the sight of the landscape around us.

For miles in each direction, all the farmland lay in ruin. Some fields were completely empty, as if seed had never been sown like those travelers had told us on our way to Canis. Others contained short, crispy corn stalks that fell over each other long ago as they baked in the summer sun, drying away into dust. The wheat and the barley too stretched across the cracked, parched earth as if it had been flattened. During a short break, I went on a small walk toward the nearest field, stretching my healing ribs. There, I took the liberty of plucking one of the dried wheat heads to roll it around in my hand like I'd done a million times, but it completely dissolved into ash to be carried away on the wind as soon as I touched it.

Not every crop year could be good. Every farmer had experienced their fair share. After all any little thing could go wrong when your livelihood sat under open sky with no protection. But my old theory was right. This wasn't a natural blight by any means. Only dark magic could have caused this. The only question was why.

My eyes met Sam's for the briefest of moments, and I could see recognition in his eyes as well. He knew just as I did that something wasn't quite right here. Then, he turned his head toward Stellan on the horizon, and anxiety seemed to age him ten years before my eyes. I tried to ask him what was wrong, but he kicked his horse into motion before I could.

We galloped along faster than before, and as we approached Stellan, my heart began to sink. Evan, who rode next to me, noticed my expression and asked, "What is it?"

I swallowed carefully before responding, "The last time I was in Stellan was when I picked up our cousin, Keera, four years ago."

Evan remained mute, a sadness masking his round face. Her death was still a fresh wound for him. Still a little for me, but far more for him, who actually raised her.

"I saw you for the first time then, too. Though I didn't know it. You were the person with the violin dropping her off," I kept rambling. "Life was so different...before. Sometimes I wonder if I would still be living with Rosetta and Keera on the farm if I'd never become the Allyen."

"Maybe if Rhydin never existed," Evan commented. "But if he hadn't existed, we would have never been separated. Our father would have never joined Rhydin. Rosetta probably never would have been born because our mother never would have remarried."

"You have a point," I mused, then turned to him more fully. "I hope you can meet her someday. My sis-...*our* sister. Rosetta."

"Me too," Evan said as he turned back to his horse. "I hope she finds her way away from Rhydin and can join our rebellion."

I chewed on my cheek. It still made me sick that she was stuck with Rhydin's people, all because of that Mikael. Sometimes I had nightmares about it. About him stealing her away and leaving the Einanhi of her body to trick me into thinking she was dead. About one of Rhydin's people killing her before she could get away. She had been so determined the last time I saw her that she could bring Mikael back to the light and leave together with him. I could only continue to hope that she was right.

My heart sank further when our entourage reached Stellan. Gone was the quaint little town that bubbled with country life. In its place was a ghost of its past, and the heavy cloud cover above certainly didn't help the grayish cast to everything. Houses and shops stood haphazardly, windows and doors hanging open like empty eyes. It was so quiet that the wind whistled, dragging dust from the main, dirt road along with it.

As we rode further into town, I started noticing something black smeared across doorways, sometimes in the shape of an "x" and others sloppily dripping down the walls to the threshold.

I'd seen this before. Memories came flooding back. Sam's eyes widened, and I knew he recognized it too, even though the two human-looking Ranguvariians, Evan, and Anne looked on in confusion. After all, the Epidemic had only ravaged Lunaka, well before the Owenses came to town.

Sam suddenly pulled tight on his horse's reins, which caused it to rear and scream in fright, before bolting down the main road to the east. James took off after him faster than my mind could compute. I would have followed if Evan and Anne hadn't looked to me with alarm.

Anne's grip on her two boys stiffened as she asked, "What's going on? What do the black marks mean?"

"I-It's the Epidemic," I answered, struggling not to stutter. "A nasty disease Rhydin told me once that he created in order to kill me a couple years before I found out I was an Allyen. He set it off in Lunaka since he didn't know where Evan was. It killed my parents and got my sister instead of me, even though she got better. The black is ink. People would smear it on the doorways of people who were infected."

What I didn't add was the reason the ink was chosen. The ink eerily resembled the disease. Infected people's veins would turn black like ink as the disease spread through their bodies. Once the blackness reached their heart, it was all over.

"But all these houses look empty," Evan replied as he lifted the collar of his tunic over his nose. As he did so, I began to smell it too. The smell of death.

"When it got bad in Soläna, they started moving sick people to a central location to try to care for them better and keep them away from others," I said as I covered my own nose.

Sure enough, as I looked around again, only the houses with the black marks stood empty like sad faces. Those without the marks were boarded up tightly, their inhabitants likely hunkered down until it passed. I wondered how long this had been going on.

"Shouldn't we get out of here then? You're not gonna gain any supporters from their death beds, and we sure can't make others come out to be exposed. Much less expose ourselves if we haven't already," Anne muttered, looking like she was ready to skedaddle at any second. Her orange turban was strangely bright compared to the gray town.

"But Rhydin is the one who did this! This illness isn't natural! I nursed my sister back to health. We could do the same for these people and save them!" I argued. "If we can save any of them, they're sure to join our cause once they know Rhydin is the one who did this to them!"

"Er, that's a lot of ifs, Lina," Evan groaned. "Especially when the biggest if is whether we'll contract the disease too!"

"Yeah, I think that might just be a disaster waiting to happen," Luke pitched in. "Sorry, Lina, but it's not worth the risk. Even if you won over a whole army from this town, it wouldn't be worth it if both adult Allyens died of the Epidemic a week later."

Abruptly, I heard the thunder of hooves racing back towards us, and I turned just in time to see Sam and James barreling back into town. Sam never stopped, his horse sprinting on by, but James skidded to a halt at the sight of a demanding, questioning look from his brother.

James gasped for breath as he said, "Sam's sister…She lives in a Rounan settlement just east of Stellan… Epidemic started there… He won't stop 'til he finds her!"

Realization slapped me in the face. I'd totally forgotten Kelsi, the pompous woman who served as Kidek in my place during the war, lived in Stellan. No wonder Sam had been so anxious and torn off so suddenly!

I gathered my reins again, steering my horse in the direction Sam had gone. "I have to help him!"

"Lina, the disease...!" Luke cried.

"Doesn't matter. Family comes first," I announced as Anne looked at me with new eyes. "Everyone else go make camp. The rest of you have never been in contact with this before. Sam and I have been exposed to it before without catching it, hopefully there's some power in that! We'll meet up with you later."

Evan looked at me gravely, but he nodded. Anne moved her horse to follow his, but Luke ushered his closer to mine as he said, "I'm coming with you. I can't let you go alone. James and B-... James will stay with the others."

With that, our group split apart. Evan, Anne, and James rode away from town to set up camp, and Luke and I took off after Sam. Stellan was a very small town compared to the capital of Soläna and the towering city of Lun. It didn't take long before we reached the center of town, and from there it was easy.

Even though the rest of the buildings in the central square were marked with ink or tightly locked up with only a glimpse of firelight to be seen through the cracks, one building stood out from the others. Every window of the schoolhouse was thrown open, flickering light visible from each one, and Sam's horse stamped the dry ground by the hitching post.

Luke and I joined our horses with Sam's and strode up the three steps to the schoolhouse door. Luke was having trouble keeping his eyes their normal color of blue. Recently, he had resorted back to his old, sullen behavior around Anne to keep his eyes from shifting color with his emotions, his one inherited Ranguvariian trait, just as he used to do around me before I knew he and his siblings weren't human. Now, however, as I placed my hand on the doorknob, his eyes flickered back and forth from the blue his siblings possessed to the daffodil color that took the phrase "yellow with fear" to a whole new level.

Compared to the firelight outside, the inside of the schoolhouse appeared dim. Oil lamps sputtered in sconces every few feet along the wall, but they weren't nearly enough to illuminate the crowd of people we found within. School benches had been pushed aside and cots set up in rows barely a foot apart, and the people still on their feet were vastly outnumbered. People of all ages, genders, and skin tones lay side by side, and even though all of the windows were open, the air tasted stale.

I untied my sash and retied it over my nose and mouth before moving through the sea of illness. Luke remained by the door like the faithful bodyguard he was. The only real sound in the room was that of whistling windpipes as these poor people tried to keep breathing. I found myself searching each of them for how far the disease had progressed.

On some of them, the blackness in their veins was still confined to their hands, and presumably their feet although those were bundled up under blankets. On others, I could see ink peeking out from the collars, and I knew that these wouldn't be alive in another twenty-four hours. Still others were completely covered up in their blankets, yet to be removed from the room. All of it jogged dark memories of my parents' final days that I tried my hardest to shove down.

I pushed my way toward the back of the schoolhouse where I thought I could see Sam's bandana hidden down between a couple cots. As I got closer, I realized he had crouched down between two cots at the end of a row, and sure enough, I recognized Kelsi in one of them. Her face was pale and clammy, and her hair had lost its shine. I couldn't hardly look at her with the same disdain as I once did, she looked so pitiful.

"How is she?" I said in a voice barely above a whisper. There wasn't enough room for me to huddle down with Sam.

My husband took a deep breath and swallowed before responding, his voice a little raspy, "Her marks are about at her elbows. Nikolas is a lot worse."

I stared confused for a moment until Sam nodded at the man in the cot next to Kelsi. He had a baby face and freckles, like he was Kelsi's much younger brother rather than whom I could only assume was her husband. I thought I remembered her mentioning a husband when she came to our compound during the war, but I wasn't sure. It only reminded me of how Sam hadn't told her about me, or really me about her, and I didn't want to dwell on that.

Nikolas was almost entirely covered in blankets to keep him from shivering, but his plague marks were nearly to his jaw, which could only mean that the ones on his arms had reached his collarbones. It wouldn't be long before they choked his heart.

I rolled up my sleeves and set off to find some materials from any of the other overwhelmed caregivers. Rags, poultices, herbs, any of the things I could remember helping ease my parents or my sister of their fevers or pain. Of course, there was no cure. Nobody knew why most people died, a few recovered, and some never contracted it in the first place. We could only try everything we knew to do and hope for the best.

Thus, we began a new routine that I wasn't sure how long would last. Sam and I spent long days in the Stellan schoolhouse caring for Kelsi and Nikolas, as well as any others that seemed to have a fighting chance. Luke would escort us to town every morning and out to Evan, Anne, and James's camp every evening. Those three made use of the extra time by traveling a few hours in different directions to look for possible places to hide a large rebellion or to speak to uncharted Gornish and Rounan settlements.

As the days stretched on, Sam became engrossed in his sister's health. It wasn't that I entirely blamed him, but it began to feel like he was in a different kingdom even though we were at least always in the same place if not side by side. Kelsi was the only thing he saw through his tunnel vision. My thoughts became my constant companion instead, and as the days stretched on, I kept coming back to one.

What did Rhydin think he was accomplishing by destroying crops and resurrecting the Epidemic? He'd won the people of Nerahdis. Why jeopardize that?

There was a new citadel among the mountains of Nerahdis, located a few miles north of Caden's Peak where it straddled the border between Lunaka and Mineraltir. While the other castles boasted nothing more than large footprints, this palace stretched high in the sky, likely the tallest fortress that Nerahdis had ever seen. Its thin spires were midnight black and delicately constructed unlike the crude, thick formations of the castles of the Three Kingdoms. Rhydin had ensured that his imperial residence would in no way resemble anything the people of Nerahdis had seen before, just as he was a leader unlike any other.

Rhydin paced the empty halls, his footsteps echoing along the white marble pillars that contained veins of black so dark they appeared to be bleeding. Very few of his Followers were permitted the right to live with him in the palace portion of the citadel, but even then, not a single one of them was allowed in certain areas. The punishment was death if they were even caught outside the door.

What was taking them so long? He pondered.

Rhydin tossed his thick, fur cape behind his shoulders as he reached a balcony facing east. The sun was setting to the opposite direction, and its light was fading from Lunaka. He could see Spenser's Lake from here, its waters growing dark. His mind turned numb at the thought that Diagalo, a town wiped from the face of Nerahdis, used to lay on its shores. His memories of that place were…blurry, to say the least.

His memories were much clearer after he gained all his magical powers. Stole them, actually. He remembered that day like it was yesterday, the most important day of his centuries-long life. Thankfully, the only witness was still an incomprehensible specter trapped in the trashed and abandoned Archimage Palace. No one could stop him now.

"My lord," a voice called from down the hallway.

Rhydin's pale hands tightened so hard on the balcony railing that his tendons stuck out. He responded scathingly, "What is it, Robert?"

The older Allyen came trotting along, his face withered and gaunt. "You will be pleased to know that we have found Prince Xavier and Princess Mira."

"And their child?" Rhydin quirked his eyebrow. Upon hesitation from Robert, Rhydin glared at him. "If we do not find their child, then Mineraltir still has a ruler aside from me!"

"I understand, my lord," Robert answered, quivering. "We will find him, I swear it. A helpless, blind toddler should be easy to discover."

"Good." Rhydin straightened and released the railing. "Put them with the Lunakan Royals in the dungeon. They will await their fates together."

"Yes, sire." Robert dipped his head, his shoulders scrunched upward.

Rhydin looked at him pitifully. How things had changed after the incident. Fear. Respect of his power was one thing. Sniveling was yet another. "What of our search for Dathian's pesky daughter? We must have *all* the former Royals if we are to succeed."

Linaria and Evanarion's father twitched. "No sign of her, my lord. She lost us in Rondeau."

Anger boiled within Rhydin, but he turned back to the scenery. He answered coolly, "No matter. She cannot escape forever. She will be executed privately if need be."

Robert continued to stand in the middle of the hallway quietly, the silence making their ears ring.

Rhydin peered at him out of the corner of his eye. "Is there something else?"

"Master, I-..." Robert stammered, "I do not understand your plan. You've won! Why subject your loyalists to economical failure, plague, and now this?"

"I..."

Something in Rhydin's mind wouldn't click. The gears wouldn't thread together. The failed crops in Lunaka, the disappearance of game in Mineraltir, the lack of fish in Auklia…the resurrection of the Epidemic… He had done all these things. He had done them for a reason. That reason…?

He had to do it. He just had to. He needed the people to *need* him to survive. He was the one doling out provisions to those who were losing their livelihoods. The one handing out cures to those who deserved it. Otherwise, they could turn against him at any moment. That made sense, didn't it? There was no other option.

"Don't question my plan, Robert, or you'll find yourself in the dungeon with the Royals," Rhydin snapped. "Everything I do is for the good of Nerahdis. You will see, someday."

Robert immediately bowed low. "I understand, Master. I'm sorry, Master!"

Rhydin spun around and marched in the opposite direction, trying to calm his fury as he announced, "Move up the execution. I want this done whether we have the Mineraltin brat and the Auklian witch or not!"

CHAPTER THIRTEEN

"What do you mean their cottage was empty?" I blurted.

It was early morning. The sun was just beginning to burn off the dew and crank up the heat for another Lunakan summer day. Luke had already transported Sam to Stellan for the day, and I had been taking my time getting ready. Weariness sapped my bones, no doubt from the days on end that we had spent caring for Kelsi and Nikolas. But when James abruptly burst into the camp from his shift to keep Bartholomiiu company while he hid from Anne, my senses were suddenly on high alert.

"I don't know! One of our people would check on the Lunakan Royals once a week, and when she arrived for the weekly check this morning, the cottage was empty!" James exclaimed, his eyes wide. "She said there were signs of a scuffle. The door was blown open and the window in the back was shattered, but there's nothing to suggest what happened!"

"They all three had feather necklaces, right? Could it have been Rhydin?" I asked anxiously, beginning to pace back and forth in front of the campfire. "They should have been impossible to find!"

"I know, Lina, but apparently they were," James responded, flabbergasted. "Maybe somebody saw them, I don't know. Our people are looking for them as we speak. We've even got a few watching Rhydin to see if he knows anything. So far, his activity appears normal."

I shook my head impatiently, frustrated.

"I'm sure Rhydin knows something," Anne remarked bitterly from where she sat with her two boys. "I've heard that he's after the Royals something fierce."

"But why?" I asked. "He's already kicked them all out of power and into hiding, what else could he want?"

Anne shrugged nonchalantly as she adjusted her turban. "Just tellin' what I know, Miss Allyen. Nothing Rhydin ever does is good, no matter what he talks himself and the people around him into."

All of a sudden, Luke walked into the camp. Another flurry of activity and arguing ensued as James relayed the report to his elder brother. Luke ripped his fingers through his hair, turning around so that Anne couldn't see the rainbow of colors through which his eyes flashed. Then, he composed himself the best he could and faced us with the best political smile he could muster as I thought to myself how much he must miss his sister, the usual leader, right now.

He cleared his throat and said, "We carry on until we hear what's happened. There's no use running off all over Nerahdis in search of them, our people can do that."

"And who are your people, exactly?" Anne asked skeptically, crossing her arms tightly. "You and your brother keep mentioning these 'people,' and while you two appear

Gornish, I highly doubt any regular Gornish people would spend so much effort searching for Royals."

A cold feeling stretched down my neck. I thought we had been so careful. Obviously, not careful enough.

"We just mean our friends," Luke responded coolly, his voice eerily monotone to keep his eyes in check. "Friends like us who want to help the Allyens succeed. That's all."

"Not sure I believe you," Anne harrumphed. "Too fishy in my opinion."

I spoke up before Luke could betray himself, "Anne, you joined our group to see if you could trust us. We're still learning whether we can trust you too. Please be patient with us and know that we'll tell you more of our secrets in time."

Anne didn't reply. She tossed her shoulders, jingling the glass baubles along her Auklian silk sleeves, and returned to packing her bag for her and Evan's daily search for a rebellion location. Her two boys watched her absentmindedly for a couple minutes before racing into the trees with mischief on their minds.

I released a breath I hadn't known I was holding and faced Luke, who had calmed himself again. He looked at me sadly, his eyes turning a bit more blue than normal. I asked, "What's wrong? I thought you handled that really well."

"It's not that," Luke answered, scratching the back of his neck. "When I took Sam to Stellan this morning, Kelsi's husband had passed. Kelsi's marks have spread as well. He's really upset."

Nodding slowly, it felt like there was a deflating balloon in my chest. "It's time for me to head in, then."

"Lina," Luke sighed and touched my elbow to stop me from walking away, "you don't have to do this. Kelsi's probably not going to make it. You hated her. Why continue to expose yourself?"

"Because it's the right thing to do, and nobody deserves to die alone," I answered, swallowing slowly. "Now, please transport me to Stellan so I can help my husband."

Rachel's brother muttered something unintelligible, likely something to do with his disagreement, but he followed me away from our campsite nonetheless. After we were a safe distance away, where Anne wouldn't be able to see Luke use his transportation magic, he took my elbow in a tight grip and hummed a couple notes to summon his magic wings. They cocooned us, and as the world flashed white, the empty prairie and small gathering of trees were replaced by an even emptier, gray town.

Luke remained silent and trailed after me as I immediately headed for the schoolhouse. He had stopped caring about where we transported since the town was as good as abandoned, so he usually dropped us in the square where the schoolhouse was located. I bounded up the steps two at a time, my short legs screaming, and pushed through the door where my nose was harassed by the stench of stale air, sweat, and death.

A few cots that had been filled yesterday were now empty. The schoolhouse only contained about half the people as it had when we arrived, although maybe three of those people had miraculously recovered. Those people were now up on their feet and doing everything they could to tend to the others since there was now no risk of infection for them. They always looked at me with wide eyes like windows when I entered. I constantly wondered what they were thinking.

Luke took up his usual post at the door as I strode to the back of the room. Sure enough, Nikolas's cot was empty, folded up, and resting against the back wall. Sam was hunkered down over Kelsi's wilting frame dabbing at her forehead with a moist cloth soaked in an herbal concoction that had seemed to help those who had recovered. My eyes grazed new spills of ink etched into the skin of Kelsi's neck as I rolled up my sleeves, covered my nose and mouth with a handkerchief, and moved to drag another blanket on top of her.

The instant the blanket left my hands, Sam jumped like he hadn't known I was there and threw a hand in my direction. He didn't meet my eyes, and his voice rasped as he said, "Please go away."

My brow furrowed. I asked, thinking I hadn't heard him properly, "What?"

"I need to do this on my own," Sam responded, his voice at a very strange pitch. He continued to blot at Kelsi's forehead, not looking at me, and she moaned unconsciously.

I opened my mouth to object, but I knew there was no point. Death was a fickle thing, and every person tended to handle it differently. Sam was shutting down before my very eyes, but he apparently had to walk through this on his own terms. As I walked away to see if any others needed tending to, I tried to convince myself that I was okay with his pushing even me away. Luke was eyeballing me, wondering what was going on. I ignored him.

I wandered over to a teenage boy several cots over, one who was thin with a wild crop of blond hair and couldn't have been too far away from coming of age. His marks had actually started retreating a little bit, leaving purple, healing bruises in the territory they abandoned. I began to focus on him, remaining in my own little world to keep from thinking too much, before I realized that he was trying to talk to me.

"Yer the Allyen...ain't ya?" he asked hoarsely, his hazel eyes foggy with illness.

As I opened my mouth to respond, I realized that the atmosphere of the room had shifted. It was like I could physically feel every conscious person's ears on me. I replied slowly, "Yes, I am."

The boy blinked at me a few times, absorbing what he'd heard. "Why're ya here?" he groaned.

Again, the entire schoolhouse went still. I willed my voice to be louder as I realized an opportunity was at hand. "I'm here to help. You can trust me. Someone evil has done this to you all."

"Who?" the boy asked. He weakly touched his wrist without thinking, which I noticed was bandaged similarly to the way Sam used to bandage his wrist with the Rounan mark.

"Emperor Rhydin," I said firmly as I stood to face the rest of the room. "He's a sorcerer who designed this Epidemic the first time to kill me. He's the one who has unleashed it upon us all again."

One of the ladies acting as a nurse gasped loudly and turned on me angrily. "How could you say such a thing about the man who freed us from the Royals and ended the war? He's done so much for us!"

"He's lying! He's tricking you all into being oppressed under something far worse than the Royals ever were!" I argued, "Someday, you'll all see! I'm the one who saved you all from Duunzer, which was also sent by Rhydin. We're forming a rebellion against him, and I hope that someday you'll all be a part of it."

While the lady and a couple others shook their heads, most of the conscious faces staring at me seemed to actually be considering what I was saying.

The boy on the cot whispered, "I believe ya."

"Thank you," I replied, feeling drained from putting myself on the spot.

"If yer really here ta help," the boy said again, his voice gruff and hesitant, "I know someone who needs it."

I looked down at him in surprise. "Who's that?"

"Some of mah neighbors. In the...ya know" – he squeezed his wrist tighter which confirmed he was a Rounan – "They got sick before I did, an' they sent their lil daughter Nathia to mah ma until they got better. As ya can see, none of us did."

"So, what happened to her?" I asked anxiously. "Where is she?"

"I dunno," the boy shrugged. "Pro'bly still in the compound. Ya gotta go find 'er."

"I will," I promised, my head bobbing up and down before I really comprehended what I'd agreed to.

"Thank ya. Ya better go!" the boy cried, "She's been alone an awful long time."

I cringed slightly, hopped up, and rapidly strode back toward the entrance of the schoolhouse. Luke gave me a questioning look before I glanced over my shoulder at Sam, wondering if I should tell him where I was going. He was still huddled over his sister, oblivious that anything had happened in the room.

I realized then that he wouldn't be missing me.

"What's going on?" Luke asked, his eyes darting back and forth between me and Sam.

"There's a little Rounan girl still in the compound who needs our help," I answered quietly. "Let's go."

"No, I meant between you and Sam," Luke clarified sheepishly, but there was nothing but genuine concern in his eyes.

I sighed, "Doesn't matter right now. We've got to get moving."

Luke stopped asking questions, and we walked outside. I removed the cover from my face and took deep breaths of air, which while still smelling off was far fresher than it was inside the building. It was mere minutes until Luke transported us once again, this time to the small, Rounan settlement just over a couple hills from Stellan. I could even see the tower of the schoolhouse on the horizon, and I felt amazed that they could live so close to a mainly Gornish town without trouble. Our compound had been a good twenty miles from Lun.

This little gathering of houses was significantly smaller than the compound Sam and I had called home for nearly three years, which was now nothing more than ash strewn along the prairie. I had also always wondered how Sam and James were able to tell that the Rounan settlement was where the Epidemic had restarted. Now that I was here, there was no question about it.

While Stellan had possessed a decent number of buildings that were boarded up with plenty of people still living in isolation within them, there was no such life within this compound. It was like every house had staggered around like a drunkard, leaning its doors and windows this way and that, and regurgitated anything inside.

People's belongings were sprinkled along the yards and road like clusters of wildflowers. They'd either been dropped by the people who ran from the disease or pillaged by those who came after it. It was hard to look at. It was all too similar to images I had long blocked out from the first time the Epidemic struck. Ultimately, the settlement was utterly empty. Not a soul left. How would we ever find this young girl?

"Lina, how do you expect to find this child?" Luke mumbled out of the corner of his mouth. "If she's been left alone for close to two weeks, she might be dead."

"I don't know," I groaned, threading my fingers through my hair. "We have to at least try, okay? I promised that boy. Please?"

"Alright, if you say so," Luke grumbled, but then a smile played at the edges of his lips. "You have a good heart."

I dropped my hands and stared at him. "Thanks. It's just the right thing to do, isn't it?"

"Yeah," he replied. "Let's get started. It shouldn't take us more than a few hours to search, and this place freaks me out."

We didn't split up. Luke was too on edge for that. So, we started walking toward the closest house and went from there. Each one of them appeared to hold a different story, and stepping inside each one was like stepping inside another person's life. While all of the buildings had been ransacked to some extent, a few of them appeared like the people had simply gone out to work for the day and were planning on coming back later. There were dishes on the table, food that had long turned rancid in a cold pot over a dead fire, gloves and tools neatly tucked away ready for a day's work.

Some of the homes belonged to young families, judging by the children's toys and certain placements that suggested a woman's touch. These things were lacking in the smaller shacks that I could only assume were the former homes of single men where order wasn't as much of a priority. Still others, seemingly the ones with the most material possessions, seemed to belong to older folk who had been living out their golden years. The absolute only similarity between them all was the splash of ink somewhere along the frame of their doors. The settlement looked to have once housed around forty people. I couldn't bear to think they had *all* succumbed to the Epidemic.

Although, knowing Rhydin, he probably started the Epidemic in the Rounan settlement on purpose. The town of Stellan could have simply been an innocent bystander with its close proximity. I wondered which of these homes had once been Sam's sister's.

A couple hours went by before we reached the last outcropping of houses. The sun was beginning to sink toward the horizon, and the wind was shifting. Luke continued to eye our surroundings more and more, and I knew the clock was ticking on our time here. Every tick was palpable, and every tick lowered my hopes of finding this little girl.

Who was I kidding? This mission had been a failure from the start.

I dragged my feet toward the next to last house, Luke a couple of steps behind me. The door was open a crack, and this one had been drenched in ink like someone had dumped an entire pot over it instead of just brushing a bit on the frame. I thought nothing of it and pushed the door open with my hand, just as I had done with all the others.

Whoosh! A plate suddenly whizzed right past my head and crashed into the edge of the door, sending broken shards raining over me. I gasped and ducked, throwing my hands over my head, as Luke jumped through the door and slashed a second plate with his sword before it could collide with my face.

I caught a glimpse of a figure hunkered down in the back of the room just as a big, black kettle zinged in our direction. Without time for a single thought, I mustered my magic and blasted the kettle back with a golden flash and a bang.

As I raised my hands to start on the offensive, the person in the back cried out in a croaking voice, "You're an Allyen! Don't fire!"

"Then stop throwing things at us!" Luke shouted, his blade still raised. He took a few more steps into the room, eyeing its upheaval. But this home's disarray was different. The table was upended and faced toward the door. The floor was absolutely covered in everything but the kitchen sink, like stepping through a minefield. This home wasn't just occupied. It was being defended.

I slowly, hesitantly, lowered my hands. The figure in the back of the room remained crouched where she was, and I inched toward her, the hair standing up on the back of my neck. I asked warily, "Who are you?"

"Just a poor Rounan woman," the figure rasped, like air was leaking around every word. "A poor Rounan woman at death's door."

As she said that, a match was struck, and a lantern suddenly illuminated her appearance. I couldn't stop the look of horror from crossing my face as I beheld this woman's emaciated frame, every inch of skin marred by the inky lines of the Epidemic. These were the advanced stages. It was a wonder she wasn't dead yet.

"Please," she muttered, "you must help me."

I opened my mouth, but no words could even trickle out. I might have been an Allyen, but I certainly wasn't a miracle-worker. At some point, I whispered, "Why didn't you go to Stellan with the others?"

"And be mocked and abused by the Gornish? I don't think so," the woman replied, her silver-haired head giving a shudder upon her frail neck. "Besides, I would be a fool to think I could be saved now. It's the child I request your help for."

As if on cue, a tiny girl crept out of the shadows, who couldn't have been more than five years old. A shock of blonde hair was tied up out of her face, which was peculiar since the rest of her little head was covered in chocolate brown waves. She stared at us fiercely, trying to mask the fear that oozed from her green eyes, while I gazed back in disbelief.

"Are you Nathia?" I asked, repeating the name that the sick Rounan boy had told me.

The girl's brow furrowed, but she nodded.

I shook my head incredulously. "I don't understand. How did she recover from the Epidemic with no resources out here?"

"She never fell ill to begin with," the Rounan woman responded, her voice becoming weaker. "A lot of power, this one. Her parents were powerful Rounans too, but that didn't help them. She's lucky."

My eyes drifted to the young girl's Rounan mark, which lay exposed. Sam had once taught me that the square shape of the mark indicated how much power a person possessed while the diamond shape, which overlay the square, represented how much of that power the Rounan could actually use. Nathia's mark was one of the largest I'd ever seen; it nearly wrapped around her wrist like a bracelet while the long, angled point nearly touched her elbow. I was about to comment on this when Luke suddenly interrupted.

"Pardon, but may I ask whom you thought we were? Why you have barricaded yourselves in here?" Luke asked, his voice deceptively calm.

"Well, what would *you* do if one of Rhydin's people arrives every day to make sure any of us who happen to survive or return are dealt with?" the old woman snapped.

Luke's knuckles turned white on his hilt. What felt like sharp claws traced my shoulders down to my spine. The sun was close to touching the horizon. We needed to go.

With the last of her energy, the woman seemed to sense the change in the atmosphere and drew little Nathia to her, instructing her to go with us and not to be afraid. Of course, she also promised that she would be fine, which Luke and I both knew was a lie. This woman had hours left, if not minutes. It was a wonder she could even use her magic to keep us from entering. But, we said nothing.

Nathia was gathering a small rucksack of possessions more akin to child's toys than actual necessities when the claws along my back deepened. Fear spread through my system, although it wasn't because I could sense one of Rhydin's Followers now that we'd been warned. It was because the Follower I sensed was a man I'd previously hoped I'd never see again.

The man whose blood, and nothing more, declared him my father.

Luke shut the door and groaned only loud enough for me to hear, "Great. And of course, there's two of you now so I can't just transport us back to Stellan."

"Just take Nathia to Stellan first. Leave her with that boy I was talking to. He's recovering and can find her a home with her people," I said quietly, my words as on edge as I felt. "Then you can transport back, grab me, and take me back to camp."

"That would require leaving you alone in between," Luke replied, grimacing.

I huffed, "It'll be fine. He won't hurt me. Just hurry."

My Ranguvariian protector nodded hesitantly, his eyes threatening to flash colors before he reined himself in. He held his rock-hard hand out to Nathia, who stared at him uncertainly before taking it slowly. I studied her closely before Luke ushered her out the door to transport. Somehow, I had a feeling that this wouldn't be the last I'd see of young Nathia, such a powerful young Rounan, whether in the near future or the far.

With a flash, Luke and Nathia were gone, and I faced the door. Before I could leave, my mind already focused on what was ahead of me, the old Rounan woman reminded me of her presence. She surprised me when she said, "It's been an honor, Madam Allyen. I have the highest of hopes that you will save us all."

I nodded at her, feeling too emotional to adequately put my appreciation into words, and I strode out the door to face my father while perhaps the one Rounan who didn't hate me drew her final breath.

CHAPTER FOURTEEN

T he sun had fully disappeared when I exited the house, and the Lunakan air was rapidly becoming still and stifling. I knew I only had a few minutes before Luke would return, so I walked quickly, hoping to take advantage of the situation. After all, I had a Ranguvariian feather and Robert did not. I knew where he was, but he had no idea I was even here.

It didn't take long to find him. He was wandering along a worn path through the center of the compound, not really looking at anything in particular. I wondered how many times he'd had to walk this route and how many times he'd actually found a Rounan. I could only imagine what he'd done with them, but it couldn't be pretty judging by that woman's dogged protection of Nathia.

I watched him for a few seconds, taking the time to actually absorb the reality of his presence and characteristics. Robert's face was gaunter since the last time I'd seen him during the destruction of our compound. Shadows clung to the hollows beneath his eyes and cheekbones, exacerbated by his unshaven jaw.

However, there was no denying that his stride mirrored Evan's. A quick one with short paces, his head hardly bobbing up and down. It was truly like looking at an older version of my twin brother. No use in still trying to convince myself that he was lying. It hurt nonetheless.

Balling my sash up into my hand to be ready with my sword at any moment, I departed from the protected covering of one of the houses and walked into his line of sight. Robert's eyes widened a bit upon seeing me, waking him up from the doldrum of the same old path. But, no malice ever entered his expression, unlike the other times I'd seen him at our compound, the Archimage Palace, and the prison tower.

He asked slowly, quietly, "Linaria? How are you here?"

His calmness and clarity were throwing me off. I'd expected another heated confrontation filled with yelling. "I..." I stuttered, unsure of how to proceed, my anger dampened, "I...I'm here to stop you. Leave this place and its inhabitants, and never return!"

Robert blinked his Allyen eyes at me a few times. Something had changed. The fire was gone from this man. I hadn't feared being alone with him when Luke left, but now, all of a sudden, I did. He repeated, as if in disbelief, "You're here."

I stared in silence, my entire train of thought thrown off course.

"Linaria, please," Robert nearly whispered as he reached toward me with an open hand. Desperation was written all over his face, and I wasn't sure how to feel about it. "Join me. Master Rhydin promised not to harm you or your brother if you join our cause."

Bile rose up in my throat. I responded loudly, "I can't believe that for a second. Besides, I would never join Rhydin after all he's done. Just look around you, Robert!"

For someone whom Rhydin had declared his right-hand man, Robert glanced around him with more of a look of sheepishness rather than that of a proud comrade. It was all too strange.

I leered at him. "Not so pleased with your Liberator now, are you? What changed your mind, Robert? The murders or the ruination of people's livelihoods?"

A switch flipped. Fury filled Robert's expression as he bellowed, "My master knows what he's doing! He will *always* have my full support, just as he should have yours! And I am your father, Linaria, and you will refer to me as such!"

Whatever softening that may have occurred in my heart toward this sad man immediately hardened once again. I barely noticed the burst of light behind me and the abrupt, hard grip on my arm as I declared, "Never."

Robert and the rest of the prairie scenery melted away in front of me, the colors swirling out of existence into a world of white before rapidly reconvening into the small, darkened woods where our camp was situated. I didn't have to see Luke's scarlet eyes to know that he was furious, even before he shouted, "Do you have a death wish or something??"

"I only wanted to see him! I knew he wouldn't hurt me. The man's my *father* after all," I shrieked defensively. "I knew you'd be there any minute, and I was ready in case he tried anything."

"I swear, Lina," Luke grumbled, throwing his hands above his head, "it's a wonder you never gave my sister any gray hairs because I'm going to have a full head of them by the time we're through!"

I opened my mouth to retaliate, but suddenly James was upon us, running from the direction of our camp and yelling louder than us both, "Thank goodness, you're back! We have an emergency!"

Luke was instantly on high alert again. "What, what is it? Did they find Prince Frederick and his family?"

James blanched even paler than he was before and gulped, "Yeah…as well as Prince Xavier, Princess Mira…even Queen Gloria. It appears that all of the Royals are in Rhydin's dungeons although we can't tell for sure. They're all going to be executed in the morning!"

"*Executed*?" Luke and I shouted in unison.

"At dawn," James warbled, like his throat was constricted, "Rhydin wants to eliminate any other claims to any of the thrones to preserve his reign. What do we do?"

"Uh, we *save* them, that's what we do!" I replied incredulously, planting my fists on my hips.

"But Rhydin's dungeons are totally impregnable! Trust me, if was possible to get in there, we'd have broken them out by now," James huffed, his pale face flushed.

"Yeah," Luke sighed, scratching the back of his neck anxiously, "those things are protected by literally every spell and charm Rhydin knows. Some of them outdate even Grandpa Arii."

I stared hard at one brother, then at the next, disappointed in their negativity. "Then we save them when they exit the dungeons!" I declared.

"They won't leave the dungeons until just minutes before the execution, and even then, they'll be on a public platform Rhydin's Followers are constructing as we speak," Luke replied skeptically. "James said we're not even sure who all is in there!"

A few seconds went by as I thought hard, the gears in my mind turning. Then, I asked the first question of the only plan I could remotely think of, "Are there any more Ranguvariians we can call upon to help us? We don't have long before dawn, and we're only going to have seconds for this plan to work."

Rhydin stood proudly on the elevated platform across from the gallows where the Nerahdian Royals would all meet their end, his pale hands splayed along the railing and his shoulders tossed back to emphasize the regality of his imperial armor and fur cape. He held his chin high as commoners from near and far trickled into the area around the gallows in the pink light of morning. They drew close first at a snail's pace, then like floodwaters as the hour neared when the sun would make its official debut for the day.

All for him, he thought arrogantly. They were all here to see him finish what he had started and cement his claim to all three thrones.

The wind began to pick up, and Rhydin knew the moment was drawing near. His Followers had constructed this arena of sorts barely within the borders of Lunaka in the shadows of his sparkling new, imperial palace. He wanted his power and leadership on full display today.

As soon as the sun barely peeked its golden face over the far horizon, Robert ascended the stairs on the backside of the platform and took his place next to Rhydin, on his right but two steps behind. Rhydin wanted no one questioning whether their new emperor was independent.

"On your command, my lord," Robert whispered, trying to conceal the shakiness of his voice. He failed, and Rhydin's amethyst eyes narrowed. If Robert couldn't come to terms with the positive change Rhydin was implementing, he would be the gallows' next victim.

"No use putting off the inevitable. Give the people what they came for." Rhydin smirked.

The older Allyen bobbed his head and trotted back down the stairs of Rhydin's platform, and the emperor turned to face the massive crowd that had collected around the gallows. Rhydin's Followers had distributed flyers throughout Nerahdis, calling for supporters of the Liberator-turned-Emperor to come to this place for a very special display to ensure the end of all wars. Rhydin knew that terminology would bring hundreds out, if not thousands, and he brimmed with dark excitement as he subtly cast a spell on his voice to project it for all to hear.

"Greetings, people of Nerahdis! Thank you for joining us here today for this momentous occasion!" Rhydin announced, his lips spread wide in the best smile he could maintain. "As I told you, in a few short moments, I will have single-handedly ensured that Nerahdis will never be abused by the Royals or embroiled in any war ever again!"

Thunderous applause. Hundreds of thrilled faces of every age, gender, and nationality.

"I assure you," Rhydin continued proudly, "you will remain under my fair and devoted rule for the foreseeable future!"

More applause and cheering. Nerahdis was an ocean of relief and happiness in front of Rhydin's platform, and he basked in it. *This* was why he had worked so hard for hundreds of years. *This* was why he would continue to remind the people of their need for him. They didn't need to know that the foreseeable future was actually the rest of time.

Of course, they could also never find out about his magical powers, his lack of aging, or his hand in their economic distress and the resurgence of the Epidemic. But, what did that matter when they all adored him? If there were any nerves among the crowd as they eyed the gallows and what it signified, Rhydin never saw them.

"Now, without further ado," Rhydin said as he gestured to the small door directly beneath him that led inside the lower level of the platform upon which he stood. "Your former rulers and abusers!"

Robert flung open the door beneath him and began leading out the former Royals. Nine rope necklaces hung from the gallows ahead of them as nine people entered the daylight in chains. The people roared with glee upon sight of the former King Adam of Lunaka first in line, a thoughtful strategy on Rhydin's part, seeing as he was likely the most hated of them all. Adam looked around at the enormous crowd, bewildered by the brightness and loudness, his crown stripped from him. When his harsh eyes landed on Rhydin, they burned like wildfire.

Rhydin kept his face relaxed as he met the gaze of the man who had pledged his loyalty to him, helped him acquire his empire even while believing it would allow him to keep his throne rather than pass it to his son. Rhydin had never once intended on fulfilling that promise. By the red hot look on Adam's face, Rhydin also patted himself on the back for thinking to gag the man magically beforehand.

Next in line drew an equal amount of cheers from the green-clad Mineraltins in the audience. The former Queen Jasmine had her shoulders hunched forward under a mountain of unruly, unkempt black hair as she marched forward slowly behind Adam. She never once looked up, her eyes still containing an ounce of shock as she bored holes into the ground in front of her. Alas, Rhydin had never intended to keep his promise of sharing his eternal youth with her either. He only needed his Royal Followers temporarily, and that time had expired at last.

Princess Ren came trampling after her mother, her elaborate pink dress soiled from the dungeons, and Rhydin briefly wondered if he should have gagged her as well. She kicked and screamed something or other about how unfair everything was, but as people tossed their hands and murmured in agreement that she deserved her ill treatment after her past behavior, Rhydin decided it was fine. However, as the audience suddenly grew eerily silent, he found himself taking a step forward to see who had walked through the door next.

As the golden-haired Queen Gloria of Lunaka exited the lower quarters of Rhydin's podium, the crowd became so still that all anyone could hear was the sound of each other breathing. Rhydin glanced about the people slowly, wondering what the big deal was. Gloria may have been a beloved queen, but she was still a Royal and one who was married to a monster at that. The people should still be thrilled, Rhydin pondered, but they weren't.

Frederick, Cornflower, Xavier, and Mira followed their parents and stepfamily out toward the gallows, and with each of them, many of the spectators' eyes grew larger and larger. Puzzling, Rhydin mused. He thought he had done better at convincing the people of Nerahdis that the younger generation was just as bad as the older. Yet, the entire gathering erupted into cacophonous yelling when Frederick's young son appeared with Eli, his Follower from Auklia, trailing closely behind to make sure the Royals kept moving.

"Yer not goin' ta hang a child, are ya??" one woman's scream broke through the chaos.

Another man's bellow reached Rhydin's ears, "Stop this! This is wrong! Just banish them or something!"

While each of the Royals were guided to their respective noose and several among the audience began to leave, Rhydin rapidly took another step forward and lifted his hands to calm the fervor. "People of Nerahdis! I know this is difficult, but this is the only way to make everything right again! *Remember* all the horrific things these people have imposed upon you! Outrageous taxes, flagrant disregard for the issues that plague you daily, the hanging of anyone who could possibly oppose-...!"

"What, so exactly what you're doing at this very moment?"

The emperor froze. That voice. Female, but strong and gritty. It could only be one person. He turned ever so slowly, carefully bringing himself away from the view of the people.

Linaria stared back at him with her Allyen eyes. A glass-like feather gleamed upon her breastbone along with her locket, the reason he had not sensed her coming. Rhydin would have never suspected such overconfidence from her as to attempt sneaking up on him.

He smirked. How foolish.

"Are you here to watch as well, young Allyen?" Rhydin cackled.

A smile played at the edges of Linaria's lips, and as gasps of surprise and fear echoed around them from the audience outside, she held her small, tanned hand out with a gesture back toward the gallows. She whispered, "No, I am not."

For once, a small inkling of anxiety radiated down Rhydin's veins, a feeling that was foreign to him. He rushed back to the railing to behold the scene unfolding below. As

197

most of the crowd now fully disintegrated in fear or disapproval, five figures had appeared out of nowhere upon the gallows, each of them hurrying to one of the Royals and working furiously to remove their noose.

Anxiety turned to anger as Rhydin absorbed every little detail of the Ranguvariians in front of him. Their stature, ears, eyes, wingspan, the two who appeared human, all of it. The very creatures that he was working so hard to capture in order to reveal all their little secrets were in front of him now, and there was nothing he could do to stop them.

As the two who appeared mostly human disappeared in the blink of an eye with the Royals they had managed to free – Dominick and Xavier – Rhydin roared to Robert and Eli on the ground, "*Do something!*"

Another Ranguvariian vanished with Princess Cornflower in the seconds it took Eli to dash over to the lever while Robert stood stock-still, his eyes pinned upward at his daughter. Time slowed down as the last two Ranguvariians worked to free Frederick and Mira from their nooses just as the first two human-looking Ranguvariians reappeared without their charges, making beelines for Queen Gloria and-…

Rhydin dove out of the way for the second Ranguvariian-human, who flew right past him, batting his shard wings and slicing Rhydin's cape to shreds. He growled in fury as the Ranguvariian swept over to Linaria to take her away as well, but that was when the deafening snap of wood reached his ears. All three of them paused. Linaria's Allyen eyes met Rhydin's amethyst ones.

That was when the wailing began, and Rhydin cracked a cruel smile.

Luke and I forgot Rhydin and rushed to the railing of the podium, desperate to see what had happened. My eyes glossed over the limp frames of Queen Jasmine and Princess Ren, not needing that mental image. But, my gaze snagged on King Adam, a third of his scalp still bald from the spell I'd fired at him during the compound attack. He had been my first enemy, who I always thought would die at my blade. The man who sold out his kingdom just so he could keep his throne away from his son. Who hunted people with magic relentlessly. Who tried to fling Frederick off a balcony and who spearheaded the war that made Rhydin emperor.

He was no more.

At Luke's gasp, a sound like he'd been punched in the stomach, I jerked my gaze away from King Adam and to the source of the wailing. Relief flooded me when I saw Mira and Frederick both alive, freed from their nooses with only seconds to spare by Bartholomiiu and a female Ranguvariian whom I didn't know, but my heart plummeted to my toes upon sight of Queen Gloria dangling from the gallows.

We were too late. We had been so close. James was right next her, clutching his hands like he'd been burned by the rope as he tried to get it off when the lever was pulled.

Mira screamed, clinging to her mother, and tears trickled down Frederick's thin cheeks as he tried to pull his sister away. Half of the few remaining audience members cheered. Whether for the demise of the truly evil Royals or for the survival of the younger generation, I wasn't sure. Others stared vacantly at what had transpired in front of them, and a few actually hurled insults at Rhydin.

Rhydin's expression had been changing back and forth between victory at the death of four Royals and fury that five had been rescued, but it turned hard at the sound of the criticisms levied toward him. Dark power began building around him, and Luke grabbed onto my arm from behind.

I shuffled him off. I could end this now. Rhydin couldn't use magic in front of people or his ruse as emperor was over.

My sword sprang forth, and I used it to cast a quick, powerful blast that should have knocked Rhydin flat. However, it was deflected back at me when a figure suddenly transported in front of Rhydin. Robert stared back at me, his sword drawn and gleaming purple as he channeled Rhydin's dark magic instead of his own Allyen power.

"Move!" I shouted angrily.

"No," Robert responded quietly, his eyes muddled but sure.

"This has to end, Robert! You *know* what he's doing is wrong!" I pleaded, gesturing with my sword all around me before I tossed furious words in Rhydin's direction, "You'll never win!"

Robert squeezed his eyes shut in frustration, rubbing his gaunt face. He whispered slowly, almost so I couldn't hear him, "It's too late for me, Daughter."

Behind him, Rhydin straightened and whirled to face us, the strips of his former cape flying about. He fixed Robert in his deathly gaze and stated clearly without emotion, "Kill her."

The former Allyen took a couple, uncomfortable steps backward. "What? No! I must have another chance to turn her to our side!"

"So be it," Rhydin spat. "Then kill her infuriating *creature* so I can conduct my experiments and crack all their secrets!"

Robert hadn't so much as turned in Luke's direction before my protector threw two tiny daggers that he must have had up his sleeve for a while. I barely saw that one nicked Robert's cheek. The other bounced off a blade that Rhydin drew from nowhere before Luke's hand abruptly grabbed my arm, and the world began to grow white and morph.

I fell hard to the ground when we arrived back in our campsite, feeling a bit of whiplash as well. Luke had landed on his own two feet, but he brushed himself off anyway before he said, "Sorry. Nothing good was going to come of that."

Sighing loudly, I conceded, "Fair enough. Although we did confirm that Rhydin still wants to capture one of you."

Luke looked at the ground sadly, his eyes tinging to a darker blue. "We can't let that happen. We have such an advantage right now since he doesn't understand how our power works, how our feathers can hide presences...any of it. If that changes..."

"I know," I mumbled, but I tapered off of what I was going to say next as the yelling from closer to the campfire reached my ears.

"How could you not get to her in time?? Why didn't you get more Ranguvariians or *something*?"

It took me a moment to recognize Frederick's voice. I had never heard him shout before, much less roar like what I heard now.

Luke and I hurried over to the center of our campsite where the others were. Mira looked unwell as she rocked a bawling Cornflower while Frederick's red face was very much in Evan's bubble. Xavier, on the other hand, appeared...happy, of all things, most of him concealed under a large cloak. Meanwhile, Anne stood off to the side with her hand firmly on her sword hilt, her olive complexion paling at the sight of Bartholomiiu and the other two Ranguvariians who had been able to join us on such short notice.

Sam, it occurred to me finally, was still absent. He didn't know any of this had happened because he'd never returned from Stellan.

Evan was as white as a sheet, trying to defend us when he hadn't been there to even fully know what happened. I jogged over to rescue him now and placed myself between him and Frederick. I said calmly but firmly, "Frederick, we did everything we could-..."

"No, you did not!" the Lunakan prince yelled, a ferocious fire in his eyes that I'd never seen before. "You could have brought just *one* more Ranguvariian with you. *You* could have stayed here and let Luke retrieve my mother instead of you! For Nerahdis's sake, I could have gotten myself out and my rescuer could have-...!"

"Stop," I replied simply, not letting his words provoke me. I reached up and placed my gloved hands on his wiry shoulders as he looked ready to crumble. "Just stop, Frederick."

Frederick gazed at me slowly, the anger in his eyes barely masking the grief underneath.

"I'm so sorry she's gone. But playing 'what if' isn't going to bring her back. It won't bring back any of the ones we've lost to Rhydin," I whispered, my voice rasping a bit.

The blond prince shook his head, his receding hairline making him appear far older than his years. He turned away from Evan and I, walking sluggishly toward his sisters when his stare happened across the smiling Xavier. I cringed, knowing what was coming. Frederick spat, "What could you *possibly* be happy about?"

"It may be a bad day in your world, Frederick," Xavier answered with a strange, dark grin, "but it's a *very* good day in mine."

"How could you say such a thing? Your wife's mother just...just suffered a terrible death." Frederick's voice broke.

"As regrettable as that is, it comes nowhere near to stifling the immense joy that the two witches who did *this* to me," Xavier crowed as he shifted his large cloak to the side to reveal his right arm, which was stiff and bent at an odd angle, "got what they rightfully deserved."

Frederick's fury burned brighter. "You got that when your arm was smashed by a rock in an avalanche when you and Sam were trying to desert."

"True," Xavier conceded, smiling nonetheless, "but the months I spent being tortured for hours on end without proper treatment did their toll. Allow me my happiness in this."

I watched Xavier move his arm awkwardly back under his bulky cape, the elbow not really bending and the fingers never leaving the tight fist, and decided to remove myself from the situation. I didn't need to witness Frederick getting all his anger out of his system as Xavier inevitably stirred the pot.

Padding away softly, I found myself a nice tree to sit by as I tuned out Frederick and Xavier's shouting. Despite my best hopes, all of their previous beef from the war came out, and I glanced back at the others in sadness only once. My thoughts wandered to Sam briefly, wondering if Kelsi was still alive, if he was still with her, and how long he would stay with her nonstop like this.

I lost myself in these thoughts so fully that I didn't even notice when Anne came to sit with me. She arranged her Auklian silk sashes, which so cleverly hid a leather vest full of small weapons underneath, and thumbed one of the shiny baubles that hung from her sleeves.

After several minutes of silence, she adjusted her orange turban, grabbed a canteen from behind her, and took a swig.

She muttered, "You wanna tell me about the pointy-eared dudes now or later?"

I chuckled in spite of myself. "Might as well do it now."

Anne offered the canteen to me, and I pulled my leather gloves off. When I reached for the sloshing canteen, every thought of mine was derailed.

My fingers. Their veins were black. As if stained with ink.

CHAPTER FIFTEEN

"No," I breathed as I retracted my hand from Anne's canteen. I rubbed the fingers of both hands against my trousers rigorously, willing the dark smudges to just be dirt. They wouldn't come off.

Anne's crimson eyes doubled in size. "The Epidemic," she breathed.

I jumped up from the ground like lightning had struck me, barreling away from Anne. "Don't touch me," I cried, fumbling with my gloves to get them back on, "I thought I was immune because I didn't get it back then, but...but..."

"It's okay," Anne said soothingly as she stood. "I got it the last time. I can't get it now."

I gaped at her. "I thought the Epidemic didn't reach Auklia? You didn't recognize the ink on the thresholds in Stellan."

Anne adjusted her orange turban, her eyes darting to the ground briefly before meeting mine with a red ferocity. "Actually, I lived closer to Lunaka briefly when I was younger. But we didn't live in a town, so I never saw those warning marks. Just…don't worry about me. I've had it before."

"But…" I stammered, panicking, "I've been around everyone else, what if I got them sick too?"

Anne leveled her scarlet gaze at me. "My father was a bit of a worrywart, but my mother always used to say 'don't worry 'til ya have to.' You've spent a lot of time in Stellan away from the rest of us, and ya can't get me sick. Only Luke has been around you, but he's been to the schoolhouse plenty of times too. You need attention first-…"

"Don't tell anybody else," I begged, fighting the urge to grab the muscular woman by the arms. "I have all the things I need to treat it from Stellan, and I'll keep my distance from the others…"

"What about your husband?" Anne questioned sternly.

My eyes slid to the ground. Sam. He still hadn't returned from Stellan. Was his sister more important than me? I shook my head and responded slowly, "Until his sister passes, I doubt we'll be seeing him."

A few moments of silence passed. Anne was strong-willed, and I could tell she was biting her tongue as to not enter the discord between Sam and I. But, to her credit, she remained silent. While Frederick and Xavier continued to argue in the background with the periodic interjection from poor Mira, sister and wife, Anne and I returned to our sitting positions against an ancient tree trunk. Anne changed the subject and suggested, "How about those creatures then?"

Anne was surprisingly receptive of the notion of Ranguvariians, although slightly less so of the Aatarilecs. I decided to go ahead and tell her about both since she seemed to have officially cast her lot with the rest of us. Plus, it kept my mind off my new predicament. She asked several questions, most notably about why Luke and James appeared human, why Bartholomiiu acted so strangely, as well as a few about the Aatarilecs. I didn't know whether the information made her trust or question us more.

She was quiet once I'd answered all her queries, and as the day went on, she left with Evan to continue scouting for a rebellion location. I tried to create a new normal for myself away from the others. I had spent every day for the last few weeks in Stellan with Sam taking care of the sick, but now that he didn't want my help and I was ill myself, I needed to find something else to occupy my time.

The Royals, too, were in the same predicament. Apart from spending the last several days in Rhydin's impenetrable dungeons, they too had to create a new normal. James and Bartholomiiu procured some new clothes for them to replace the dirty, tattered ones they had worn their entire stay with Rhydin as well as to make them look less conspicuous.

It was decided that the Royals would stay with us since we were close to finding a place to conceal and build our rebellion against Rhydin, so James was sent to pick up Taisyn, Xavier and Mira's blind son. They had narrowly secreted him away with a maid just moments before they were captured, and I was immensely thankful. We'd lost Queen Gloria because we hadn't had enough help or enough time to rescue everyone. I couldn't imagine who else wouldn't have made it if even one more Royal on our side had been present at those gallows.

Frederick and Xavier kept their distance from each other, using Mira and Cornflower as go-betweens, while I kept my distance from absolutely everyone else. Every evening, Anne aided me with the herbs we had been using to treat the infected in Stellan, yet each day the ink that stained my skin spread.

Within twenty-four hours, it had stretched halfway up my forearms. After two days, my elbows were beginning to turn black. All of this, I kept hidden under my sleeves. There was no point in stressing everyone out if we were already trying everything we could.

Sometimes, I wondered if the treatment would work for me. Other times, especially as each meal and night went by with no sign of Sam, I wondered if it mattered.

As my energy started fading and food lost its flavor, Anne became my sole confidant. While Luke, James, and Bartholomiiu busied themselves with guarding us, searching for a hideout, and keeping tabs on Sam in Stellan, and the Royals kept to themselves to avoid arguing, Anne tried to keep Evan from me. However, it wasn't long before he began to study me from across the campfire and question Anne more intensely when she made up some sort of excuse for my avoiding him.

At the end of the second day, Anne plopped down next to me with two bowls of stew, pushed the fuller of the two into my hands, and eyed the ancient book in my lap that now appeared waterlogged too after the shipwreck. Thankfully, the spell that preserved the book's interior was still working because the pages were intact even after everything. Even though I had learned everything I was ever going to learn from the book, I still paged through it every once in a while. I kept hoping maybe it had one more shred of wisdom to share, and it wasn't like I had anything else going on in my life at the moment.

"Well, ya won't believe it," Anne announced as she took a slurp from her stew, foregoing her spoon entirely. "I think yer brother and I might have stumbled across something great!"

"Really?" I asked as I tried to stealthily place my bowl of stew away from me, its aroma nauseating.

Anne raised one of her eyebrows, catching me instantly, and she unceremoniously nabbed the bowl and stuck it back into my hands, taking my book in the process. "Yeah, but you have to eat to find out."

I groaned, staring at the bobbing chunks of squirrel and carrot in the brown liquid which threatened to choke me. It looked a whole lot more like vomit now that food had lost all appeal for me. My dry throat became a hard ball as I forced myself to slowly fill my spoon with nothing but the broth and ladle it into my mouth drop by drop. It burned like poison as it went down.

"What is this?" Anne asked breathily.

The anxious tone of her voice set me on edge, although I gladly plunked the bowl of stew down several inches away from me as I turned back to her. Her orange turban was tilting forward as she stared at my book, still open to the illustration of a young Rhydin with Emperor Caden. But, to my surprise, it wasn't Rhydin that she fixated on.

"What is this book?" she repeated, her eyes wide. "How does it know about the Archimage? It's supposed to be erased from history."

I measured her expression warily, confused. The fact that the Archimage position was covered up in all the history books was not common knowledge, even after Rhydin created the falsehood that Dathian was some sort of puppet master behind the Royals' actions and the war. I answered hesitantly, "Well, I found this book in the Archimage Palace. It seems to have been written a few hundred years ago before the position became secret. I was surprised too when I found it."

Anne continued to gaze at the book, her eyes darting back and forth as she read the text vigorously, ignoring the illustration completely. I studied her with new eyes. The average commoner would have struggled to read the book, if they could read at all. Even I had to ask Frederick for help. Anne scanned and flipped the pages with ease, devouring everything the book had to say about the Archimage.

Abruptly, she seemed to realize that I was staring at her. She cleared her throat and gestured back to the illustration. "That's pretty crazy, ain't it? That Rhydin was the First Archimage? I'm not sure I believe it."

"It's true," I replied cautiously, wondering what the real reason behind her interest was. "Rhydin said so himself right before he murdered Dathian."

The color vanished from Anne's tanned face. Her voice was reduced to a whisper, "The rumors are true? Rhydin was the one to kill him?"

"Yeah. For once, the rumors are true," I answered bitterly, and then looked over her saddened expression. "Did you know him well? When your mother was a maid there?"

"Oh, no," Anne responded quickly, shaking her head and her turban wobbling, "Servants aren't supposed to be seen. I knew him from afar, I guess. He just always seemed like a nice person, even if he was a bit erratic."

I smiled at her, remembering Dathian's weird, flighty behavior. How Arii had made fun of him for thinking there was a ghost in the palace...although Dathian may have been right all along. Yet, his disapproval of my marriage to Sam had ultimately soured him for me.

"He had his moments," I mumbled as I took the book back from her. Even though I wanted to probe her for more about Dathian and her strange reaction to the book, I asked instead,

"So, there's a good spot for an underground rebellion somewhere?"

"Yeah, actually," Anne answered too quickly, like she wanted to change the subject, "yer brother and I were out scouting closer to Spenser's Lake when we stumbled across this really great cavern. It's like this huge dome underneath one of the foothills, it could easily house several hundred people. Plus, with the water source nearby-..."

Anne kept talking, but I no longer heard her. My senses had taken over to alert me to the arrival of a presence I knew better than any other, and my heart jumped into my throat. I scanned the campsite until Luke entered the clearing accompanied by none other than Sam.

He looked disheveled to say the least. I had never seen him with such tired eyes or so many days gone without a shave even in the thick of harvest, aside from perhaps when he was Rhydin's prisoner of war. It had only been a few days, yet my eyes clung to him. I'd forgotten how much more red was in his beard versus on his head. It was becoming hard to see the boy who had been my childhood friend within the man ravaged by war and sickness.

I jumped to my feet before I thought better, and while I didn't fall, the world spun a little. Anne stood next to me, concern in her eyes as she watched me and glanced at Sam. My heart began to hammer as fast as a mockingbird at its favorite tree. What would I do if he came over here? He'd never had the Epidemic, although he'd certainly exposed himself to it enough already. But, if he tried to kiss me, could I push him away?

My thoughts raced and raced, but it turned out to be in vain. Sam's eyes were hollow and absent with exhaustion, and without so much as a look around, he plopped down by the fire and started shoveling stew into his mouth. My jaw went slack. Had he only returned for food?

I made sure my sleeves were still tucked into my gloves and took a few tentative steps forward. Anne mirrored me, saying nothing. She acted as my shield, ready to keep others from getting too close, or perhaps a shield for everyone else, to allow me to get closer to Sam. I came just near enough to him that he would be able to hear me but I wouldn't have to raise my voice for the whole camp to hear. I asked timidly, "How's Kelsi?"

Sam finished pulling a piece of squirrel meat apart with his teeth and answered grumpily, "Her marks are nearing her collarbone."

"I'm so sorry," I responded hesitantly.

At that, Sam glanced at me very briefly before giving the entire camp a look as he smashed a stewed carrot between his lips. "When did the Royals get here?"

"A few days ago," I replied bitterly. "You've been pretty out of the loop. We had to rescue them from Rhydin's public execution. King Adam, Queen Jasmine, Princess Ren, and Queen Gloria were killed."

Confusion claimed Sam's face. "Rhydin executed some of his own people?"

"Yeah. I guess he must have decided he didn't need them anymore. He's got what he wanted," I answered glumly.

Sam nodded slowly, turning back to his stew. Silence ensued for a few seconds, and it took every fiber of my body not to run forward, knock the bowl out of his hands, and demand his complete attention. Was he not even going to apologize for totally abandoning us? Abandoning me?

I tensed as I asked, "Sooo, are you back then? Y'know, so we can move forward with creating our rebellion? Fighting Rhydin?"

"No," Sam answered quickly with a strange stare. "Or...not yet. I can't just stop trying to save my sister."

"Sam," I groaned, throwing my hands toward the ground, "if her marks have reached her collarbone despite all your best efforts, there's no way-..."

"Don't say it," Sam interrupted me before eating the last few spoonfuls of stew. "Until her heart stops beating, she still has a chance. I just need to work harder."

"Sam," I repeated, quicker with more frustration seeping forth, "I know it's hard, but you can't stop her from dying. You're not all-powerful!"

My husband bolted to his feet and tossed his empty bowl to the ground, shouting, "Maybe I can! I just have to keep trying. If you can't see that, then there's no point in my being here."

I felt like I'd been slapped. My cheeks burned. He looked straight at me, yet while he of all people should have been able to see through my ruse, that I was sick and could barely remain on my feet, he either ignored it or couldn't see it because of the distance and discord that had been blossoming between us since the end of the war. We kept trying to fix things, yet we kept coming back to this.

Sam began to stomp away back toward the direction of Stellan. Whether Luke took him or not, he was on his way out. When the thought brushed my mind that this might be the last time I'd see him, I knew I needed to say something. Something to help him understand, even if that understanding came too late.

"Everything I've done," I said louder to reach his turned back, my voice quivering, "was done to protect you. To keep you safe. Every secret I've kept from you, every lie I've told you. Perhaps I should have shared with you more. I'm sorry."

Sam gave me one last glance before he disappeared into the trees. That look was slightly confused but mostly stoic. He gave a heavy sigh, uttered a simple "me too," and disappeared.

My eyes began to sting, and heat flushed my face. How could he be so blind? Suddenly, I became very aware of everyone's eyes on me. Luke, James, Evan, Anne, even Bartholomiiu. It felt like I was a tiny rock millions of miles underground away from the air. I couldn't breathe.

Adrenaline shot through me, giving me the energy to turn and jog – to say I could run would be a grievous overstatement – away from the campsite. Evan called after me, but I didn't stop until I ran out of steam at the shore of the river that led to Spenser's Lake several miles away. I heard footfalls behind me, and a brief glance over my shoulder confirmed that Anne, as well as probably at least one Ranguvariian, was following me.

Collapsing on the riverbank, I dragged my fingers through the dirt, mud, and silt. I raked them through the miniscule root systems of tiny green plants that certainly didn't deserve what I was doing to them. When I brushed a large stone, I chucked it into the gurgling river and watched the ripples disrupt the stream and the quiet waters along the edges. My life was in upheaval, and I needed the river to reflect that.

"You know he'll come 'round, Madam Allyen," Anne announced from behind me with a cheery tone like it'd make me feel better. "He's just grieving. Everybody does that in their own way, and you know it."

"I know!" I whined, too exhausted to even turn in her direction. "It might be stupid, but it still hurts."

"Eh. Not entirely stupid. He's still being yet another foolish man," Anne chuckled and shook her head as she walked a bit away from me along the riverbank.

After a couple minutes of staring at the stream and listening to it wash everything away, I turned to her and said, "You've become a good friend, Anne. If there's anything you still want to know, just ask."

"Actually," Anne replied hesitantly, her crimson eyes darting to the ground as she skipped a rock, "there's something I should really tell you."

I leaned toward her to listen more carefully but never got the chance. It was like needles pricked me when my senses suddenly screamed Robert's presence. While I opened my mouth to say something, Anne's eyes registering it too, I realized the situation I'd put us in. A sick, exhausted Allyen and a magic-less commoner?

We were sitting ducks. Sam wasn't the foolish one. I was.

I tried to get to my feet, but my knees sank back into all the mud I had dredged up, weary from the effort. Fearful, I scanned every direction unsure of Robert's location, my senses muddled by illness, bushes and trees obstructing my view. Terror rippled through me when I felt a hand on my shoulder. I tried to summon whatever magic I could muster, but the golden orb I managed to create fizzled out.

Robert breathed hot and heavy in my face, his expression desperate, "Come with me, Linaria. Please, join me, so we can be together!"

"No!" I cried, trying in vain to push him away from me when a geyser of water appeared out of nowhere. It gushed into Robert alone and dragged him a few feet away from me, hitting him square in the chest and churning around his ankles. Confusion rocked me until I turned to see Anne with her turban askew and her hands outstretched. Sprigs of wiry, emerald hair poked out from her turban.

She was an aguamage. I'd never sensed it in her, not even once. To have magic, she had to be at least nobility. But between her green hair and her knowledge of the Archimage and his palace, I knew better.

Anne was Lady Sabine.

Abruptly, I was staring at a stranger, even as Luke burst through the brush on her left, sprinting toward me. Anne/Sabine conjured another wave to crash toward us in Luke's wake, but Robert was quicker. The older man darted back to me, beckoning Rhydin's dark transportation magic, as Luke dashed in from the opposite direction. Before I knew it, a hand grappled each of my arms and the world sliced in two.

CHAPTER SIXTEEN

P ain ripped through me. Half of my body was sucked
toward Luke while the other half was swept toward
Robert. I screamed, Luke yelled, and Robert shouted. The
riverbank and Anne disappeared into a sea of white, but the
world couldn't decide what it would form next.

One moment, long lines of trees would begin to materialize
only to be struck from existence as dark stones tried to take
their place. It was like an indecisive artist was sitting at his
easel drawing and erasing, drawing and erasing, over and
over. I was on the brink of losing consciousness, every one of
my cells shrieking with pain. Finally, Luke gave a yelp, and
the blackened bricks overcame the serene trees.

I felt the slam of the ground against my body as we landed,
and both of the hands that nearly tore me in two were blown
away from me. My ears rang with a deafening roar, and all my
joints moaned together. I would have been content to lie there
on the cold, damp floor for hours if my vision hadn't suddenly
cleared enough to reveal that we were in a dungeon.

"Well, well," Rhydin's voice mused from what sounded like a deep tunnel, "Robert, you have certainly outdone yourself this time."

I shot forward with a burst of panic. My head responded with a wave of nausea, and I ended up tripping over my own feet. My eyes were still hazy, but there was no mistaking the bars lining either side of the corridor in which we had landed. The most eerie part, however, was the fact that all of these cells were completely empty.

After all, Rhydin wasn't exactly the type who took prisoners.

Luke was instantly on his feet, and I could only assume he must have used his magic to come along with us when he wasn't strong enough to take me away. He drew his sword, huffing a couple notes of one of his musical spells before sending a bright ribbon of power in Rhydin's direction.

Rhydin never moved a muscle, but Robert sprinted over and threw up a glowing hand, thwarting Luke's spell. Beads of sweat dotted Luke's brow, his energy already being sapped by Rhydin's presence, and I knew this fight was over before it even started.

Rhydin chuckled, "You've brought me not only one of the treacherous Allyen twins, but a *Ranguvariian*! Now, I can finally discover how they can thwart me so."

Luke gritted his teeth. To my surprise, he never tried to transport away again. I didn't know if he had the power to do so around Rhydin, but he still didn't try. He stood his ground. He couldn't leave me behind. He shouted angrily, "You Archimage traitor!"

The cruel grin vanished from Rhydin's face. He said sternly, "Take him to my laboratory."

Several guards trotted down the stairs and into the dungeon. They were fools if they thought Luke would come willingly, I thought. Even through his weakness, Luke knocked them left and right with his blade, his magic too limited now to allow for spells. He fought with everything he had, and after he had disposed of most of the guards, he tried to make his way toward me. I struggled to my feet, my head woozy. This was our only chance to escape.

Rhydin frowned and moved into Luke's path, not drawing any weapon. Luke hopped from one foot to the other, desperately trying to get around the sorcerer without the possibility of being touched as his strength ticked away with every second. He was starting to wheeze Rhydin's power was affecting him so much.

Finally, Luke made a dash for me, unable to wait any longer, but Rhydin moved with some superhuman speed of his own, clamping a hand on Luke's exposed bicep, just above his forearm guard. Luke growled with pain and threw off Rhydin before he dropped to the ground. His chest heaved as he sucked down air, his teeth gritted. The flesh of his arm was now angry red and disfigured as pieces of skin flaked away from the burn.

"Intriguing," Rhydin commented as he stared down the length of his nose at Luke. "I intend to discover why that is, and so much more. Take him away."

More guards hurried forward, and when Luke tried to fight again, Rhydin simply reached out and brushed his knuckles against his cheek. Luke cried out again and slumped into a heap as each guard grabbed a limb and began to usher him away from me.

I had reached for my magic several times by now. To help, to hinder, to do something. Several times, it failed me.

"Luke!" I wailed, dropping to my knees again as another wave of nausea overcame me. "I-... I'll come save you! I promise!"

Just before he disappeared from sight, for the briefest of moments Luke's eyes flashed yellow with fear as he stared back at me. Then, they tinted blue momentarily before becoming as black as night. He wasn't done fighting, I told myself. He would be okay. I would escape, or the others would come. He would be okay.

The heavy dungeon door closed with a deafening boom on Luke and the five guards who carried him. As silence seeped back in around the three of us who remained, Rhydin turned and strode toward me. "I have wanted to do this for a *very* long time."

I pushed away from him the best I could, but I wasn't capable of anything that could stop him at this point. Rhydin reached down, his freakishly cold fingers looping underneath the chain around my neck, and stripped me of my locket. My magical amplifier. What made me capable of everything I could do. "No!" I whimpered.

"Oh, yes." Victory gleamed in Rhydin's eyes as he straightened and marveled at the locket's silver face. Then, he scooped it up along with its chain and tucked it neatly away in his waistcoat. He looked back to me, about to say something, when abruptly his expression changed. He seized my leather gloves and yanked them off, exposing the ink of the Epidemic in my veins. He then grasped my collar and pulled it aside. More ink. His grin grew even wider.

Robert's expression, in contrast, grew frightened. This crinkled the scab on his cheek where Luke had nicked him with a knife at our last meeting during the Royal executions. He took a few steps toward us, his hands outstretched like a beggar. "Master, your antidote! Please, you must give it to her! She will join us now and not cause any trouble, I promise!"

I never thought I'd ever do this, but... I looked to Rhydin with a shred of hope. That he would honor the vow he made to Robert that he'd allow me to live with him after taking my locket and defeating me. That he would give me the antidote to the contagion that he had designed, that he would cure me of the ache in my bones, the wheeze in my chest, the nausea in my belly. Of the ink that traipsed nearer and nearer to strangling my heart.

I knew it was a lost cause within only seconds of seeing the look on Rhydin's face. An expression of disbelief that Robert still expected him to keep this promise likely made decades ago. After all, it was to kill me that he designed this Epidemic all those years ago in the first place. Robert, however, continued to gaze at his master hopefully, and I wondered if he realized that he was about to be betrayed just as King Adam and Queen Jasmine had been.

"Oh, Robert," Rhydin chided as he shook his head. "You know she would never join us whether her life depended on it or not. Besides, I simply cannot allow either of your children to remain alive. They're symbols of hope. Of rebellion against my rule.

"But, Master, you promised-...!" Robert cried, his gaunt face paling more than normal.

"Which is why," Rhydin cut him off sternly, the grin fading from his face, "I created the Epidemic to kill them. That they would *happen* to die of an illness rather than directly at my hand. They could never be allowed to survive, Robert. You must know this to be true."

Robert swallowed hard. He couldn't look at me. After a few moments, he nodded ever so slowly, his fight sucked away leaving only a shell behind.

Disgusted, I glared at Robert. "You want me to call you father, yet you give in to his every command? Even to end my life? You're pathetic."

The older, former Allyen stared at his toes. Rhydin brushed his hands together, wiping them of me, and turned toward the exit as he declared, "Throw her in a cell. No need to schedule her execution now. She will be dead in a matter of days."

Two more guards clothed in midnight uniforms came forward and grabbed each of my arms. I let myself become a deadweight, not having the strength or power to fight them but not wanting to make it easy for them either. They threw me into the nearest cell, which smelled of mildew and rat droppings, and slammed the bars behind me with a loud clang. My head collided with the cold stone of the floor, which was also damp with a substance of which I didn't want to know the identity, and the fog of the Epidemic claimed my mind.

It was suddenly a battle to remain conscious. The rancid odor of the cell made me retch, which only made me more nauseous. I tried to lean forward in order to study the lock on the door, the hinges, the tiny window in the opposite wall, *anything* that could lead to my escape to rescue Luke. Dizziness overcame me, and I desperately hoped that the others were putting together some sort of plan to save him.

Just to save him. Not me. He deserved to be saved. I'd gotten him captured because I was stupid and ran off.

Me? Rhydin had my locket. My power was halved. My children were in Caark, safe and sound, not needing me. My husband was in Stellan, ignorant of my plight and of me in general.

As I lost the battle for my wakefulness, I wondered if it would be best if I simply never opened my eyes again.

The prisoner screamed and writhed on the examination table when Rhydin entered his laboratory. The place was as clean as his servants were capable of with many big windows filled with clear glass to allow as much light as possible. Every spare inch of shelf space was filled with jars of herbs, minerals, and specimens as well as various scientific instruments that Rhydin had kept from the old days.

His old favorite was a lengthy telescope sitting in the corner of the room pointed at the largest window near the ceiling. Yet, he hadn't bothered to look at the stars since the day he gained his power and banished his ignorance within the Archimage Palace.

"You're not going to get away with this!" the prisoner, called Luke Rhydin seemed to remember, shouted from his spot strapped to the table with magically-enforced chains.

"I already have," Rhydin mused as he withdrew Linaria's half of the locket from his pocket. He waved it in front of Luke's face menacingly, making it dance along its chain, and then set it upon his desk. "Now, I just need Evanarion's half, and I will reign over Nerahdis for the rest of time!"

And destroy that pathetic ghost of my past in the Archimage Palace at last, Rhydin added to himself.

Rhydin gathered a few materials and tools as Luke fought until he was truly exhausted, his energy drained just because of Rhydin's presence. Rhydin *so* looked forward to discovering the reason for this, as well as why and how the infuriating beasts couldn't be sensed. With Luke on his table, every Ranguvariian secret was now ripe for the picking.

Luke tried to throw himself around when Rhydin approached him, but that just made the insertion of the needle more painful. As crimson blood filled the vial, Rhydin mused more to himself than anyone, "Even Ranguvariian blood is red, I see."

The beast boy growled as his eyes flashed a rainbow of colors, another secret Rhydin wished to unlock, "Why are you doing this??"

Was the boy a dolt? Rhydin stated monotonously, "To learn your secrets."

"No, why are you doing *all* of this?" Luke responded, his eyes red and angry. "Why do you think you need to be emperor? Nerahdis was better off without you!"

Rhydin paused. Again, the gears in his mind weren't clicking. He shook his head, trying to formulate a response, but nothing would come. He shook his head as he withdrew the needle from Luke's arm. The words hesitantly spilled out of his mouth without his meaning to. "...I'm doing this."

Luke's brow furrowed like he was now studying Rhydin instead of the other way around.

"You are not in a place to ask questions, boy," Rhydin snarled angrily as he reached for his next tool. "Everything I do is for the good of Nerahdis, and that only comes through my rule, not the Royals'."

"Stars above," Luke breathed in exclamation, his eyes wide and copper-colored in a kind of horrified surprise. "There's no logic behind what you do, only that you must do it. You don't age. You crack like marble instead of bleed. You're not human, are you?? You're-...!!"

Rhydin lashed out like lightning and caught Luke's throat. The boy screamed in agony as his skin boiled, and Rhydin screeched, "You know *nothing* of what I am! What I did to become what I am! I am more human than any of you revolting creatures!"

Luke choked and sputtered for moments more before becoming silent. Still, Rhydin clung to his neck until he heard a door open and close behind him. It was minutes more before Rhydin could manage to unlatch himself from the boy, and he stared at his hands briefly prior to curling them into fists. He turned, still seething and trying to regain control, to see Robert standing timidly by his desk. He roared, "What do you want?"

Robert faltered before answering, "To inform you that the camp where I found Linaria has been abandoned. I imagine they are on their way here."

"What does it matter?" Rhydin grunted as his steam cooled. He reached for his tools once more, preparing to begin his experiments.

"They are likely coming to free her and this boy."

"Forget them. They will never get through my charms and defenses," Rhydin scowled as he conducted his work.

Robert, again, looked terrified to even clear his throat. "Forgive me, Master, but Lady Sabine and my son were in that camp too. They are likely part of the party heading this way."

The dark sorcerer froze. Considered it for a few moments. Then spoke, "Give me half an hour. Then we destroy the rest of the Royals and the Allyens."

"I can't thank you enough for coming with me on such short notice," Rachel said quietly. "Just your presence should be invaluable."

The sun was dipping toward the western horizon, causing Rhydin's palace to grow darker and darker until it was nothing more than a silhouette with the sun's brilliant light behind it. A small group of people was inconspicuously approaching from the east as fast as they dared. Chelsea, an Aatarilec banished to Caark that Rachel was slowly but surely coming to respect as a person, strode next to her. Rachel ardently hoped that their hypothesis was true.

That having an Aatarilec present would allow her Ranguvariians to fight Rhydin's magic unhindered.

Aside from that hope, Rachel was beside herself with worry. James had transported to Caark frantic for help because both their brother and the person they'd vowed to protect their whole lives had been abducted by Robert. Jaspen stayed in Caark with all the children so that Rachel could come help, and she couldn't imagine what horrors Luke and Lina could possibly be going through in Rhydin's dungeon. The sooner they found a way in, the better.

"Oh, I am looking forward to this," Chelsea whispered in response as she tied her mint green hair back into a ponytail. "I hope Rhydin shows his ugly face, so I can shred it myself." Briefly, her human hand transfigured into its true form: a more petite, lavender-skinned hand with lengthy, sharp claws.

Rachel nodded. They could agree on that, at least. The light was fading fast, and the trees were beginning to thin out as they approached the palace. She hoped they would be able to at least get to the dungeon before they were detected.

Her eyes wandered between the others in their group, making sure each of them was being cautious. They might have all been wearing feather charms, but those didn't make you invisible. Aside from a handful of extra Ranguvariians sent in by Grandpa Arii, Evan was toward the front with her, anxiously leading the group forward to find his sister, while James and Bartholomiiu flanked the back.

In the middle were a few of the Royals that Rachel couldn't dissuade from coming along, Frederick, Mira, Xavier, and, to Rachel's shock, none other than Lady Sabine. Rachel had been astounded to see that her brothers had in fact located her. She had to admit she hadn't thought they would succeed, but there appeared to be more to that story which would be told after Lina and Luke were rescued.

Sam was with the group as well, and while Rachel had been happy to see him again and that he was well after being around so much illness, he seemed to be acting strange. He reminded her of a deer caught off guard by the snap of a twig, like a rug had been pulled out from under him so hard that he was still flailing in midair even now. James had quickly briefed her of the situation that had unfolded over the last several weeks, that Sam had stalled the mission to dedicate his time to his ailing sister. Rachel had a feeling her youngest brother had left out a few details.

When Sam came to the camp shortly after she had arrived and learned of not only Lina's kidnapping but her suffering of the Epidemic according to Sabine, he initially denied that it could be possible. This told Rachel all she really needed to know, but her friend's marriage was none of her business. Only her safety.

Rachel was shaken from her thoughts by the sounds of clanking metal growing ever louder. Her brow furrowed. They were still at least half a mile from the palace walls. Why would soldiers be all the way out here?

"Hide!" she hissed, and the entire crew rapidly found a tree or some other brush to take cover behind. Rachel carefully peered around her chosen tree with James glued to her side. She fingered her sword hilt as she numbered the entire regiment marching toward them.

This wasn't some happenstance scouting force. Rhydin had known they were coming and from what direction. Something was wrong. Something had changed. Rachel felt it in her bones, and she feared the reason.

James gasped, bringing her attention back, "Rhydin is with them! Why would he be here himself? What's going on, Sis?"

Rachel studied the regiment harder, and sure enough, Rhydin was behind his flanks dressed in an overly-adorned, black military uniform. As if on cue, he raised his pale hand, safe because his soldiers faced the opposite direction, and emitted a purple beacon of magic.

Instantly, Rachel's arms and legs began to tingle, losing feeling swiftly. Her lungs suddenly felt constricted, and she fought to keep her breaths regular and quiet. Normally, she wouldn't be experiencing this kind of reaction to Rhydin's magic until she had been around him for some time, not immediately. James, too, groaned and raised a hand to his forehead, his eyes trying to focus. Rachel glanced around. Bartholomiiu and the others weren't immune either.

Panic entered her system. Rhydin had done it. There was no other explanation. He'd cracked all their secrets. That it was the use and presence of his magic that made them weak and how to sense them beyond their feathers. There was only one way he could have done that.

"Luke," Rachel breathed, her face becoming hot.

James turned to her innocently and moaned, "Luke? Where? Do you see him?"

Rachel didn't answer. Couldn't answer. Couldn't speak the words. She still incredibly hoped that she was wrong, but she knew better. Luke had to have been subjected to unspeakable horrors for Rhydin to glean this information. Her grief would have to be acknowledged later. Her fury would reign for now.

Chelsea left her tree several yards away and ducked low as she sprinted to where Rachel and James huddled. As she grew closer, Rachel felt her symptoms improve to the point of being barely noticeable with the Aatarilec right next to her. Chelsea's golden eyes had the decency of being concerned when she asked, "Are you alright? Is it not working?"

"Oh, it's working," Rachel responded snidely, trying her hardest to keep her voice even and her tears from falling. "I just should have recruited about a dozen more of you apparently."

Chelsea drooped and then grew frustrated, "How is this happening? I thought you said we had the element of surprise!"

"We lost it," Rachel answered tersely, her jaw tight. "We were too late for our brother. We may not be too late for the Allyen yet."

James gaped at her, realizing what she had realized, but there was no time for that now. The regiment marched toward them, having no idea that their illustrious leader was performing magic behind them, the very thing they believed they fought against.

Rachel turned to her own people and put on her leader's voice, the one her grandfather had taught her since she was very small. She proclaimed, "This isn't going to be pretty. Rhydin has unlocked all our secrets. We've lost all our advantages. I wouldn't fault any of you if you want to leave, but I will be pressing onward."

"Me too!" declared James, his eyes glassy.

Behind him, Bartholomiiu, ever his shadow, nodded his shaggy head as he agreed, "Lina, must save."

Likewise, the other Ranguvariians all bobbed their heads, which didn't surprise Rachel. Her people were fierce warriors and had been such for centuries. Rhydin's victory meant death for them all, so she truthfully would have judged any Ranguvariian that turned tail now. Even Frederick, Mira, Xavier, and Sabine seemed to be able to put aside their differences in order to stick with the cause.

Xavier cackled, hoisting his bum arm into the air, "You all would die without me!"

"I'm not leaving my sister," Evan said fiercely, and then shot a hateful glance at Sam.

"What?" Sam responded defensively, "Why are you looking at me like that?"

"It was after your argument that she ran off. If you hadn't been so rude and distant to her all this time, none of us would be in this situation!" Evan growled lowly.

One by one everyone looked at Sam. It was very clear that a plethora of excuses and thoughts were running through his mind, thinking of which to say, but Rachel acted quickly to shut it down. "Now is not the time, gentlemen! I suggest you ready yourselves for battle."

Evan and Sam continued to glower at each other, but Rachel was done dealing with that. She blocked everything else out aside from the soldiers marching toward them that were within arrow's distance now. This battle was personal for her now.

She drew her blade, and the rest of the Ranguvariians followed suit. James gripped his tight with both hands. The Royals, Evan, and Sam all brandished their weapons. Chelsea transformed into her full Aatarilec appearance, shrinking down, turning purple, and sprouting fangs and her claws once again. Rachel said to her, "Stick close to us, and we might stand a chance."

"Only long enough to get to Rhydin. Then you're on your own," Chelsea replied, and Rachel couldn't tell if she was angry at her or Rhydin.

"Fair enough," Rachel responded, and then announced louder, "On the count of three."

As they charged forward on three, Rachel bellowed, "For Luke!!"

Chapter Seventeen

M y head was still throbbing when I came to, but the musty smell of mold and blood immediately reminded me of where I was. I groaned, my dizziness not subsiding, and grasped at my collar to pull it aside.

My eyes were foggy. When I squinted, I could see the Epidemic's ink rotating around my heart like a vulture circling a beast close to death.

Not long now, I thought to myself. But, you have to try.

Standing was out of the question at this point, so I leaned forward onto my hands to crawl over to the locked, barred door once more. There had to be some way to break out. With movement, however, my vision became clearer, and I could suddenly see that there was an unknown object between me and the door. Like a big, lumpy blanket or something.

Ever so slowly, my mind registered that it was not a big blanket or even a pile of blankets. It was something wrapped in a dirty sheet. Something that was long and lean and had shaggy hair at one end. My mind reached clarity all at once, and I scrambled on my hands and knees over to the unmoving, blanket-clad lump.

"No, no, no," I mumbled over and over, my clogging throat distorting my voice. "Wake up! *Wake up!*"

Luke was unnaturally still. My eyes played tricks on me that his chest was moving up and down, but it wasn't. I gripped his rock-hard shoulders and shook him with all the strength I could muster, ignoring the fact that the sad sheet he was wrapped in was stained a rust-colored red in multiple places.

Old blood. Dead blood.

"Luke, wake up," I repeated, my voice unrecognizable now. I felt my face breaking. "You can't be dead. You can't be."

Injured, sure. You could come back from injured. But not dead. Death was permanent. My mind spiraled.

Why is he dead?

Because you ran off like an imbecile. Like a child. Away from your protectors who have promised to guard you with their lives. And now, one of them has fulfilled that vow.

It's. All. Your. Fault!

I broke. My wails echoed throughout the dungeon and back to me until my own noises were all I could hear. Memories of Luke played through my mind. His taking me back and forth to Stellan each day. How he saved me from drowning when our ship went down. How he'd helped me to find Sam during the war. Everything all the way back to that trip we'd taken over the mountains to Mineraltir, just the two of us, before I even knew what he was. How he'd gotten me back out of that kingdom just before Duunzer's Darkness claimed it. And now, I would never see his eyes change colors with his emotions ever again.

I rocked back and forth with Luke's head in my lap, quiet once it crossed my mind that Rhydin had his body thrown in here to illicit this exact reaction from me. So, I sat there silently with tears flowing in rivers down my cheeks, imagining the most painful way I would take my revenge upon Rhydin. It was due to this stillness that I jumped when the big door to the dungeon creaked open softly.

I quickly wiped my face and shook my head, trying to clear it. I couldn't bear to let go of Luke's broken body, but I situated myself to face the bars with as fierce of a look I could manage. A posture and expression that argued I was tough as nails rather than the shattered soul I was. I figured it was Rhydin coming down to see me, to rub his victory in my face. But it was Robert who suddenly stepped into the frame of my cell.

Anger flared through me. I snarled, although my ferocity was dampened by a couple of nasty coughs, "What do you want?"

He appeared anxious. He kept darting looks over his shoulder back to the entrance of the dungeon. He replied gently, "Please, Linaria, you must listen to me."

"I will do no such thing," I wheezed, and then gestured to the bloody sheet in front of me and the body it covered, "You've done enough."

"Linaria, I… I'm so sorry. I never meant for any of this to happen," Robert pleaded, his voice growing quieter and faster. "Rhydin lied to me. All I've ever wanted is to be with you and your brother."

"I don't believe you!" I accused furiously before having to stop and cough again.

At this, I heard a jingling noise and then a metal clang. I opened my eyes from coughing to see Robert standing in front of the open cell door. He had my full attention now as he hurried in, knelt by my side, and began searching his pockets. His eyes looked different. They were clear with no trace of the delusional rage that had often occupied them every time I saw him. Robert withdrew a small, glowing vial from his cloak pocket along with a terrifying looking contraption that had a needle on one end.

"What are you doing?" I mumbled, starting to lose consciousness.

"Saving my daughter's life," he responded quickly, still appearing to be hurrying for whatever reason. "I joined Rhydin because I wanted my children to grow up in a world free of Royals. It seems to me that a world ruled by Rhydin is far worse, and I will not let him kill my children."

Robert fumbled with the needle device for a few more seconds, snapping the vial onto it, and then reached for my arm. I probably would have still fought him if I'd been at full strength, but at this point, my body was as limp and unresistant as a noodle. He injected the glowing blue solution into my arm, and then threw the needle to the side.

Its effects were almost instantaneous. My fever broke, my head cleared, and my lungs felt clean again. A rush of energy flooded my limbs, and before my very eyes, the ink of the Epidemic faded from black to indigo to royal-blue to finally the pale blue-green that veins are supposed to be. I flexed my normal-colored fingers and hands, absorbing what had happened.

Robert stood and held out his hands to me, "Come along. We must go before Rhydin discovers what I've stolen."

I laid my hands upon Luke once again and asked, "Is someone really going to miss one vial?"

"No," Robert breathed anxiously as he dug around in his pocket once more, "But this *will* be missed."

My jaw dropped open as Robert dangled none other than my locket in front of my face. I stuttered as I took it, "H-How?"

"That doesn't matter," Robert replied rapidly, and then he held out his hands to me again, "We need to go. Now!"

"I..." I stammered, looking back down at Luke anxiously, "I can't leave him."

Robert responded edgily, "Linaria, if we take him with us, I won't be able to transport us away! As it is, we need to get outside to do so. We can only transport in to the palace, not out of it."

"But Robert-..." I tried to plead.

"He's dead, Linaria," Robert replied firmly, taking hold of one of my hands as he tried to pull me away from Luke. "I'm sorry, but you can't help him now!"

"Please," I whimpered, gazing into Robert's Allyen eyes, "Please, Father."

Robert huffed in frustration, but there was no denying the softening of his features at the sound of the name he'd yearned most to hear. In only a second, he bent down and grabbed Luke's lanky body, heaving it over his stout shoulders. Luke's fingers and toes almost touched the ground due to Robert's short stature, but he was aloft nonetheless. Then, he shoved me gently toward the open door. Before I knew it, we were running.

I hopped up the stairs out of the dungeon and nearly tripped over two knocked-out guards posted outside the door. No wonder Robert had been so jittery. It was obvious to anyone walking by that something fishy was going on.

"This way," Robert breathed as he jogged through the door with Luke. He led us down a southern hallway built of black onyx stones and amethyst decorations, although we were running far too fast to truly take in how Rhydin had decided to decorate his imperial palace. Part of me took a moment to relish how strong and sure my feet felt underneath me. It was like a breath of fresh air after how weak the last few days had left me.

The surety left me when Robert and I rounded a corner to where three hallways joined together, coming face to face with none other than Eli and Kino, the former Auklian advisor and the Lunakan woman who answered Rhydin's every beck and call. Both of them were clad in the sleek, black uniforms of Rhydin's new military, and confused expressions crossed both their faces as they took in the sight of Robert and I together.

"Robert!" Eli sneered after a swift glance at my unbound wrists, my health, and the locket around my neck, "How could you? Master *trusted* you!"

"You've betrayed us all!" Kino screeched as she drew her blade.

"Rhydin betrayed us first, and if neither of you can see that now with how he rules over Nerahdis, then you are both truly lost!" Robert argued. Then, in a swift motion, Robert let Luke's body slide down his back to the floor while he began working his hands.

After a few milliseconds, the brightest golden orb I'd ever seen materialized in his hands, and he chucked it squarely at Eli's chest. The Auklian man only narrowly avoided it, his large glasses askew on his face, and I looked on in awe at my father.

He was using his Allyen magic. After at least two decades of ignoring it and only using the power given to him by Rhydin, his birth magic was still alive and stronger than ever before. Once an Allyen, always an Allyen. A smile cracked my face.

Kino rushed toward me, and I barely summoned my sword in time to block her ruthless blows. Kino was much taller than me and moved like a predatory cat, so I stayed in a defensive stance for a few minutes. When she paused to make some sort of verbal jab, I took my chance and fired a magical charge.

It slammed into her shoulder, leaving her uniform burned and ragged as she yelped. She growled as she flipped her blonde-tipped hair out of her face, "Oooo, I'm gonna make you wish you'd died!"

She threw one of her hands into a circle motion, and a magical wind sprang forth and knocked me backwards. I tried to remain on my feet, but the gust was too strong and the midnight tiles beneath my feet too slick. Sliding backwards, I reached out and hooked my arm through the nearest window, holding on until Kino's spell stopped. Then, I darted forward, and our swords clashed once again.

"Open your eyes, Kino," I pleaded as we pushed against each other, "It's only a matter of time before Rhydin betrays you, too! He killed Adam and Jasmine, and he lied to Robert for decades. Can't you see?"

"All I can see is that my master would *never* betray the one who brought him your head on a platter!" Kino responded silkily.

I engaged with her again, sending two magical charges in her direction, when I heard Eli mock my father, "You were his right hand, Robert! You had it *made*! *All* of us wanted to be you!"

"What, a puppet?" Robert spat derisively as he thrust another spell in Eli's direction, sword-less, "Rhydin isn't all that he seems, Eli! There's something not right with him. You need to get out while you can!"

"Why?" Eli cackled as he mustered another wave of aguamage power to try and sweep Robert off his feet like an undertow, "Your position is officially open, and I'll deserve a promotion after this! You've lost everything because of that rotten daughter of yours!"

"You're wrong," Robert nearly whispered as he jumped to the side of the flowing water, "I was empty as Rhydin's second. She's saved me, but you'll never understand."

I was having trouble concentrating on Kino, my heart full, when abruptly, Robert's voice became a lot louder as he called to me, "We don't have time for this, Linaria! We need to leave before Rhydin returns!"

I grunted. Did he think we were fighting just for fun?

"Come here!" he shouted again.

Confused, I parried a few more of Kino's blows before blasting her in the chest with such a quick spell that it more exploded her backwards than really hurt her. In the same moment, Robert tripped Eli and thrust him forward into a suit of decorative armor centered in the junction of the three hallways. I rushed over to him, and in only seconds, he grabbed my shoulders and planted me right in front of him. Then, he took one of my hands and said, "Do as I do."

Robert began a series of movements. Stepping out with his right foot, raising his right hand and stretching it outward in an arching movement, and then turning his whole body as he thrust it toward Eli. A small orb materialized and shot at the Auklian, who easily doused it with his water magic as he sprinted back toward us.

"Now!" Robert cried, his gaunt face showing some color for the first time.

He began his movements again, and I mirrored him. He stepped out with his right foot; I stepped out with my left. I followed his right arm with my left, channeling my magic and his due to our joined hands through the amplification of my locket, and a much bigger orb than I'd ever seen emerged.

Eli's eyes grew wide as the light of the spell flashed over his glasses, and he tried to turn and run. However, we released our combined power upon him, and he was blown off his feet and hurled to the ground.

Suddenly, the halls became silent. We ran over to Eli, his chest charred and ragged. Squeaking noises came from his mouth as he struggled to breathe. He stared up at us helplessly, unable to move, his thick lenses shattered and his wavy hair in disarray. The man who had guarded Sam's cell in the war and fought me at the Archimage Palace. The man who tricked me into going to Lunaka Castle the night my magic awakened by disguising himself as Sam, and the man who tried to hurl Frederick off a balcony to fake his death. The man who threw the lever that killed the Royals. That same man lay here broken at our feet, and rage filled me at the sight of him.

"This is for all of us," I said quietly as I raised my blade and touched its point to his chest. "For Sam. For Frederick. For Queen Gloria. For Luke. For me."

Then, I pushed on my sword, and his sputtering stopped.

Robert hesitantly placed a hand on my shoulder, "We need to go."

Suddenly, panic filled me, and I glanced in every direction. "Where's Kino?"

Robert looked around briefly as he trotted back to Luke's body and heaved it back over his shoulders. "She must have gone to find Rhydin. All the more reason to hurry!"

I took one last look at Eli and sealed him away in my memory. Between his and King Adam's deaths, it was beginning to feel like the end of an era. But this era would only end once it was Rhydin that my blade punctured.

The two of us took off again, racing down the next hallway as fast as was possible with Robert's load. The sunlight was disappearing fast, and this added to my anxiety. We needed to get away from this palace before darkness fell, or we'd be easy targets out in the open. After all, it was my insistence on bringing Luke that meant we couldn't simply transport away once we got outside.

Once we reached the end of the hallway, Robert began to breathe a little easier when the petite, wooden door came open in his hands. We left Rhydin's palace of cold, dark stones behind for soft grass, silent trees, and the faint smell of pine. However, the feelings of tension and fear didn't leave me.

I called ahead to Robert who jogged in front of me, "Where do we go now?"

"We keep moving," my father responded over his shoulder. "Hopefully, the battle will keep Rhydin distracted, and he won't come after us. Our presences will disappear if we can reach the mountains."

"Battle?" I repeated. My mind hinged on that one word as my feet slowed. "What battle?"

Robert appeared to inwardly regret his words as he stopped running and turned to face me. He hesitantly answered, "There's a small skirmish occurring just over that hill. Between Rhydin, as well as some of his forces, and several of your friends." He pointed in the opposite direction.

My heart wanted to sink and lift at the same time. They'd come to rescue me, but now they were battling Rhydin without my help.

"We have to help them," I declared as I spun on my heel to march the other way. Once I turned, my ears could pick up the faint clangs of swords and booms of magic.

Robert paused, but he must have decided it was no use trying to argue with me because he simply started trotting toward the hill without a word. We spent the minutes it took to reach the hill in silence, and I couldn't help but study my father's back as he ran in front of me, Luke's limp arms and legs bobbing.

I'd never known I was capable of the magic that we performed together to end Eli. There was so much about being an Allyen that I hadn't gotten to learn from Grandma Saarah before she died. Before she was killed trying to protect Keera, Rosetta, and I from Rhydin. Perhaps now I would be able to fill in the missing pieces of my magical prowess from my father.

As we rushed toward the battle, Rosetta continued to flash in my mind. Her oval, freckled face framed by her straight, sandy hair. The last time I'd her, she'd helped lead Sam, Rachel, and I to freedom outside of Rhydin's prison tower in the Great Desert. She refused to come with us, insisting that she could save Mikael, the boy who'd essentially faked her death to kidnap her to go follow Rhydin. She promised me she'd join me when she could…but that had been over a year ago.

I called out uncertainly, "Father…?"

Robert halted in his tracks so rapidly, I thought he might trip under Luke's weight. He stuttered, "Y-Yes?"

"Is my sister okay?" I mumbled.

A gray hue overtook Robert's face. I imagined it wasn't easy to think of the love of your life having a child with someone else after you left. I was almost fearful his anger would return, but he answered stoically, "Yes. She's fine. She lives in the citadel around Rhydin's palace with that boy."

I released a breath I'd never realized I'd been holding for over a year. Rosetta was still alright. She could still join me someday. I could only nod my head in thanks, and the two of us started up our hurried trek once more.

It was twilight by the time we crested the hill, and when I witnessed what was below us, heat flooded my body and adrenaline kicked into gear. This battle looked like it'd been going on for a while. Everybody was spread out in a tiny clearing in the trees. I saw all my friends, minus Princess Cornflower and An-...*Sabine*'s two boys, as well as perhaps half a dozen Ranguvariians and four dozen of Rhydin's soldiers.

There were also dead lying in the dirt in black uniforms alongside those whose uniform had been faith and hope in our rebellion.

We wasted no time and edged down the hill, remaining hidden in the trees. Once we were within several yards of the main action, Robert chose a larger tree to set Luke against, and I hoped no one would disturb him while we were forced to leave him alone. My throat was starting to swell up again, so I pushed myself away from him. There was a time to grieve and a time to fight. This was the time for the latter.

My eyes scanned the battle when we reached the last tree. I sought Sam first and saw him dueling three of Rhydin's soldiers, using his Rounan powers to knock them over or pull the swords out of their grips. Evan, too, was fighting a few of these soldiers, and I realized quickly that all these soldiers were commoners. Rhydin was still trying to keep up his ruse of not having magic, and it was getting these poor innocents injured or killed. Our people were dealing with being drastically outnumbered, but the soldiers were really no match for them one-on-one.

Robert abruptly touched my arm and then pointed a little further north from where I'd been looking. There stood Rhydin, one of his hands up in the air emitting a purple beacon out of sight of his soldiers as he sternly watched the action. I had no idea what that was all about, but it hit me that this was my moment. This was the time I could show the soldiers his use of magic. Seeing me alive, well, and free was the perfect bait.

I moved to step forward into the fray when a firm hand grabbed my shoulder. Robert said to me earnestly, "Wait. I need to tell you something."

"Now?" I asked, a hint of a whine in my voice. "Can it wait?"

Robert spoke rapidly, "Rhydin, he… He isn't what he seems, and neither is the nature of his magic. I think I've figured it out."

"Okay," I answered impatiently, eyeing the battle still thundering just yards away, "Is now really the best time?"

"This is important, Linaria!" Robert chided, his haggard face sincere as he clung to my shoulder. "Rhydin's power was created by man, just as Nora's was as the First Allyen centuries ago. He wasn't born with it like the Rounans and Gornish Royals are. There is a link between our magics, and we must be very careful because I believe this could be problematic later on. On top of that, I don't think Rhydin is hu-…"

All the hairs on the back of my neck stood up on end, and Robert's eyes and the trees behind him took on a purple sheen. I was turning to look when Robert dove forward, colliding with me and knocking us flat on the ground just as a large violet blast soared over our heads and crashed into the tree closest to us. It went up into an amethyst blaze, and Robert rolled off me, got up, and assumed a defensive stance like lightning.

When I stood and joined him, I noticed that the clearing had fallen silent. All the fighting had ceased as everyone, my friends and Rhydin's soldiers alike, stared in our direction. My ears rang in the silence. A few of my friends' faces lit up upon sight of me, but it was upon Rhydin my eyes landed. As he glared at Robert and I, I had never seen him so filled with fury.

Of all the different versions of the future Rhydin had likely seen, it looked like this one had never once crossed his mind as one that could even possibly come true.

CHAPTER EIGHTEEN

"Robert!" Rhydin roared, his voice distorted by anger.

My father visibly gulped, his gaunt throat bobbing. He didn't respond, but he did start walking away from the burning trees and toward my friends, hugging the edge as he remained facing Rhydin. I followed him slowly.

Rhydin unleashed another barrage of purple fire in full view of his commoner soldiers and screamed, "*What have you done?*"

I jumped forward to help my father block the attack, our feet spread shoulder-width apart and our hands outstretched like flat blades to divert the fire around us with a flash of our golden light. When the fire ceased, I noticed Evan gaping.

Robert took a deep breath, gathering his courage, and said loudly, "You betrayed me first, Rhydin! I gave up everything to join you and make a better world for my children. You promised to rid Nerahdis of corruption. Instead, you've only plunged it deeper into darkness and threatened my children's lives. No longer will I stand by and aid your wicked ways!"

As Rhydin growled and started charging another attack spell, all of his remaining soldiers began to turn tail and run. Every single one of them dropped their blade and dashed into the trees in the opposite direction of Rhydin's palace.

When a Ranguvariian I didn't recognize made a move to follow them, I saw Rachel firmly shake her head. They had been just as fooled as Robert and were innocent of Rhydin's crimes. I briefly smiled at the sight of my red-haired friend, but then deflated when I remembered I had returned with the body of her brother who had died because of me.

All of my friends turned to face Rhydin now that all of their opponents had run off. He was outnumbered now, but I knew he wasn't going to go quietly.

Rhydin's nostrils flared as he watched his soldiers abandon him. He let out a snarl and continued with his spell, unleashing it in Robert and I's direction again. This blast was much larger, but I gritted my teeth, hoping the two of us together would be powerful enough to at least keep from being killed.

We readied ourselves, but suddenly fire, water, and wind came to our rescue. Xavier, Sabine, Frederick, and Mira cut off Rhydin's spell with all their powers combined, and I couldn't help but gape in amazement.

This is the way it was meant to be. All three elements together just like the Three Kings – two kings and a queen now – should work in harmony.

"Lina!"

I turned at the sound of my husband's and my brother's voices calling my name. The four Royals continued to combat Rhydin with the help of Rachel and what looked to be Chelsea, the Aatarilec from Caark, as Sam and Evan rushed up to Robert and I. Robert stared at Evan with such longing that it actually broke my heart, although I could tell that Evan was on pins and needles just being near him. I was about to help them say something to each other when Sam threw his long, lanky arms around me.

"Lina, I'm so so sorry," Sam gushed as he crushed me tight and then released. "Are you okay?"

My heart put up a wall, afraid of being hurt yet again. I mumbled, "Yeah, I'm fine."

Sam's brow crumpled at my short, quippy response, and he replied quietly, "I've been a fool, Lina. I shouldn't have blocked you out, I'm so sorry. I keep thinking that I'm protecting you, either from Rhydin by getting you to Caark or from getting sick, which you did anyway. But, I only end up hurting you."

"Yeah," I breathed, continuing to eye the battle just yards away from us, "Look, Sam, now isn't a good time for this…"

"Please, you have to forgive me," Sam begged, clinging to my hands. "I love you. You're the most important thing in my world, and I've done a crummy job of showing it."

"Later," I insisted as the battle grew louder, but I squeezed his hands. "I'll always love you. In plenty and in drought like we vowed, remember?"

A relieved smile relaxed the muscles of Sam's face as I turned to Robert and Evan. Robert looked like a bashful four-year-old while Evan stood with his arms crossed firmly. I approached my brother, touched his elbow, and said, "He saved me, Evan. I'd be dead if it weren't for him."

"He abandoned us," Evan hissed at me, which only resulted in Robert shrinking further away.

"He was just as misguided as the rest of those who serve Rhydin. I won't say it's not his fault," I replied slowly, and then met my father's gaze, "but he's ready to make it right."

Evan jutted out his jaw as he considered it, then sorrow overtook him. "Is it true? About Luke?"

My heart sank. I didn't bother asking how they could have known already. I warbled and pointed, "He's gone. Robert helped me bring his body. It's over behind those trees."

Both Evan's and Sam's shoulders slumped, and they both stared at me thoughtfully. Even after all the close calls and losses we'd had in the last several years since Duunzer, none of us ever expected to lose one of the Owenses. Evan looked at Robert with a new light in his eyes, and I hoped Robert's service would help redeem him to my brother.

A particularly loud boom brought our attention back to the others battling Rhydin, and he asked, "So what do we do now? How do we defeat him? He's alone, now's the time to do it."

He had questioned me, but Robert was the one who responded.

"Not defeat. Destroy," he clarified quietly. "I know how."

All three of us turned to the older man expectantly, surprised to hear those three little words.

Robert continued, "There is a spell that has been handed down for generations. Linaria and I performed a small part of it just a small while ago. Nora was able to defeat Rhydin using this spell because she was far more powerful as the first Allyen, but she wasn't able to destroy him by herself. It requires three Allyens to fully perform."

"Then let's do it!" I cried, my hands in fists.

"It's not that simple," Robert replied, sadness in his face, "You two haven't had any practice with it, and the full spell isn't an easy maneuver to teach."

"We have to try," I maintained. "Besides, Rhydin isn't going to let us go quietly into the night."

Just as another round of magic roared with the final disappearance of the sun's light, Xavier suddenly flew back to us and skidded to our feet, his clothes lightly steaming. He groaned loudly, his face and arms covered in small burns from narrow misses, and then he hopped to his feet and fixed us in his blue, fiery gaze. "Are you Allyens ready to help us, or what?"

"Actually," I responded as I leaned into his bubble and poked his chest, "we need you to distract Rhydin a little longer so we can practice this spell to destroy him."

"*Distract*, huh? Because that's definitely all that we're doing right now," Xavier huffed as he turned back toward the action, "We're barely holding our own, but whatever!"

"I'll come help," Sam said before turning and pulling me close again. "Be careful."

"I'm always careful." I grinned in spite of myself.

"Says the girl who leaped off a castle parapet to shoot Duunzer," Sam chuckled, and then jogged off after Xavier to join the clash.

I watched them for a few seconds and marveled at the power and skillset of all our friends, but also of Rhydin unfortunately. Frederick, Mira, Xavier, Sabine, and Sam all fought him with their various magics while Rachel led her small troop of Ranguvariians, some of whom lay dead around us. Chelsea, in her Aatarilec form, stuck very close to them, and I knew this was the only reason they weren't all dead.

Rhydin, even if only barely, kept them all at bay with his vast powers, and I knew then that it was definitely going to take something special to truly destroy him. I also realized that we probably only had mere minutes before his magic-bearing Followers showed up to reinforce him.

"Alright," I announced, feeling time ticking, "where do we start?"

"You both have the halves of the locket?" Robert asked, meeting each of us in the eyes. It was still so surreal to see how clear he seemed, no longer clouded by the rage Rhydin instilled in him.

Evan and I both nodded.

"Then," Robert took a deep breath, "I dare say it is time to create a third piece."

"A *third*?" Evan gasped, "Why?"

"The Allyen locket was divided into two pieces when I was your age," Robert answered, his eyes on the ground. "My mother, your Grandma Saarah, made it her life's mission to discover why Nora couldn't completely destroy Rhydin three centuries ago even with all her prowess. She decided it must take two Allyens, and she magically split the locket with Clariion Arii's help so each of us could benefit from its power. The two of us tried to perform the spell together when Rhydin attacked us the night of your birth."

Evan glanced at me anxiously. We had never heard this story before.

"We wounded him. Nothing more. That's why he laid low for nearly ten years before he tried to kidnap you both, but that night was also when he tricked me into joining him a couple months later, which is a story for another time." Robert grew quiet, ashamed of himself. "My mother's experiments were brought to a halt once I left, but she was sure that three Allyens, each with the amplification of the locket, would do the trick."

"So how do we split it now?" I asked.

Robert held out his hand to me, and I handed my locket to him. Evan's half was simply a disc that fit inside the two flaps of my piece, so it would have to be my half that was split. He replied slowly, "I remember how my mother and Arii did it. Feed your power into me, children, and we'll do it together."

Evan and I each took hold of one of Robert's arms, and I mustered the warmth of my magic, siphoning it into Robert. I felt Robert draw upon his own magic, and he cupped my half of the locket in his hands until brilliant white light streamed from the crevices between his fingers.

As he worked, I watched the battle on the other side of the clearing. Frederick and Xavier were working together, using wind magic to guide a long rope of fire at Rhydin, while Chelsea and Rachel were working their way closer and closer to him even as he continued to throw them backwards with big, purple charges. Sabine was trying to flood the clearing to slow Rhydin down when my eyes picked up figures in black behind Rhydin racing this way.

His Followers would be here any second, and we wouldn't have the upper hand anymore.

"Hurry up, Father," I muttered, and Evan stared at me for the use of that name.

When Robert opened his hands, my half had been split in two between the face of the locket and the back. He handed me the piece still attached to the chain that Sam had given me at the Winter Ball just before Duunzer struck, the last Lunakan winter holiday I'd attended. I looped it back over my head, trying to get used to feeling half its usual weight, as Robert unthreaded the leather cord that kept his collar cinched shut and used it to tie the new piece around his neck.

Three Allyens with three thirds of the locket between them. This was it.

Again, Robert stated, "Do as I do."

This time, it was easier for me since we didn't have to hold hands now that we all had our own locket piece. We stood in a widely-spaced circle, and Robert began to lead us through a similar series of movements that he and I had just performed, although it was more detailed this time now that we had both hands free. I mostly kept up with the movements, but Evan limped through them, this being his first time.

As Robert moved to run through the three-person spell a second time, the noises of shouting and magic colliding increased as Rhydin's Followers arrived and started drawing my friends' attention. When I looked over my shoulder, Rhydin was now unoccupied, and he had Robert fixed in his amethyst death glare.

I grimaced as Robert tried to gently critique Evan on one of the positions and said, "It's now or never, guys! Time's up."

Evan and Robert both panicked at the sight of Rhydin stalking toward us and took their positions. All of us stepped out with our right foot and arced our right arms over our heads. A small star of magic appeared in my hand as I brought it back to my center and continued the movements of the spell, now stepping and arcing my opposite foot and hand. Then, I started the more complicated hand movements, building and building upon my little star until it grew into an orb the size of a cantaloupe as I marched toward the center of the circle.

Robert and Evan were doing the exact same things and matched my pace toward the center of our circle, growing closer and closer until we were nearly in a huddle. Rhydin's expression was filled with fury as he recognized what we were doing, and he hustled toward us faster as he built his own charge of violet energy. It felt like ants were crawling on the back of my neck as panic threatened to overtake me.

I thrust my right foot forward for the last time and pushed my cantaloupe-sized ball of golden magic into the dead center of our imaginary circle, and my father and brother did the same. No sooner did the three orbs combine into one colossal globe when I abruptly heard a bloodcurdling shriek of pain.

Instinctually, my eyes shot back to Rhydin as our magic began to fizzle, losing its power. While the dark sorcerer now grinned with evil joy, his violet ball of magic was still in his pale, deadly hands. When I looked back at what we were doing, our magic nearly completely gone now, I was now able to see the head of a spear erupting from the middle of Robert's chest, crimson leaking around it.

"*No!*" I screamed as I ran forward and caught Robert under the arms, easing him to the ground.

Several feet behind him was none other than Kino smiling cruelly and empty-handed. Rage filled me at the sight of her. Red burst through my vision. I growled and was about to jump up to separate her head from her body when a weak hand touched my arm.

"Linaria, Evanarion," Robert whimpered, his voice croaking. The light that had returned to his eyes had disappeared once more. "Don't let anger be your guide."

"No, you're going to be okay!" I warbled as I tried to hold the blood in with my hands. Evan, too, did his best to help me.

"It's too late for me," our father answered, stilling our hands with one of his. "Just please. Remedy everything that I've done. All I ever wanted was to be with you both in a better world. I love you."

As Robert's breaths ceased and Kino cackled in the background, I am ashamed to say now that I almost immediately disobeyed the first of my father's final requests. I was instantly up, drawing my sword and letting out an angry scream as I sprinted toward Kino. She grinned wider as I approached, and she drew her own sword just quick enough to stop my first blow from slicing her in half.

I swung several more two-handed strikes with all the strength I had, and each time Kino's smile waned a little more as she had to use more and more of her power to block me. I screeched at her, "*Why*? Why did you kill him? Why can't you see you're being used and lied to like he did?"

"Because that's what traitors get!" Kino sneered, her exhaustion becoming obvious. "Robert was delusional, we all knew it! I support my master in *all* he does!"

"Then I have no guilt for ending you," I stated plainly as I began another barrage of magic and swipes of my sword. I furiously struck blow after blow, giving Kino barely enough time to defend herself, much less fight back.

Finally, she stumbled backwards, and the tall woman fell to the ground. She inched away from me in a sort of crabwalk, the gray eye I could see beyond her blonde-tipped hair open wide in fear. She backed up as I pursued, and I swung my sword, leaving a red gash along her jaw when she moved out of reach. I raised my sword again to finish her.

"Lina!" I heard my brother squeal. "Help!"

I dared to turn away from Kino long enough to see Evan dueling Rhydin all by himself, and terror shot through me like lightning. For a split second, I debated between helping Evan and finishing Kino off when I saw a puff of purple smoke out of the corner of my eye. Anger filled me to the brim.

The cowardly woman had transported herself away.

Enraged, I threw myself toward Evan and Rhydin, my fingertips tingling with magic aching to be used. Rhydin was beating Evan backwards with charge after charge while all Evan could do at this point was hold his sword up to keep diverting the deathly magic around him. I threw my own blast in Rhydin's direction, and he stopped attacking Evan just long enough to knock my golden ball of energy away from him and into the trees.

As he did, his face suddenly went slack, a horrified look in his amethyst eyes, and all at once, he let out a circular charge that slammed both Evan and I to the ground. For a brief moment, Rhydin was frozen, his gaze transfixed on the trees where he'd deflected my magic. I gripped my sword, my head aching from the blow, but when I looked up, a grin spread across my face.

The trees were full of people.

CHAPTER NINETEEN

S tanding alongside the trees were at least a few hundred, if not more, of Rhydin's common folk soldiers. Their dark uniforms camouflaged them in the trees' shadows, but their looks of shock, terror, and confusion were undeniable.

They had seen their great emperor wielding the very thing they feared the most. The very thing they had been fighting all this time.

By now, all the fighting in the clearing had ceased. Rhydin threw furious looks at his Followers, who had likely brought in the soldiers as more reinforcements without realizing that Rhydin would be caught compromising his fake identity.

Joy radiated through me. This had been my goal for nearly a whole year ever since Rhydin became emperor! There was no taking back what they had seen, regardless of Rhydin's smooth-talking, political speeches. As I got to my feet, I dusted myself off – possibly giving myself a pat on the back in the process – and turned to see how Rhydin was going to try and work his way out of this one.

"My people!" Rhydin declared with an embarrassed smile totally unlike his personality, like he was trying to play off an innocent accident. "How good of you to join me on this battlefield! Come-....!"

An overweight man who appeared to be in his upper forties with a thick mustache moved forward and bravely interrupted Rhydin, shouting, "You're a bloody sorcerer!"

The fake smile on Rhydin's face became smaller and truly political as he responded, "That may be true, my good man, but lest you forget, remember that I am still your Liberator from the tyrannical rule of the Royals!"

"But you *lied* to us!" the mustached man yelled in return. "No one with magic can be trusted! *You* said that!"

Just as Rhydin opened his mouth to spout another remark to spin the truth, Frederick rushed forward to address our newfound audience, his calm, kingly voice returned, "It is not magic itself that makes a person good or evil. Magic is merely a tool. It all depends on the heart of the person who is wielding it, which is why you all must see the darkness in Rhydin's heart!"

"This *Royal* lies to you like always!" Rhydin sneered. He picked up the edges of his cape and began to circle Frederick like a vulture, a cruel smile on his face. "This boy is from a long line of Royals who have abused you all since Nerahdis's beginning. He will only return you to the system of which you fought so hard to be free! *I* am the one who has freed you!"

"Free?" Xavier scoffed. He sauntered forward to join Frederick in the center of the clearing. "You sure have a funny definition of freedom, Rhydin, if it includes sickening your people and blighting their land."

Rhydin cackled too loudly, "You are both fools if you think I am behind such natural phenomenon!"

As our battle quickly evolved from one of muscles to one of wits, I found myself piping up after Rhydin's ridiculous answer, "I've been a farmer for years, and there is absolutely nothing 'natural' about what's going on in our fields with the perfect weather we've been having! And the Epidemic, the worst plague in a century, reappears when you become emperor? That's highly coincidental, don't you think?"

Our words were beginning to work, but it was hard to gauge their effect. The hundreds of war-seasoned men and women among the trees wore a variety of expressions as they looked to each other and whispered comments, questions, or exclamations. There were people of all the Three Kingdoms in Rhydin's uniform, although it was harder to tell their nationalities apart without the aid of their usual clothing. The Mineraltins and Lunakans were mostly indistinguishable while the Auklians could be identified by the rainbow of their hair colors. The thick, mustached man appeared to be Mineraltin himself due to the fading red in his hair and the bit of green I could see just above his collar.

"Even so," Rhydin remarked, crossing his black-clad arms over his chest, "I refuse to return to a world where Royals sit on the thrones of Nerahdis, flaunt their deadly magical powers, ignore the needs of their people, and sentence to death whomever they so desire. I know *all* these good people agree with me!"

Several of the people in the audience began to nod.

"Hey," Xavier shouted angrily, "*you're* the one who's a dictator!"

Just before the debate could devolve into more arguing and name-calling, Frederick declared rapidly, "I don't want to return to that world either!"

The people in the forest froze.

"I won't deny that how our fathers ruled was wrong," the blond prince continued. He looked from his audience to Xavier hesitantly. "Our fathers ran their households the same way they ran their kingdoms. You must believe me when I say that there is no one who wants change more than we do."

Xavier's mouth turned into a thin line. I remembered old King Morris and how he shut down, letting Jasmine drive his kingdom and family into the ground. Xavier bobbed his head to agree.

"This is ridiculous," Rhydin interjected. He took a few elegant strides toward Frederick and Xavier, which made them stiffen. Then, he accused, "You *boys* are just making empty promises to reclaim your fathers' thrones! Besides, the entire Kingdom of Auklia would fall into chaos if you should have your way!"

Every colorful-haired soldier that surrounded us abruptly straightened a bit. It was like lightning in the air that only they could feel. Each of them stared a little harder at Rhydin with eyes that covered the entire spectrum from scarlet to violet. Even Evan, raised in Auklia by our aunt and uncle with Keera, twitched before hesitantly looking over his shoulder at Sabine, formerly known as Anne.

I never had the chance to talk to her about her true identity. Was she even interested in claiming her throne?

To my surprise, Sabine walked forward to join Frederick and Xavier. She looked so different without her orange turban; her emerald green hair was short, cropped just below her ears, and it made such a fierce woman even more intense-looking. Rhydin became so furious that he looked like he could kill her on sight as she strode past the boys and stopped just short of hand-shaking distance to Rhydin. She announced in a clear voice, "I am Lady Sabine. Daughter of Archimage Dathian, niece of Queen Maria, and cousin of King Daniel. Auklia is my home, and I will rescue her for my people."

Then, she turned to Rhydin and declared, "Your reign of darkness is over!"

Instantly, the crowd around us erupted into a thunder of chattering and murmuring. I couldn't make out any of it, but I hoped it was in our favor. Anger heated Rhydin to the point of steaming, and I clutched my sword tighter. Any second this sort of halftime debate session was going to dissolve back into full warfare.

"Ha!" Rhydin crowed, "What good could the daughter of the man who wrought Duunzer upon Nerahdis possibly do? You will only become a puppet master and lead Nerahdis into darkness just like your father!"

"My father did no such thing," Sabine grumbled, and she pointed the tip of her blade at Rhydin, stopping just inches from his throat. "I believe in a *free* Nerahdis where the people help govern themselves alongside their monarch. Not where kings and queens rule from above with no checks. The people deserve a voice!"

Nearly all of the Auklians in attendance roared in approval, and when Frederick and Xavier let out a cheer as well, Lunakans and Mineraltins joined them. Now, about half the huge mass of people around us suddenly had smiles on their faces, including the mustached man who had been the initial spokesperson.

Rhydin, never once losing his cool, jeered, "You say that now, but once you have taken your thrones back, we all know you three will lapse into the habits of your dictatorial ancestors!"

Even as some of the people continued to grin, the other half of the army continued to stare at the Royals in disbelief and hatred. It was then that I reluctantly accepted that the Royals' dark history was too much for them and every one of Rhydin's lies still maintained a shred of logic.

Before I knew it, the half of Rhydin's army that were swayed by Sabine's speech began to cross the clearing to stand with us. As they did, many of them ripped Rhydin's flame insignia from their sleeves or stripped themselves of sashes emblazoned with it. At the sight of at least a hundred people unifying with us while just as many solidified their positions behind Rhydin, I suddenly realized that our war against Rhydin was no longer secret.

This was a full-blown revolution now. There would never be a person in Nerahdis who didn't know of our fight again.

"So be it," Rhydin responded firmly, his anger finally showing. Then, he turned to his faithful soldiers and his Followers who led them, and he shouted, "I will not allow the Royals to corrupt Nerahdis ever again! You must follow me and fight if you truly want your freedom from these oppressors!"

Before any of us could remotely begin to address or even thank the people who had just abandoned their previous jobs and beliefs to join us, Rhydin ordered his loyal soldiers to attack. They ran out from the trees like lines of ants, their swords raised and their shields glinting in the light of the rising moons.

Time seemed to freeze and the world fell silent as all the people on our side, common folk and mages alike, took a collective deep breath as we watched our attackers advance. The former soldiers drew their blades, the Ranguvariians leapt into the air as Chelsea's presence allowed them to use their wings, and the Royals, Evan, and I brought our magics to our fingertips, ready to be used at any second.

In the middle of it all, Rhydin stood back and watched, smirking from ear to ear.

I wanted to be the one to wipe it from his pale, youthful face.

Swords clashed and magic boomed on both sides as hundreds met each other in the now gigantic fray. I ran between a Ranguvariian taking one of Rhydin's magic-bearing Followers and a duel between one of his loyalists and one of our new rebels. My head spun at the amount of noise that now filled the clearing.

As I neared Rhydin, I noticed that Frederick had picked the same target I had, so we unified our powers and sent a massive, glowing torrent of wind straight at Rhydin.

Rhydin created a quick shot of violet energy that imploded our spell just feet in front of him, and then he burst through the smoke, suddenly with two thin, black swords angled at the two of us. One of them screeched down the razor edge of my blade and crashed into my hilt, and it took all of my strength to keep my sword in my hands.

Rhydin gave another hard shove before he mocked, "This will not be a victory for you, Linaria, by any means. You have only written more death sentences for whoever leaves me for you!"

Frederick cast another gust of wind to knock Rhydin off balance and shouted, "This is only the beginning, Rhydin! More people will join us, and you'll lose your power with them!"

"After today, *no one* will ever be foolish enough to betray me again!" Rhydin yelled as he raised both of his hands in unison.

I stalled, staring at him intently as I waited to see what kind of spell he was conjuring, but then suddenly Frederick was screaming my name as he struck down two Einanhis that had materialized out of nowhere, "Lina, behind you!!"

I turned too late. A plain Einanhi had popped up behind me as well, looking the least human of any of the ones I'd seen before with its black orb of a head and stick-like arms and legs. Before I could respond, pain exploded along the side of my head, and my ear felt hot and wet. The ground rushed up to meet me, and my arms felt numb when I tried to raise them to defend myself. The strange, alien-looking being raised its twiggy arms and its thin, rapier-looking weapon to finish me.

"*Lina!*" I heard Sam call from a distance, but he was too far. The flat of my blade slid downwards to rest upon my sternum, and I could only hope in those milliseconds that my death would at least not be easy.

Just as the Einanhi thrust its razor-sharp weapon downwards, Frederick rushed between it and me, skewering the being with his sword before it dissolved into sand. Then, the Lunakan prince parried another few blows from other Einanhis around us before hauling me to my feet.

My world spun from my aching head, the wetness and hotness running down my neck. I tried to speak and ask, "Why did you do that?"

"Because you're my friend," Frederick replied swiftly, his blond hair darkened with sweat, "and it's not your fault that my mother died. I sincerely apologize."

"Call it even," I groaned. My whole hand was crimson when I pulled it away from my head. This wasn't good.

Frederick couldn't release me or I'd hit the ground again, so he fought one-handed, desperately just trying to keep a multitude of Einanhis from getting within a few feet of us. Apparently, Rhydin had created nearly a hundred of them as they swarmed through the clearing, and we were now ridiculously outnumbered. Many of them tried to approach us; it was like they were sharks detecting blood in the water. All the while, Rhydin simply watched us, sneering, before he finally turned away, deciding that we were not worth his attention.

"We need to get out of here," I mumbled barely over the roar of the battle, "or we're not going to make it out of this one."

"I couldn't agree more!" Frederick shouted sarcastically as he shoved one Einanhi backwards and reduced another to a pile of sand. He then thrust his arm into a circular motion which created a small vortex of wind that threw all the Einanhis within six feet of us away.

My world was becoming hazy as Sam's voice abruptly sounded again, much closer now, "Oh, Lina! Lina, are you okay? Can you hear me?"

I bobbed my head, which sent a flurry of painful shocks radiating along my scalp, ear, and face. Sam began to aid Frederick by picking up and throwing any Einanhis that came near with his Rounan powers. There were simply too many of them to even try fighting.

I could only assume that he spoke to Frederick now as I fought my own fight in keeping the blackness that encroached upon my vision at bay. He yelled over the chaos, "Rachel and the Ranguvariians are putting together a plan to get us out of here!"

"What about all these people? They can't transport all of us, and we can't leave our new supporters behind!" Frederick called back as he threw another draft of wind at two more Einanhis.

"I know, she said she was working on it!" Sam replied as he used his Rounan powers to maintain some sort of buffer between us and death. "Just be ready to move when you see our chance, or we may not get out of this one!"

Frederick and Sam fell into silence as they battled side by side, keeping the Einanhis at bay taking all of their attention. My head began to turn numb, which I wasn't sure was a good thing or a bad thing, and I pushed at Frederick to let me stand on my own two feet.

I kept my balance, but the point of my sword remained firmly planted in the ground, too heavy to wield. My magic, too, was sluggish in its path to my fingers, but I did my best to help even as each shot left me more winded.

Around us was total mayhem marked by random blinks of different colored lights and magics throughout the darkness of the night. Rhydin was nowhere to be seen, likely watching from afar triumphantly. Instead, the clearing was overrun by the eerie, unnatural Einanhis that moved and struck unlike any human. Rhydin's loyalists attacked alongside them, looks of amazement on their faces that they served such an almighty emperor while the soldiers who had joined us appeared absolutely horrified that they ever served such a sorcerer.

As I continued to survey the battle and watch for any chance of escape, the Ranguvariians arranged themselves in a close-knit cluster toward the front of our lines, Chelsea in the center of their group to boost their magic. I could hardly fathom how Rachel was going to possibly get us out of this one without the help of transportation magic.

I stumbled over my disoriented legs as more Einanhis kept coming, pushing us and the rest of our supporters toward the edge of the clearing. The wall of trees behind us suddenly felt like a corner rather than where freedom lay. We were too overtaken to hold our frontline, and the number of casualties was rising.

Would our rebellion form and be wiped out on the same day?

Despite my blurry vision, a massive amount of light started coming from the imaginary line between our people and Rhydin's. The Ranguvariians, at pretty much full magical capacity in the presence of Rhydin for the first time in all of history with Chelsea's help, had spaced themselves out at the very front of our line and were performing an enchantment that I had never seen before.

Each of them had one foot firmly planted in front of them with their hands lifting to the midnight sky, a chorus of staccato war songs emanating from them as they cast their magic. A brilliantly-lit wall of glass-like magic was rising in front of them to divide our forces. It mimicked their glass shard wings, except it was huge, solid, and a rainbow of bright colors pulsated through it like a solitary heartbeat breaking through the cacophony of the battle.

Frederick, Sam, and I gaped as this wall built itself crystal by crystal between us and our foes, frozen and mesmerized. It wasn't until my mind finally registered Evan's voice screaming at us to run that I could wrench myself away from the immense sight. Frederick did an immediate one-eighty and burst into a run toward the forest away from Rhydin's palace, following a couple hundred others doing the same.

Sam grasped my hand and pulled as he shouted over the deafening vibrations of the magic wall, "Come on, we need to go!"

I looked over my shoulder one last time at the glass wall that beat like a heart, and while it could have been the pain of my head, I could have sworn that Rhydin stared back at me from the opposite side, his violet eyes glowing in simultaneous victory and fury.

Transfixed, I put every ounce of energy I had left into one final attack spell, balling the glowing power up into my hand. I had to end this. I had to try. I couldn't simply turn tail and run without trying even though a small part of what was left of my thinking knew it was preposterous.

Nonetheless, I fired that shot at Rhydin, and while it hit him smack in the face, it actually futilely bounced off the Ranguvariians' wall. Rhydin cackled at my stupidity and desperation, while Sam tugged on my arm hard to get me to follow him. But, my strength utterly spent, I finally lost the battle against the darkness that infringed upon the edges of my world. Rhydin's hateful face, eerily lit with the light of the Ranguvariians' magic, was the last thing I saw.

CHAPTER TWENTY

T he smell of damp dirt permeated my senses. My heavy eyelids blinked sluggishly, struggling to focus. It was so dark. Where was I?

Ever so slowly, the ceiling of a patchwork tent appeared above me, and I could feel the ache in every one of my muscles as I lay upon ground that felt like rock rather than earth.

I tried to roll my head along the rolled-up blanket serving as a pillow, but I grimaced when a lightning bolt of pain struck the whole side of my head and along my left ear. Confusion plagued me until I spotted my sword lying a couple feet away from me, dirtied with blood and grits of sand.

The battle. The Ranguvariians' spell. Rhydin's face. Robert. Luke. It all came back.

I sat up in spite of the throbbing pain, and suddenly I noticed Sam sitting in a dark corner of the tent. His eyes were overflowing with concern as he moved forward and whispered, "Take it easy. You took quite the knock."

"What happened? Where are we? Did everyone make it?"
I blabbered like a waterfall of anxiety.

"It's been a couple days since the battle. The
Ranguvariians' wall allowed us to get away. Everyone who
survived the battle made it here," Sam replied hesitantly
before he grasped my hand. "We're in the Dome."

"The Dome?" I asked confusedly before wincing as the
raising of my eyebrows sent another shock through my ear
and scalp. Reaching with my fingers, I was relieved to find
that ear still attached beneath a mountain of gauze.

Sam gave me a slight, lop-sided grin. "It's what we're
calling it. The rebellion location Evan and Sabine found.
You're gonna love it."

I nodded gingerly, and the tent fell into silence. It had been
months since I'd had so much of Sam's attention, and I didn't
know what to do with it. I found myself grasping at the first
thing I could think of to say. "Did Kelsi make it?"

Sam's mouth turned into a thin, grim line. I didn't need to
hear the answer. He spent a couple seconds licking his lips
and weighing his words before saying, "I'm so sorry for
derailing our mission. She's my sister…I had to try."

"I know," I sighed, folding my hands awkwardly in my
lap. "I would have done the same thing if it was Rosetta."

My husband huffed, lowering his bandana-ed head to his
hands, "Perhaps, but you wouldn't have pushed me away like
I did to you."

"Hmm," I replied, "I don't know about that. But what I do
know is that we both seem to get ourselves into sticky
situations or arguments while trying to protect the other."

"It sure seems so," Sam grumbled before meeting me in
the eyes again. "I was trying to protect you, but I never should
have tried to trick you into going to Caark without me or keep

you from helping me in Stellan. I really am so sorry, I'll never shut you out again."

"I know. I'm sorry too," I answered quietly as I reached for his hand. "Don't forget, it was my trying to protect you that led me to keep my dream of you dying a secret back during the war. That only got you drafted and down that path in the first place while if I'd just told you, we might have avoided it altogether."

Sam chuckled, "Looks like we've nearly gotten each other killed a few times in the three years we've been married."

"I guess we really can't protect each other...can we?" I asked sadly. My fingers drifted to my aching scalp. Another battle scar to add to my collection.

"We can try," Sam whispered. He pulled himself closer and lovingly wrapped me in his arms. "But we need to trust in each other's strengths. And no more secrets."

"Okay." I smiled, and my pain numbed a bit. "In plenty and drought, in plague and blessing, until my coal goes out."

"Until my coal goes out," Sam repeated, before kissing me.

"Ahem," a low, feminine voice sounded.

Sam and I glanced up to see Anne...*Sabine* holding the flap open to our tent, letting in a small amount of aquamarine-tinged light. She was wearing nicer clothes than anything I'd seen her wear before: a beautifully embroidered, sapphire tunic that had long tails draping to the ground with the tiny golden baubles typical of Auklian nobility. Overtop her best trousers and boots, of course.

She cleared her throat nervously, "Lina, can I speak with you?"

I nodded, and Sam gave my hand a squeeze before he stood and ducked out of the tent. Sabine remained in the back corner, uncertainty written all over her face. In a good mood for the first time in ages, I grinned at her and spoke first. "I understand why you lied."

"You do?" Sabine asked shakily as she rubbed the back of her neck, brushing the ends of her short, emerald hair.

"Yeah, and I don't blame you one bit. I was surprised, sure," I chuckled, "But, you made it clear from the beginning that you wanted to journey with us to learn if you could trust us."

Sabine inched closer to me, looking a bit more at ease as she knelt at the foot of my blankets. "You have to understand. Even after everything my parents did, it seemed like I was the most hunted woman in Nerahdis after my cousin, Daniel, died."

"Everything your parents did?" I repeated confusedly, drawing myself upward to hug my knees.

"I was only a few years old when my father became Archimage. I don't remember anything from that time, but I remember moving from Auklia to the Archimage Palace and losing everything remotely Auklian," Sabine answered, her crimson eyes drifting to the dirt. "I lost my friends, the rest of my family. My entire heritage. Just because of the rule that Archimages are stripped of their nationalities to be impartial among the Three Kings *and* even their previous lives to keep the position a secret from the people. History was rewritten to remove my parents and I from existence."

"Wow," I breathed, "I can't imagine. It was certainly difficult for us to figure out who you were."

Sabine snickered suddenly, "Yeah. I did tell you some of the truth though. I did grow up in the Archimage Palace, although my mother certainly wasn't a maid. She left my father when I was twelve and took me with her. She hated living a life away from any sort of society. Just the three of us, all the time, except for the rare meeting among the Three Kings when they were arguing, in which we could have no part as ladies. We made a quiet life for ourselves when we left, so I fully expected to still have fallen off the map. Apparently a select few remembered my existence when Daniel died."

"I'm sorry," I responded as I imagined such a lonely existence. "I can't say I liked Dathian very much, but he must have really loved and missed you. We found out about you from the tiny portrait miniature he'd been holding when he was murdered by Rhydin."

Sabine smiled sadly. "It's okay. You can't change the past. I missed my father, but there was definitely something strange about that palace I won't miss. You might think I'm crazy for this, but...sometimes I wonder if it's haunted."

My face went slack. Was I finally not the only one who could sense some other presence in the Archimage Palace? The seemingly helpful spirit that had warned me of Rhydin's arrival at the palace, led me to the book that revealed his past, and more? I was about to gush these sentiments and ask what she'd experienced when Sabine suddenly continued her train of thought.

"Eh, I was just a kid, it was probably nothing," the green-haired noblewoman mused.

"R-Right," I stuttered, my cheeks in flushing in embarrassment. The last thing I needed was for Sabine to think I was nuts, regardless of how certain I was that there was more to that palace than anybody was willing to think. "So," I stammered, "did you really mean everything you said to Rhydin? You're going to join us and give Auklia a future?"

"Oh, I definitely meant it!" Sabine enthused, her eyes shining bright. "I've always dreamed of returning home and helping my people! I never once thought it'd be as queen sitting on my cousin's throne…but you can count me in for the long haul. I'm looking forward to shaking up the monarchy. We're even making it official today."

Just as I was about to ask her what she meant, blue-green light flooded my tent once again as the flap opened. Rachel hurried in with something under her arm, dressed to the nines in orange and yellow Ranguvariian garb with beautiful beads woven into her gleaming red hair. Her face lit up upon sight of me conscious and exclaimed, "Lina, you're awake! And just in time, too. We're about to begin."

My heart panged at the sight of her. At the memory of Luke's broken and bleeding body. I desperately hoped that Evan or Sam remembered where I'd put him and brought him home. My throat swelled to the point I could hardly swallow, and heat flooded my face. I tried to speak, "Rachel…I am so *so* sorry!"

My red-haired friend's smile vanished, but she held up one pale hand to stop me. Grief was etched into every nook and cranny of her freckled face, but most would never see past her steely eyes. She cleared her throat and replied firmly, "Don't be. Every *Alyen nou Clarii* takes the same vow to lay down their life to protect the Allyens. Luke fulfilled his warrior's vow and died the most honorable of deaths."

"But-…!" I interjected.

"Do not take that from him. There is no way to know what would have happened if things had played out differently. It was his destiny," declared Rachel firmly. Then, she strode forward past Sabine and extended her hand.

I slowly took it, trying to accept Luke's death, and Rachel pulled me up, my head throbbing. Once she did, she gingerly placed her small bundle in my hands, and I gave her a confused look. "What's this for? What's going on?"

"The end of one chapter and the beginning of a new one," Rachel answered cryptically with a shadow of a grin. "Just put it on."

She left quickly before I could protest with Sabine in her wake. Alone now in my small, dark tent aside from a puny lantern sitting on the ground in one corner, I unfurled Rachel's bundle. Inside a drab tarp was a dress cut to my short stature, but it was unlike anything I'd ever seen before. It looked like it was made of silver thread that shined in the firelight of my lantern; every inch of it sparkled as if it was a jewel.

I ditched my tattered tunic and trousers that were still soiled with Luke's and Robert's blood and smelled of Rhydin's dank dungeons. However, it felt like an insult to the dress to put it on while my skin and hair still stank of memories I wished I could forget.

Thankfully, in one of the other dark corners of the tent was a small basin of water, so I spent several minutes doing the best I could to wash myself clean. I scrubbed every speck of dirt and blood long after it had disappeared, leaving my skin red and raw, yet I still felt dirty. I didn't realize how long I was taking until I heard a soft but impatient "hurry up" from Rachel just outside.

Finally, I donned the dress, and I inwardly thanked Rachel that it was sleek and not poofy like some Royals' dresses I'd seen. It hugged my collarbones and had long sleeves that draped at least a foot downward from my hands. The hemline dragged the ground a little bit, but not nearly as bad as most dresses that were loaned to me. The entire thing was silver except for a thick border of scarlet etched with black Ranguvariian patterns around the neckline. I couldn't help but wonder what kind of occasion was occurring outside that necessitated such attire in a hole in the ground.

I smoothed the fabric of the dress, grabbed my sword to re-conceal it within my trusty sash, and reached up to touch my locket – an old, nervous habit – to make sure it was still there. I panicked for a split second when it felt lighter against my fingers, until I remembered that I only had half of my usual necklace. There was another piece somewhere that I could only hope Evan had recovered from Robert.

My, how things were changing.

Rachel lifted the flap, blinding me with the blue-green light yet again. "Come on, they're all waiting for us!"

I stepped out of the tent and waited for my eyes to adjust. When they did, my mouth dropped open. "The Dome" was an apt name for this place. We were in a gigantic, rounded cavern that was several stories tall, and I could hardly see the edges of it. It had to be an entire mountain that was hollow or something.

At the zenith of the cavern was a bright cluster of what I could only describe as some sort of crystals that gave off several different colors of light, although the end result was the aquamarine color in which everything on the floor of the cavern was bathed. Patchwork tents, a few small campfires, and a few bigger areas where people could meet or were filled with some crates of supplies. I had only been out for a day or two, yet the Dome was already turning into a quaint community of revolutionaries.

The most amazing part? There had to be enough tents to account for a few hundred people down here with us.

Gaping, I turned to Rachel and breathed the only word I could manage, "How?"

"Our cause is growing every day," Rachel replied, beaming with pride. "The news of Rhydin's lies and his execution of the Royals has spread coast to coast. The people's responses to the news are varied. Many remain loyal to Rhydin, either due to fear or because they are just *that* fed up with the Royals, but we are gaining a few numbers here and there all the time. It's very slow, but far better than I expected so soon."

"Wow," I exhaled, unable to fathom it. Then, after another quick look around the empty tents surrounding us, I added, "If there's a few hundred people down here, where are all of them?"

"Waiting for you," Rachel groaned yet again. The tall redhead steered my shoulders to my left and would have pushed me along the whole way if I hadn't started walking faster.

"Why me?" I responded anxiously. "Where did Sam and Sabine go?"

"You'll see," my friend said quietly. "They're already there. On time, I might add."

There was a hum in the air as we grew closer to whatever event was transpiring, and the flicker of fire appeared around the next corner in a blue-green hue. We started seeing a person or two as we approached, a man in Auklian silks and a woman in Lunakan leather. Soon, we were pushing through a crowd like sardines until we reached an abrupt clearing in the center of the Dome. All the while, the humming became louder and louder, but my heart plummeted when I beheld the scene around me.

People watched, some stoically, some wide-eyed, from the sidelines of a big, open space like a canal between two landmasses. I saw faces young and old, male and female, pale and dark, of all three of the Three Kingdoms. With our appearance, all of them had their eyes on me, and I tried not to panic at the sudden attention.

At one of end of the large, empty aisle among all the people was a big pile of logs, which we were closest to at the moment. The other end seemed to mostly consist of a small stage from what I could see at this distance. A few people were standing upon it, but I couldn't tell who from so far away.

Just when I thought the humming couldn't get any louder, several Ranguvariians came forward from among the humans, evenly spaced down both sides of the aisle. Each Ranguvariian spread its wings wide, casting a colorful glow upon the people around them and the empty aisle.

However, I couldn't help but notice the gaping holes in their wings where several feathers were missing, like frayed holes in a quilt. My brow furrowed, wondering why so many had sacrificed so much. Surely not every person down here could be wearing a feather? Especially since I'd heard that Rhydin knew how they worked. I would have to ask Rachel about this later.

One of these Ranguvariians was banging a wide, animal-skin drum rhythmically, a *thump-thump* like a heartbeat. Another Ranguvariian was bearing a tall, golden torch with ornate designs, but it was unlit. Without missing a beat, Rachel walked toward her and took the dead torch, then my skin erupted into goosebumps when she then handed it to me.

I stared at it for a couple seconds, then whispered, "What do I do with this?"

"Light it," Rachel murmured under her breath, "with your magic!"

"I have *light* magic, not fire!" I hissed.

"Allyens have done this hundreds of times. You can do it," Rachel answered unhelpfully.

My eyes scanned the audience desperately. Sam, Sabine, Frederick, Xavier…none of them were to be found. The beat of the drum echoed the sound of my pounding heart in my ears.

When I looked down the aisle to the other end, I noticed that one of the people on the stage had started jogging my way. I recognized Evan as he grew closer, and he was huffing slightly when he finally reached me. He was dressed in an elaborate tunic made out of the same silvery material as my dress with leather trousers and a braided belt. His Allyen eyes seemed heavy as he held my gaze, and he repeated our father's words, "Do as I do."

A lump rose in my throat, and I mirrored Evan as he reached to the top of my torch with one hand. He closed his eyes, and I did the same, thinking of my magic to draw it forth.

Evan muttered again, "Concentrate your power. So bright that it's hot."

I did as I was told, focusing everything I had on the rough little wick between mine and Evan's fingers. I had never used my magic constantly for this long, and the usual warmth that I felt soon grew warmer and warmer until my fingers felt like they had been severely sunburned. I opened my eyes, afraid of truly being burned, and the wick was smoking a little bit. After only seconds more, Evan executed a rapid twist of his fingers, and fire burst to life.

As soon as the torch ignited, the humming and drumming ceased. Evan remained by my side as the Ranguvariians began to sing long, choral sounds echoing throughout the Dome in harmony. Rachel gave me a little shove toward the pile of tree limbs and logs, and then started to sing and translate for the sake of us humans, "*Uny calou, etne clarii, uny calou.* Well done, my soldier, well done."

I approached the pyre hesitantly, but I froze in my tracks when I saw what it was for. Stretched out upon it was Luke's long, lean body, which had been re-wrapped in a clean, orange linen blanket with gold decorations.

"*Anoet'v vas naeran dii ntae nten, etne clarii.* You vowed you would die for us," Rachel continued to sing.

I gulped hard and looked to Evan in a panic. Why were they making me do this? I couldn't do this!

Evan scurried over to me and walked me closer to the pyre. He whispered, "You're the one he died for. It's part of their ceremony, you have to be the one to do it, or you'll disgrace his memory."

"*Aiin'v ran, nten. Ba eht raniin iiba Alyen. Iiba C'calou chaldnii.* You gave your life song. So the Allyen may live. The greatest sacrifice."

The chorus of Ranguvariians, the beating drum, and Rachel's chanting all faded into the background. It was silent in my head as I stared at Luke for the last time. I wanted to keep looking. I couldn't tear my gaze away. This couldn't be the last time I'd see his long, pale, freckled face.

But it was already over. I would never see his rare smile again. I would never see his eyes flick through the colors of the rainbow again. I would never be scared out of my wits as he plucked me off the ground and flew me around again. All I had left were the memories and the fierce resolve that Rhydin would *never* get away with this.

With that notion powering every fiber of my body, I leaned the torch forward to ignite the pyre.

"*Eht anet iivan dii jaenou, eten shnetran.* May your blade remain sharp for eternity," Rachel finished the traditional words solemnly.

The Ranguvariians' song ended on a high note, and the drum ceased once again. Everyone along the aisle watched the fire for several moments in complete silence as it spread through the pile of logs. Smoke began to rise toward the top of the Dome where there must have been a small opening for it to exit and air to enter.

After a few minutes, just as the fire was about to reach Luke, Rachel held out her hand for the torch, and I gave it to her. She announced in a loud, clear voice, "One chapter has come to an end. It is time for a new one to begin."

Immediately, every head in the audience shifted from our end of the aisle to the stage on the opposite side. I could make out three vague shapes down there, but it was too far and the air too smoky to really tell what they were. Rachel lifted the torch and then struck the ground with it loudly. The Ranguvariian drummer struck up another beat, this one a much more traditional, Gornish cadence rather than the tribal heartbeat of the funeral.

Rachel and Evan both started walking at a brisk pace down the aisle toward the other end, and I had to jog a few strides to catch up with them. The people all followed us with their wide, star-struck eyes, but their silence unnerved me. There was no chattering, whispering, or even fidgeting. Everyone stood stock-still, in awe of everything transpiring in front of them. A Ranguvariian funeral was certainly a rare and moving event, so I couldn't help but wonder what the second ceremony entailed.

As we approached, I realized that the three shapes on the stage were chairs. Like rickety, kitchen chairs. Why were there three sad-looking chairs on a stage?

Rachel slowed and came to a stop, planting her torch in the ground once again. Evan and I halted beside her, and my nerves finally began to relax when I spotted Sam walking forward out of the crowd. He was in much nicer clothes as well: a navy, satin tunic with a purple sash embellished with gold overtop his nicest trousers. As always, he wore his Kidek bandana proudly tied around his head.

Several audience members smiled and silently cheered by raising their arms over their heads. Rounan marks were upon each of them. Perhaps, we had gotten through to more of the Rounans whose compounds we'd visited than I'd thought. Sam winked at me and mounted the stairs on the east side of the stage. However, he didn't approach any of the three chairs and remained standing off to the side.

Likewise, on the west side of the stage, Clariion Arii himself strode to take a position symmetrical to Sam's, bedecked in a similar outfit to Rachel's. He clutched a silver staff embedded with amber beads, and his centuries-old eyes glowed pink as he beamed at Rachel, his successor.

"Heirs of Nerahdis, come forward," Rachel announced loudly.

Frederick, Xavier, and Sabine suddenly came forward from the back center of the stage, and each of them trod confidently toward one of the three kitchen chairs. They remained standing solemnly as their families quietly appeared behind them.

Xavier brooded uncertainly as Mira and Taisyn, their small, blind son, came to stand by his chair. Sabine seemed so strong she could slash someone's throat just by looking at them while her two small boys, orphans of the war, fidgeted by her chair.

Dominick clung to Princess Cornflower's skirts behind his father's chair, terrified even with his aunt. Frederick looked like he was bearing the weight of the world on his shoulders, his blond hair so thin I could pretty much see his scalp.

This was new, as far as what I knew about Nerahdian coronations. The Three Kings were always presented as fierce, lone monarchs who were god-like. Not human beings who had families just like everyone else.

Then again, there was a lot about what was going on right now that certainly was not traditional. Like having a half-human, half-Ranguvariian woman running the show.

"Prince Xavier Rollins," Rachel began, "do you so swear to lead, serve, and protect the people of the Kingdom of Mineraltir, to the best of your ability, until your final breath?"

Xavier took a deep breath, the magnitude of the situation weighing upon him, as I could only imagine what memory of his father he was thinking about as he declared, "I so swear."

Rachel continued, "Lady Sabine Cedal, do you swear to lead, serve, and protect the people of the Kingdom of Auklia, to the best of your ability, until your final breath?"

"I so swear," Sabine answered passionately, a grin toying at the edges of her mouth.

"Prince Frederick Tané, do you so swear to lead, serve, and protect the people of the Kingdom of Lunaka, to the best of your ability, until your final breath?" Rachel asked, finally smiling herself.

Frederick answered confidently, and I knew how much he was looking forward to putting right everything King Adam had done, "I so swear."

James jogged out of the crowd toward his sister with an ornate, wooden box. There were tearstains on his cheeks, and my throat swelled once again at the thought of Luke's absence. He should have been here for this. James opened the box in front of the three of us, and upon burnt orange velvet were three very plain, silver crowns that I'd never seen before. They were likely the best the Ranguvariians could come up with due to our limited resources in the Dome, but they were still beautiful in a simple way.

Evan took the middle crown, one that looked like a single, gleaming wave, and Rachel took the one on the left, which was straighter with shining leaves springing from it.

When I looked at her funny, she responded in a whisper, "What? My grandmother was Mineraltin, remember?"

It was then that I understood. Rachel would crown Xavier, Evan would crown Sabine as someone who grew up in Auklia, and the final crown on the right was mine to give. It was to be Frederick's, and it looked like a chain of sparkling wheat heads.

My breathing became erratic when I gingerly touched it with just enough fingertips to lift it from its orange bed. It felt very strange to be holding a crown. A plain, farm girl like me had never even touched one of these in all of time, much less been the one to place it on a prince's head to make him king.

Evan and I trailed after Rachel toward the stage and up the creaking, haphazard steps. As Rachel began the traditional words of the monarch vows, with a few tweaks to allow for more freedom and less fear, I numbly stepped in front of Frederick, still holding the crown out from my body like it was a poison-dipped dagger.

Frederick smiled sadly, and I could see the whirlpool of anxiety in his blue eyes. He murmured, "I'm sorry for blaming you for my mother's death. It wasn't your fault."

"It's okay," I replied nonchalantly. "Trust me, I get it. You were grieving."

Frederick nodded almost imperceptibly as he stared at the crowd over my shoulder. He was a great big ball of nerves, and I'd never seen him like this before. He whispered, "I've thought about this day a thousand times since I was a boy. I never once dreamed it would play out like this."

"Believe me," I chuckled, "neither did I."

"It seems right for you to do it though," Frederick said quietly, his expression warming. "After all, it was you who made me realize I wanted to be king as a boy, instead of running away from my father."

I smiled as the memory came to me. Frederick had told me this story while we were marooned in the basement of Luke's livery. He had run away as a child and I had unknowingly told him that he could right all his father's wrongs if he became king. My fingers became surer and steadier on the silver wheat crown as I answered, "It is my honor."

When Rachel came to the end of the words, Frederick knelt before me and bowed his golden head, which sent goosebumps up my arms. I slid the crown over his temples, and he smiled at me as he stood once more as Rachel crowned Xavier and Evan crowned Sabine.

Rachel declared happily, "We now dub thee King Xavier of Mineraltir, Queen Sabine of Auklia, and King Frederick of Lunaka! Long live the Three Kings and Queen!"

"Long live the Three Kings and Queen!" the crowd roared all around us as Xavier, Sabine, and Frederick sat upon their bare, wooden chairs, surrounded by their families.

Sam and Arii remained off to their respective sides, having done nothing but clapping. It made sense now. They symbolized the Rounans' and Ranguvariians' support of the new monarchs. While they had done nothing but stand there, their doing so spoke volumes as to how we would all move forward.

As I looked out to the cheering people, the few hundred rebels who had joined us against Rhydin underground in the Dome, I realized that the warmth bubbling up in my chest was none other than hope. Hope that destroying Rhydin was closer than ever before, that it was actually within our grasp. For the first time, our battle was now public, and we were gaining more help every day. Out there, Gornish, Rounan, and Ranguvariian stood together.

This event was a glimpse of the future. A future where instead of basic chairs underground, Frederick and the others sat upon their rightful thrones in the castles of their ancestors. A bright future free of Rhydin and the oppression and prejudices of the kings of old.

It might not happen tomorrow, but it was coming. I could feel it in my bones.

The days of Rhydin's reign of darkness were numbered.

Chapter Twenty-One

———⟨✦⟩———

Middle Autumn 24ᵗʰ, Year 1 of King Frederick's Reign (Year 3 of Rhydin's Reign of Darkness),

Today, Evan and I laid our father to rest. We waited a few days after Luke's funeral and the coronation ceremony out of respect, but this event was secret. Most people probably wouldn't understand. Heck, I wouldn't have understood my own presence here this time last year. So much has changed.

We buried him just outside the Dome where the open grasses of Caden's Plain kiss the foot of the mountains surrounding Lunaka. Sam and Cayce, who recently joined us from Caark now that her and Evan's son is old enough to be without her, were the only other people there. While I miss Robert and am eternally grateful for his decision to save me, Evan seems to be mourning more than I am. I had gotten to know Robert a little bit there at the end, but Evan never got the chance. He keeps asking me about him. I hope someday he will feel at peace.

The only thing we have of him is the third piece of the locket that he created from my half, which we've decided to hide away so that even if we are captured, Rhydin won't have all three pieces. If Rhydin can only be destroyed by three Allyens performing the *Alytniinaeran* spell (as the Ranguvariians are now calling it - "All-yuh-tnee-nigh-rahn," "death by three lights") - our only choice now is to wait for when Rayna is older.

It makes sense now why Archimage Dathian saw the destruction of Nerahdis when it appeared that no future Allyen would be born to us back during the war. We would be lost without her now, unable to ever perform *Alytniinaeran*, even if we must wait until she is old enough to wield the magic she has been given. To Cassandra, for giving us her and Frederick's daughter on her death bed, we must be eternally grateful.

Even though we must wait to destroy Rhydin for good, our rebellion has by no means been idle! Our civil war is nearly in full swing as we work to undermine Rhydin in smaller scuffles and reconnaissance to gain as many resources and people as we can while we wait. As the rumors and news of Rhydin's slaughtering the Royals and his possessing magic spread from coast to coast, more people seem to find their way to us all the time, whether they join us in the Dome because they fear for their lives or serve as spies afar. After wondering for so long if our rebellion would ever even get off the ground, it's thrilling to watch it grow.

The Dome has become a haven for everyone. Gornish, Rounan, Mineraltin, Auklian, Lunakan, Ranguvariian - every type of person is represented down here in a way that is totally unprecedented. It makes me hope that the Nerahdis we're working to build will be a much more cohesive place than how it's been for my whole life.

To that end, we've created a new council to spearhead our efforts to adjust the existing monarchies to be more open. It consists of Frederick, Xavier, Sabine, Sam, Evan, me, and James, who sits in as his grandfather's ambassador. It is our hope that one day, we'll have someone from the Aatarilecs as well to represent the immense help they have already given us. For now, I am just thrilled that Frederick and Xavier have buried the hatchet. Sabine seems to be exactly the cog that was missing to keep the boys from working together.

Not only is the Dome diverse and unified, but we're protected from Rhydin down here. Rhydin may have cracked most of the Ranguvariians' magic from his capture of Luke, like how to sense individual feather charms, but the Ranguvariians were able to make something work. The cluster of crystals at the very top of the Dome weren't crystals at all, but hundreds if not *thousands* of Ranguvariian feathers magically sealed together. Sheer number restored their power of invisibility, and so the large, aquamarine fixture keeps our rebellion not only undetectable, but aglow with the light of their magic. Now, whenever I see a Ranguvariian whose wings are riddled with holes where feathers were taken to build the crystals, small parts of their power gone, I can only imagine the magnitude of that sacrifice. Apparently, Ranguvariian power does not rejuvenate like Gornish magic does, even when given willingly and not stolen.

The Dome may be safe at the moment, but Rachel still doesn't want the lock and key to be housed in the same underground cavern. Therefore, our children, Kylar and Rayna, and Evan's son, Aron, will remain in Caark. When Rachel returned to Caark with Chelsea to rejoin Jaspen, she promised me that once we were more certain the Dome was truly safe and that Rhydin wouldn't engineer a way to sense more feathers, she would bring our children to live here with us. Sam and I are truly hoping this will only take a year or two tops, but until then, Rachel and Jaspen will try to give our kids as normal of a childhood as possible. We busy ourselves with leading recon missions - as well as studying the book I found in the Archimage Palace, the magic that preserves it, and the strange presence that led me to it - so that time will pass quickly.

Thus, I will continue to spend my days stealing from Rhydin and giving to the poor, whether they oppose him or not, until Rayna is old enough to help Evan and I destroy him. Rhydin's iron grip around Nerahdis's throat grows tighter with every passing week, so bringing food and supplies to people cut off from them either directly or indirectly by Rhydin has become another way to try and change people's opinions of the new, underground kings and queen. All these years, it was Rhydin who had the advantage of working in secret, and now the tables have turned. Down here, we can build our strength while Rhydin has no idea what's coming.

Our war isn't over. It may take a few years, but we've got the spark now. Once that day comes, this spark will be a blazing fire that nothing and no one can stop from burning Rhydin's imperial palace to the ground.

For the first time, our hope outweighs our fear.

The night sky was vast. Twinkling stars dotted it from horizon to horizon while the twin, Lunakan moons hovered just above the dark tree line. The typical Lunakan wind that Lina used to love so much couldn't reach the extreme northeastern corner of the kingdom where the Ranguvariian Clan lived, but Rachel could smell the salty stench of the ocean just over the mountains.

She delicately placed a frayed, red ribbon back onto the magically-preserved page to save her spot, then gently closed the stiff, leather volume. It was the Allyen journal, the one in which Lina wrote all of her adventures, just as every Allyen before her and after her had done, and Rachel still guarded it like a precious jewel.

A child's voice rattled off in Ranguvariian, "Aw, please, Clariion Rachel, don't stop reading yet!"

"That is the end for tonight, children," Rachel responded as she adjusted her immaculate, orange Clariion robes. She and about a dozen Ranguvariian children were huddled around a campfire under the open sky for their weekly tale. "Lina stopped writing for some time until her daughter joined her in the Dome."

"Allyen Rayna," Sunlii cheered. The young girl with hundreds of braids in her hair was a descendant of Bartholomiiu, if Rachel remembered correctly.

Rachel chuckled, "That is correct. We will continue next week."

Several of the children groaned. An older boy called Reviin gushed, "But we need more! Is there really a ghost in the Archimage Palace?"

"Did our people really give up so many of their feathers?" another child spurted.

"How long do they stay in the Dome? Do they defeat Rhydin? We want more of the story of the Allyens!" Rachel's own great-great-great-grandchild burst.

The first human-looking Clariion leveled her gaze at the girl. She was about nine with long, brown hair done up in a series of braided buns. She was also dressed in orange as a member of the Clariion's house, and Rachel remembered the day she was born clearly.

All those years ago when Grandfather Arii had been grooming Rachel to take on his role, she hadn't really considered the anti-aging portion of the job. She never once dreamed she would meet this child, much less have to watch every one of her friends and family pass from this life, especially Lina.

Some of them died. Some of them were killed.

As a young woman living in Caark and watching over her friends' children, she never once imagined that their civil war against Rhydin would play out the way it ultimately did. It was a wonder she had walked away from it after everything.

Rachel took a deep breath, letting the happy and the dark memories sift into the background before they could overtake her in nostalgia or anxious tremors. She rose from her seat, which was a side-lying log near the fire, and stretched her weary limbs. Then, she said cryptically, "This is not the story of the Allyens."

A boy with long ears and buttercup-colored eyes tilted his shaved head in confusion as he asked, "Then what story is it?"

"The Story of the First Archimage," Rachel replied with a sly grin. Then, she returned to her log and thumbed her long fingers through Lina's journal once more. "Settle in, young ones, we're only halfway through the story. It will all make sense soon."

END OF BOOK THREE

Acknowledgments

I can't believe I'm already writing my acknowledgments for the *third* book in this series! These characters were born in my mind well over ten years ago at this point, and I am so thankful and blessed that I have been able to share them in print. Many people deserve acknowledgment because there is no way I could have done this by myself!

To my readers, you all are wonderful. Every time I receive a message or hear from you about how much you've enjoyed my stories; it truly makes my week. Your words keep me going, just as you anxiously anticipate mine. I hope *Reign of Darkness* follows through on everything you've loved about *The Allyen* and *The War of the Three Kingdoms*. You guys make my writing dreams come true!

To my husband, Olin, who doesn't judge me for sitting in front of a laptop for several hours every day and who thinks my being an author is super cool. I could never do this without your support.

To my family, the blood ones and the non-blood ones, who support me in everything I do. You guys rock, and I wouldn't be who I am today without you. Thank you to my parents, my brothers, and grandma, who have all believed in me since day one.

To Rachel Evans, my Ranguvariian linguist and cultural expert. You are the mastermind behind the Ranguvariian language and the original song, *"Uny calou etne Clarii,"* which you wrote when we were either in junior high or high school. I'm glad I could honor that in this book!

To Hannah Robinson, my writing-partner-in-crime who helps me bust through the toughest of writer's blocks. Thanks for being just a text away.

To Daphne Olson, my faithful, merciless editor, who keeps me on the grammatically straight and narrow. Your skills amaze me.

To my mother, Cynthia Riley, who eagerly awaits being one of my first readers and keeps things flowing. Thank you for being my biggest cheerleader.

To Magpie Designs, Ltd. and L. N. Weldon, who turns my pencil sketches and rambling, OCD-filled emails into gorgeous covers and fantasy maps. I couldn't have asked for a better designer for my stuff.

Last, but certainly not least, to my daughter, Cassidy, who is the same age as this book. I will always remember learning I was pregnant with you at the very beginning of the drafting process. You may only be a few months old now, but this will always be a precious memory.

Thank you to everyone! I appreciate you all! I can't wait to continue on to Book 4, so find my author page on Facebook or visit my website to stay in touch on future publications!

Visit my website to learn more!
www.michaelarileykarr.wordpress.com